POST CARD

TEA ROSE ROMANCE...FROM JOVE BOOKS.

ENCHANTING NOVELS THAT CAPTURE
THE BEAUTY AND SPIRIT OF ENGLAND.

Dear Reader . . .

There's no place like England when it comes to romance. From the glorious cliffs of Dover and the lush green hills of country estates . . . to the grand courts of royal intrigue and foggy streets of London . . . England is a beautiful and timeless place that fires the imagination.

Tea Rose Romance is a wonderful new line of novels that captures all the passion and glory of this splendid nation. We asked some of our favorite writers to share their most romantic dreams of England—and we were delighted with their enthusiastic responses! Whatever the period and style—adventurous, playful, intriguing, lusty, witty, or dramatically heartfelt—every *Tea Rose Romance* is a unique love story with an English flavor and timeless spirit.

We hope you enjoy these special new novels. And please, accept the *Tea Rose Romance* postcard as our gift to you, the reader, who makes all dreams possible.

Sincerely,
The Publishers

P.S.—Don't miss these Tea Rose Romances, coming soon from Jove Books . . .

Garden of Secrets

by Eileen Winwood . . .

A spicy tale of passion and royal intrigue. A clever beauty uses an herbal potion to kidnap England's most notorious spy—but then risks her life for his love.

(Available in September 1994)

Stolen Kisses

by Karen Lockwood . . .

A rousing story of love, passion, and adventure. A hot-tempered Scotsman crosses the highlands to steal his daughter away from his English in-laws—but the child's willful governess stands in his way.

(Available in November 1994)

SWEET IRIS

AILEEN HUMPHREY

JOVE BOOKS, NEW YORK

SWEET IRIS

A Jove Book / published by arrangement with
the author

PRINTING HISTORY
Jove edition / July 1994

ISBN: 0-515-11381-6

A JOVE BOOK®
Jove Books are published by The Berkley Publishing Group,
200 Madison Avenue, New York, New York 10016.
JOVE and the "J" design are trademarks
belonging to Jove Publications, Inc.

PRINTED IN THE UNITED STATES OF AMERICA

10 9 8 7 6 5 4 3 2 1

Author's Notes

- The medical and scientific references are accurate for the period, which shows that truth is stranger than fiction.

- References to the proper reading materials for females are also correct for the period. Egad!

- There really was a GPIUB. I saw a photograph of one made of rubber.

- Profound and groveling thanks to the staff of the Ann Arbor, Michigan, Public Library system, who have never flinched at a request.

- C.Y. struck again, thank goodness.

- An Honorable Mention to Therese's big toe.

- Three cheers for the *Friends of the Library* and their book sales.

SWEET IRIS

· One ·

"*Do you suppose anyone else knows what she's*
done?"

"I hardly think so," came the tremulous reply.
"Her father took her away from home as soon as
her mother discovered what had happened."

"Thank God for that!" said the old man. "Who
would have thought that Iris, dear, sweet Iris,
would have behaved like a Jezebel, a harlot. And
a French one at that! Fifteen surviving in that
brood and she's the only one who would forget
her duty and bring disgrace to the family!"

"But surely you remember what two of her
older brothers did in Venice when—"

"Boys will be boys, Prudence."

Lifting her chins indignantly, Prudence said,
"They were not boys, they were young men, and
what they did was perfectly shocking!"

"Don't try to change the subject! The only
thing that's shocking is what Iris has done!"

With a flip of the hand Prudence snapped shut
the volume of Culpeper's Herbal that lay on her
ample lap. This mute act of defiance shook the
cage crinoline she wore beneath her voluminous
skirts.

Obediah Huntington, squire of Huntington Manor, ignored his sister's dissenting opinion and concentrated on the lifting of his bare right foot from its resting place atop the stuffed head of a tiger-skin rug. The flattened beast stared through unblinking glass eyes as the man left his elephant-tusk chair to hobble across the room. The trip was painfully slow. His destination was the mahogany sideboard that stood against the far wall. Above it was a display of African masks and crossed spears.

In an attempt to dull the burning pain in his gouty big toe the squire poured himself a generous measure of scotch and tossed it down in one fiery gulp. Tears spilled from his eyes, and his mutton-chop whiskers bristled. His voice had a rasping quality when he said, "So much attention has been lavished upon Iris. A small fortune laid out to groom her for high expectations. Now we learn that the ungrateful girl is little more than baggage. When the opportunity knocked her up, she answered the wrong damn door!"

"Obediah, you can't be serious! You must remember that young people are sometimes given to an occasional lapse in judgment."

"Egad! What Iris has done can hardly be given such a simple description! If the Marquis of Bumpsted ever gets wind of what's happened, there will be absolutely no hope of a match between them. A gentleman has every right to expect an innocent young wife. I certainly can't call Iris innocent *now*."

Plump hands worried a delicate handkerchief as Prudence said, "You are too hard on her, Obediah. I doubt that the incident, if I may call it such, meant very much. Given a discreet amount of time the affected . . . umm . . . the affected anatomy will surely return to normal and—"

"Return to normal?" roared the squire. "What's done is done, you silly woman! Such outrageous behavior cannot be undone, even when no one can see it! The girl's mind must have come unhinged by the suddenness of her good fortune." He frowned and fidgeted with his empty glass before putting it aside. "My son should have broken the news to her by degrees. Female brains can't stand to be loaded like hay wagons, you know. I've always said that too much thinking will weaken them. Haven't I always said that too much thinking will soften a female's brain?"

"Yes, Obediah, you've always said that," replied his sister. "Now, however, it's important that Iris be distracted from the problem. That's why I was so pleased when we were invited to Westbourne Hall yesterday for tea. It gave Iris an opportunity to become acquainted with Glorianna Rutherford. You do recall that Glorianna is Maxwell's wife. . . ."

As her brother made no response, Prudence chirruped on. "Iris and Glorianna are somewhat alike, I think, as neither one has a special friend near here, you see. They are of a similar age, too, I believe. Proper companionship is so important. My goodness, everyone knows that."

Prudence needed another breath before she could say, "Then there is Elgin Farley, Maxwell's friend, who is once more a guest at the Hall, so he had tea with us as well. Of course you will remember Elgin. He has that lovely old place down in Kent. The Rutherfords dote on him, you know, for he's been running tame about the place since he was a boy." She took another breath and said, "We knew his parents, though they were of a younger set—she was so terribly pretty. It wasn't an intimate association, for we only met them socially, but we knew them and they knew us. Do you recall them? They were considered rather odd, even then. I've wondered how his mother is, of course, though I never knew her well enough to write to her and ask. If she had been a friend I would have asked, but she wasn't, so I didn't."

The squire's only comment was a disinterested grunt as he hobbled back to his elephantine throne, taking care not to bump into anything. Even a stocking or slipper would have been agony against his toe.

Undaunted, Prudence said, "Dear Iris so enjoyed yesterday's visit that I invited everyone from the Hall to call on us this afternoon. It was a shame that they would be otherwise engaged today, except for Elgin, that is, and he accepted. Still, even one person is more company for Iris than no one at—"

"Elgin Farley is coming here alone?" the squire asked suspiciously.

"He's coming to see Iris. It's all quite proper I assure you, as I have left my own maid to watch over them from the terrace."

"I can hardly believe that Farley has the slightest interest in either Iris or the garden. I think he's got wind of my latest shipment of antiquities and is looking for an excuse to hang about! I just don't know how he's managed to learn of them so soon." Thin fingers drummed polished ivory before the squire finally decided that:

"Farley undoubtedly has some connection with the shipping line that carried the crates from Egypt. He's probably a spy for one of my rivals, who is trying to acquire a more notable collection of antiquities than mine!"

That possibility stuck so firmly in the squire's brain that it took the form of fact in no time at all. Having become quite agitated, the notion prompted him to say, "I'll tell you right now, Prudence, I won't see Farley under any circumstances. That way he won't be able to winkle out anything about my Egyptian treasures. He'll find out everything when I'm ready to make it all public and not a moment before!"

After that outburst had spent itself, the squire sagged lower in his chair, glowered at his offending toe, and muttered, "Spy on me, will he? I'll show the blighter that it can't be done!"

Shaking her head so determinedly that the lace on her cap wagged around, Prudence said, "Obediah, you must be mistaken. I do believe Elgin's presence here is above reproach."

"And perhaps your invitation fits right in with his nefarious plans," her brother grumbled.

"Do your antiquities truly need so much guarding?"

"Guarding!" he cried, the finger of enlightenment skewering the empty air. "I'm glad you reminded me of it! I'll have to inspect the locks on the Egyptian Room myself. And then there's the fire hazard. Those mummies are so full of resin that they'd burn like hell itself."

Thoroughly exasperated, Prudence said,

"Obediah, I'm only trying to point out that Iris has had nothing but family and tutors to keep her company for much too long. Concerts and operas are all very fine, but they are no substitute for society. Iris has grown into a young woman. She needs friends of her own age. Girls in convent schools must be better prepared for life than she is."

"Iris doesn't need to be ready for life. She only needs to be ready for Bumpsted!" The vigorous nature of the squire's reply jarred his toe, which was instantly reflected in a wince of pain.

Prudence was all sympathy. With a new direction for her thoughts she stood, clutching the herbal to her well-corseted bosom. Thus prepared, she said, "The ointment of sage in goose grease doesn't seem to be easing your gout as well as I had hoped, so I shall prepare you an infusion of violets. When you feel more the thing, you might be inspired to view the world in a kindly light."

The garden looked much like a tapestry in greens and browns with a sparkling fountain splashing in the middle of it all. A closer look revealed rows of yellow dots where marigolds had been set out as border plantings along the garden plots. Iris's Great Aunt Prudence especially liked marigolds. As the danger of frost had passed in mid-May, the greenhouse was emptied of the annual plants that had been so carefully raised during the winter months.

In this same garden, at a comfortable distance from the house, was a place where the low-growing marigolds would complement the tall yellow gentians that would soon be in bloom. All the specimens in this particular section, even the roses and lilies, would be of some buttery shade when their petals unfolded. A growth of any other description was promptly removed. The reason was that these were Aunt Prudence's favorite plantings and had received her special protective care for years. And because it was Prudence's own spot in the garden, a stone bench had been placed so that she could sit and contemplate these golden botanical delights.

But the bench had another occupant today, the anticipated blossoms being incidental. The attraction was that this place was blessedly private—or as private as Iris was able to be, away from the attention of curious servants. And because this garden bench wasn't in London, it didn't matter that the round hat she had borrowed from Aunt Prudence, and her own blue mantle with bell sleeves, had been out of fashion for several years. Regard for fashion was often thus in the country, and Iris was comfortable that way.

In fact Iris had been quietly comfortable for the entire week she had been at Huntington Manor, though the household had been knocked askew by her unexpected appearance. Her angry father had stayed only long enough to deposit her in the front hall and have a brief, private conversation with her grandfather.

Yesterday at tea, however, Iris's quiet reserve had been replaced by a faint smile. She was still smiling today. To keep herself occupied while she sat smiling, she drew a bit of knotted string across the grass to entertain Pussycat, Aunt

Prudence's marmalade kitten. But when Pussy-cat quit the string to dash under her hooped skirt and attack the tassels hanging from her boot-tops, Iris pushed the little fellow out. Then she scooped him up and tucked him into the crook of her arm. Yawning, he closed his eyes. Iris continued to stroke the silky baby long after it slept, the lazy, repetitious movements and the warm sun lulling them both into a pleasantly drowsy state.

That's why she was so startled by the male voice that purred, "Good afternoon, Miss Huntington."

Recognition dawned in an instant, and Iris looked up into the smiling face of Elgin Farley. He tipped his bowler hat, and the breeze rumpled his hair. Rather nice blond hair, she thought. But not truly blond, actually. More of a light gingery brownish blond, but not nearly the color of the cat. And his eyes were almost the color of the vase on the chimney piece that came from—

"Miss Huntington?"

Iris returned a radiant smile. "Good afternoon, Mr. Farley. I'm afraid I didn't hear your approach, though I'm no less happy to see you."

Elgin jabbed a thumb toward the wide grassy path and said, "That green stuff could muffle an advancing regiment. And considering your hat, I doubt very much that you could have seen me coming, either. Am I interrupting anything?"

"Not at all." Iris moved over as far as she could to make room for him on the other end of the bench. Even so, her monstrous skirt simply didn't allow for additional seating. As it wouldn't

do for a gentleman to push the intrusive garment aside to sit down, Iris said, "Perhaps we
should walk." When Elgin extended a hand to
help her up, Iris put the limp kitten into it.

Thus unencumbered, she adjusted the big hat
with the sloping brim that shaded her face.
While retying the wide ribbons more securely beneath her chin, a string dropped down from the
front edge of the brim. It was the hold-down that
kept the hat from lifting off on a blustery day.
Iris patiently tucked the dangling string into the
band around the shallow crown.

Though he'd had years of experience with five
sisters, Elgin was unprepared for the cat that
was thrust upon him. It looked quite dead. Even
so, he thought it best to wait for Iris to finish
battening down her bonnet before expecting her
to explain what she intended to do with the unfortunate animal. It occurred to him that he
might be asked to dig the poor thing's final resting place somewhere nearby. He looked around
for a spade. But when Iris finished with her hat,
she only said thank you, took the little cat and
put it into her mantle pocket. Then, giving Elgin
a cherubic smile, she turned to lead him down
the garden path.

Elgin followed, though he did suffer a moment
of doubt about the disposition of the cat. He
quickly assured himself that all would soon be
revealed and absently wiped his impeccably
gloved hand on his new coat. The act would have
appalled his Savile Row tailor, who had declared
this particular suit of muted plaid fit for the
Prince of Wales.

They were strolling past stocks of unopened

lupines and mounds of peonies with fat buds when Iris said, "Mr. Farley, I'm especially glad that you've come to call today so that I may thank you for yesterday."

This wasn't what Elgin had expected to hear. Neither could he remember saying nor doing anything that required an expression of gratitude. He was finally compelled to say, "Do refresh my memory, Miss Huntington. What was it that happened yesterday?"

"Nothing. That's why I want to thank you. When we were introduced yesterday you didn't mention that we were already known to one another. If you had, Aunt Prudence would surely have asked how it had come about, and you know very well that it wouldn't have been the thing to tell her. Besides, I'm in enough trouble as it is."

Elgin stole a speculative glance at the lump in Iris's pocket. "This trouble," he began, trying to sound profoundly wise. "Has it anything to do with a rather small cat?"

Iris looked puzzled. "It hasn't anything to do with any cat of any size. The thing is, I've been banished from my father's house, but that's not exactly the problem. My father says I'm disgraced and hopes that he was able to remove me from Town before my maid found out and began to gossip."

"Would that explain the watchdog?"

Iris stopped and looked toward the house to see the woman to whom Elgin referred. Swathed in black bombazine and a heavy shawl, she was seated on a bamboo settee on the nearest edge of the terrace. There appeared to be knitting needles in her possession, along with a ball of red yarn that had rolled onto the flagstones. Iris sighed and started walking again. "That's Lydia, Aunt Pru's maid. I'm never left alone. Not now."

"I see." Elgin's tone was deceptively casual. "That seems to leave us wanting only the description of your latest folly, or is it too ghastly to be spoken of?"

"There was nothing ghastly about it," said Iris. "I simply refused to agree to become engaged to the Marquis of Bumpsted. When I finally expressed my dissatisfaction with the arrangement, my father escorted me here to repent. He said he has often repented of being at Huntington Manor." During this convoluted reply Iris conveniently left out any mention of what else she had done.

Elgin said, "Bumpsted has asked you to tie the knot then?"

"The marquis hasn't proposed, though we were introduced on one occasion late last summer." When Elgin's brows rose in question, Iris said, "It was when our carriages met ever so briefly in Hyde Park. The marquis had praised the fine day to my mother. Of course mother agreed enthusiastically, but she would have done so had the heavens been pelting us with fish. Afterwards I received quite a scold for having had so little to say on a subject as simple as the weather. Mother thought I had been terribly unaccommodating. Do you think I'm unaccommodating?"

There was a tactful pause while Elgin poked at a wayward twig with the toe of his shoe. After rolling the thing over a few times he said, "I haven't found you to be so; however, my experience is limited."

"Yes, I suppose it is," said Iris thoughtfully, having waited for Elgin to finish his twig rolling. Then they started walking again. "It was only last week that I was told I must accept the offer of marriage as soon as the marquis makes it. That's also when I learned that my training for the position of marchioness has been going on for over two years."

"You're wide of the mark there, my girl. Two years ago Bumpsted still had a wife."

"Yes, but two years ago it became known that she would never recover from the illness that consumed her. Ever the practical one, my mother reasoned that the poor woman couldn't survive more than a year and added another year for mourning. Then the widower would be free to marry again." Iris gave a resigned shrug. "His time is long since up."

Iris had been surprisingly matter-of-fact in the telling of it. That tone continued when she said, "I do think it was unfortunate that my parents embarked upon this venture without telling me of its direction. Their efforts began shortly after my introduction to the polite world. When the marquis withdrew from society due to his wife's illness, I was removed as well. At the time I didn't know why, of course. I was only told that I would benefit from a broader education before marriage, and I found nothing objectionable in that."

"Wouldn't surprise me to find more schemes afoot to attach Bumpsted," said Elgin. "Pots of money with the title, you know."

"So I've been told." Iris folded her arms around herself as though she had taken a chill. "The security and comfort that a fortune can provide is obvious. The title, however, is another matter. Even if the money pots were empty, there's a certain prestige that surrounds a title, and it rubs off on those close to it. That's very important to some people." Iris withdrew into silence. Elgin simply kept pace beside her.

Had she sniffled? Feeling awkward, he cleared his throat and studied the shrubbery. Birds hopped in and out of the branches. When the lack of conversation had gone on long enough, he said, "I had wondered about your meteoric appearance and disappearance from the ballrooms of London. If you had been out long enough, we would have been properly introduced by now." Then he shook off any sentimental inclinations and became more practical. "Perhaps you should reconsider those marriage plans. After all, you must marry one day, so why not marry Bumpsted?" Iris looked at him as though his mind had gone completely 'round the bend and left his empty head behind.

He noted her expression and held up a hand. "Don't be hasty. I'm aware that Bumpsted's children are all older than you are, but that needn't be a bad thing, you know. The man has learned patience by now. And he's an awfully decent chap, actually. Honest, loyal, that sort of thing."

As Iris didn't seem to be taking his advice seriously, Elgin said, "Consider how sensible it would be. I should think that the education you've been given has prepared you to enjoy the finer things in life. If you marry Bumpsted, you can have them."

Iris agreed that she had learned a great deal about fine things. There was the poetry she'd memorized, the great works of art she'd contemplated, and the music she had come to understand through diligent practice on the flute. To this she added:

"French. We mustn't forget that there has been intensive instruction in that language. You see, Father discovered that the marquis liked to have his late wife read the French classics to him as they were originally written. My accent, I'm told, is now quite up to the task, which pleases my parents to no end, as the marquis holds refinement in high regard."

"I'm glad to hear of your refined accomplishments, because you'll need every one of them to make up for what your brothers lack."

Iris gasped and spun to face Elgin. "Don't say you know about that awful affair in Venice!"

"That awful affair in Venice is common knowledge," he answered. "With the speed of a mail train the smallest details of their expedition have reached the furthermost billiard rooms in our island home."

"Even the part about the gondola?" It was almost a whisper.

"Especially that part," came the hushed reply. Iris cringed and started walking again. Elgin sauntered after her, saying, "I'm given to understand that this particular gondola had been a rather elegant craft, but quite beyond repair once the remains of it were raised. Something about fire damage, as I recall."

Iris regretfully confirmed that rumor and added, "It cost grandfather a tidy sum to keep my brothers out of jail, even though he sent the funds to pay the hotel for a new chandelier. Of course, those same brothers would insist that it wasn't so awfully bad because the girl they carried away was only someone from the hotel kitchen. I think it was all quite horrid."

"Does anyone know how this kitchen maid felt about being carried away? I should think that her thoughts on the matter might prove rather interesting."

"Oh, do be serious!" Iris said irritably. "This merely illustrates the fact that the male of the species can behave badly and escape with little more than a slap on the knuckles, while I, being female, must pay the piper for every note he plays. I'm punished for even the smallest transgression."

Elgin considered what that small transgression might have been. As to punishment, he wouldn't have been surprised if the Huntingtons had locked their lovely daughter in some remote castle tower to keep her safe from herself.

That same lovely lady then said, "I have a generous supply of brothers and sisters. If you recall, I'm the twelfth of fifteen." Elgin indicated that he did recall. Iris said, "With so many of us, plus nieces and nephews in and out, there isn't room to breathe, much less think. I suppose that's why I've usually given in to the plans of others—to maintain tranquillity."

Elgin made a muffled choking sound that might have begun as a laugh. Iris shot him a withering look that told him what she thought of such an emission. "I've given in most of the time, until last week," she told him primly. "And do keep in mind that I've never sent a gondola to Valhalla, or laid waste to a hotel with a Viking raid, yet there's such a fuss because I've objected the littlest bit to becoming engaged."

Very politely Elgin said, "You still haven't explained what you actually did that caused such an uproar."

"Well, I didn't kidnap anyone!"

"Iris, this is important!" Elgin locked his hands behind his back, which made him look wiser than he did with his hands jammed into his pockets. And, looking wise, his attention was on the ground upon which he trod. The sun had come out, but the grass was still damp, So were his square-toed shoes. Damp shoes were not conducive to frivolity. Perhaps that explained his mood. "Miss Huntington," he began again. "I must confess that our previous encounters have left a deep impression on me, for you are a remarkably pretty woman, but pretty isn't enough and you know it. If you hope to get on in the world, you simply must behave!"

Perhaps Iris's shoes were damp as well, because she wasn't the least bit amused when she said, "I am nearly twenty-one years of age and am still kept on a lead like a tame monkey! At the same age my brothers had considerable freedom. It isn't a just arrangement!"

"That doesn't change the rules, especially for a woman! I can do as I like and you can do as I like—or as your father likes until you take a husband. Then you must do as he likes. That's how it is. Even without this latest kick to your gallop, it will be extremely difficult for you to find a proper husband if he ever learns of the other things."

"Surely you wouldn't—"

"Of course I wouldn't! But whatever you've done to get yourself removed from London must stop. Bumpsted, or any other fellow, wants a pleasant, quiet home, with a docile, respectable wife. Someone cheerful and obedient."

"Like a spaniel or a poodle?"

They faced each other like gamecocks. Iris, standing tall, came up to the knot in Elgin's tie. He nearly shouted. "You must know—" Then lowered his voice to repeat, "You must know that the best chance you have is to hurry Bumpsted to the altar before he finds out what he's getting. If you do it fast enough, he won't know until it's too late that he'll never have a peaceful day for the rest of his life!"

Indignation gave a sapphire sparkle to the icy blue glare Iris gave Elgin, though she'd had to tilt her head back to see under the brim of her hat to do it. She said, "Mr. Farley. I do thank you for the depth of your concern; however, you forget that I don't want to be *married* to Bumpsted. I want to be *saved* from Bumpsted. My family is determined that I marry a title, because a title in the family would be so grand, and Bumpsted, the poor man, seems to be the only hope they have. It's only a matter of time before the subject of my engagement is resurrected, and I don't know if I can put it off again!" What had begun soft and low had ended considerably louder and an octave higher.

Wisdom having left him, Elgin jammed his

hands into his trouser pockets and said, "Give me one good reason why you won't marry Bumpsted!"

Iris glared at him. "He hasn't any teeth!"

"But only in front! He has more in back!"

"I don't give a hoot where he keeps them!"

Silence hung over them like a sword until Elgin said, "You're set on avoiding the whole thing, aren't you." It was a statement, not a question.

Iris started along the path again. "Your powers of perception exhaust me. I had supposed that by now you might have thought of something to effect a rescue."

Elgin looked stunned. "Me? Rescue you?"

"Of course!" said Iris, turning around to speak to the man who had ceased to move. "That's the way we've always done it. It's become a custom, a tradition, and that's so British."

"British my foot! How the devil was I supposed to know that I'd be expected to save you today? I'd had this notion that I might just pop by to see how well you were doing, how at one with the world. How foolish of me! Besides, there hasn't been a single occasion when you wouldn't have been able to get yourself out of whatever-it-was by yourself."

"Elgin, your face is frightfully red. I suppose I should have given you some time to consider this rescuing business, but it just occurred to me. By tomorrow you'll have thought of something wonderfully clever."

Elgin closed his eyes, but wishful thinking didn't help. When he looked at Iris again, he said, "This rescuing business really isn't in my line, but I'm sure you'll come up with something remarkable. I have tremendous confidence in your ability. Now we've got to call a halt to this before I get sent away in disgrace."

Iris began to object, but Elgin raised a splayed hand to cut her off. He said, "You're lovely. Truly you are. And charming, too—in your own peculiar way. You're even intelligent, and I shall remember you forever. Would be difficult to do otherwise, actually. Now I'll take my leave before anything else happens."

"Won't you even stay for tea?"

"Thank you, I think not."

Iris gave him a pinched smile. She had never seen his eyes such a stormy gray. For a moment he looked as though he might say something, but he just shook his head and strode away. All she could do was stare at his back until he disappeared through the arched doorway cut into the tall yew hedge. She felt strangely bereft. Had she truly expected Elgin to come to her rescue again? With a bit of elementary arithmetic and her fingers Iris decided that it had been thirteen or fourteen years since she had first met him. It had also been the first time he had saved her. She'd been stuck in a tree.

Though a child at the time, Iris's recollection of the event was dramatically clear. The problem that day hadn't been the tree, actually. It had been the wind. Well, the wind and her dress. A dress of a pink and white stripe muslin, with a full horse-hair petticoat and several flounced petticoats beneath. Young Iris had especially liked that dress because it seemed to float, and all that fine fabric was why it had blown so far out that the hem of it got snagged on a branch where she couldn't reach it. Even so she hadn't panicked. Just when she'd decided that she would have to unbutton her dress and wriggle out of it, Elgin Farley had come along and saved her. He just happened to be walking through the orchard with his friend Maxwell and a dog. That memory was especially vivid.

Now Iris found the incident rather amusing, though it hadn't been the least entertaining at the time. Fright would best describe the feeling she'd had when Elgin climbed to a higher branch in that tree. He'd hung by his knees to reach the place where her hem was caught. She had hardly been able to watch, afraid he would fall. She thought he had been positively heroic, like a knight. Knights, after all, did that sort of thing. They fought dragons and rescued ladies in distress.

For this boon Iris supposed she should have given Elgin a fine silk handkerchief to tie around his arm, if only she'd had a fine silk handkerchief, but all she'd had was a square of plain cotton stuff and had already wrapped a caterpillar in it. The thing was tucked inside the crown of her straw hat where it wouldn't get squashed. Because it was a yellow caterpillar, she thought Aunt Prudence might like it in her garden.

Today Iris's thoughts didn't linger on caterpillars, for Elgin Farley had gone and he might not come back. The garden lost its appeal. Slipping a hand into her pocket, she gently rubbed the kitten's head. It stirred, licked her fingers with a scratchy tongue, and went back to sleep as Iris

made her way into the house and up the back
stairs to her bedchamber.

"Yes, it's hot enough," said the squire to Prudence between sips of violet tea. Bits of crushed
petal still clung to the inside of the porcelain cup
that he put down on the small table beside his
elephant-tusk chair. He stared at his toe. Then
he stared at Prudence, who sat across from him
on an ordinary sofa.

Prudence smoothed her skirts and said,
"Obediah, whatever else has happened, you can
rest assured that Iris conducted herself quite
nicely in the garden with Mr. Farley, though he's
gone now. Gone to Westbourne Hall, that is. Not
back to Kent."

"Iris turned the villain out with her silence,
did she?"

"Heavens, no. Lydia assures me that their exchange was quite animated. She wasn't actually
able to hear what they discussed, of course, but
she thinks it included my dear Pussycat. Mr.
Farley seemed to like Pussycat and even held
him for a time, you see. I'm so pleased that—"

"You say Iris had been talkative in Farley's
company?"

"Oh, yes. I myself observed such intercourse
only yesterday at tea, though I can't say that it
was particularly interesting."

Huntington sat in somber contemplation, then
lifted his brows to make room for the new
thought that chugged around inside his head.
Looking terribly pleased with himself, he said,
"Iris talks to Farley, does she? Perhaps he's what
we need to get the girl out of herself, to give her

a bit of polish. She hadn't a word to say to Bumpsted the time they met. God knows he finds shy simpering females more annoying than lice."

"Obediah—"

"Prudence, for once you might be right. Iris has been kept so isolated that she could benefit from a bit of chaste male companionship—if Farley doesn't put her off. Odd-looking chap. Shaves off all his whiskers. Face as bare as a soup pot. Damned if I know why he does it. Heard that he once wore a red necktie in public! Strange man." After considering that strangeness for a moment, he went on to say, "If we continue to keep Iris cloistered, Bumpsted might think there's something wrong with her, and there is, but we don't have to tell him so."

"Obediah—"

"Farley is playing right into our hands, and he doesn't even know it!" chortled the squire. "I'll just let him think that he might get a peek at what's in those crates in the Egyptian Room if he hangs about the place long enough. While he hangs about, he'll visit with Iris, and Iris will get herself a bit of sophistication. Farley has outsmarted himself!"

Prudence opened her mouth again, but her brother frowned her down. "It's this simple. A man like Bumpsted wants dialogue with a woman, not a tongue-tied girl. Farley will remedy all that for us." Clasping his hands on top of his head, he said, "It's absolutely perfect!"

Folding her hands on her lap, Prudence thought it was absolutely ridiculous, though she liked Elgin Farley well enough. She said,

"Obediah, perhaps you've forgotten why Iris has been brought to us."

"Egad! Who could forget? Even without Farley on the prowl we'd have to take care not to let that London tempest out of the teapot. Iris would be ruined if so much as a drop of what happened leaked out."

At last Prudence agreed with her brother, for what the girl had done would spread like the plague and prove just as deadly. Their only hope was that no one would ever find out that dear Iris, *sweet* Iris, had shaved her legs.

· *Two* ·

Elgin retrieved the horse and trap he had driven over, impatient to be away from Huntington Manor and Iris. Taking his place at one side of the hard seat, he gave a snap to the reins and set the sleek animal off at a smart trot. Leaning back, he propped one foot on the dashboard and wondered how he could have become so entangled so often with Iris.

And he wondered why she wouldn't simply marry Bumpsted and be done with it. Then he wouldn't have to worry about her anymore. He was certain that someone so small and delicately made, someone like Iris, for instance, with all that raven hair curling around such a pale angelic little face, was just the thing to bring the old boy to his arthritic knees. After that she would be his problem, and he could bloody well worry about her! And when she looked up at him with those great pansy eyes, he would probably forget all about whatever escapade she'd been up to. But when Elgin tried to give a name to the shade of blue that best described those eyes, he became inexplicably irritable.

On the other hand Elgin had to congratulate

himself for having done such a remarkably good job of it yesterday at teatime. He hadn't even flinched when he'd walked into the green salon at Westbourne Hall and discovered Iris sitting there with a cup of Earl Grey in her dainty hand.

Much to his relief it had all gone remarkably well. After introductions were made there had been wonderfully insipid conversation. The most memorable thing he had said was how do you do. In fact the entire event was remarkable by its very nothingness. It was everything he could have hoped for. And he wondered why he hadn't just let it go at that, why he hadn't simply minded his own business and stayed away from Huntington Manor today.

During this clip-clopping reverie, Elgin came to understand that nothing had really changed since the first time he had set eyes on that provoking female, young as she was at the time. Back then he had simply addressed her as Iris, not Miss Huntington. And back then she had been perched in a tree. That was years ago on another occasion when he had been staying at Westbourne Hall. He and Max had taken off for the day with sandwiches in their pockets. He couldn't remember where they were going, but they were cutting through the orchard to get there. And if the dog hadn't stopped beneath a particular tree and started to bark, they would have missed Iris altogether.

Elgin remembered that Iris had looked as though she might cry. Not from fright, mind you, but from the humiliation of being found in a tree with her petticoats blowing about her knees. It hardly mattered. He and Maxwell were adventurous young men of fifteen summers or so. They had begun to shave and weren't impressed with a little girl who had yet to see her eighth birthday. They were interested in older girls. Older girls with their hair up and their bosoms out. Elgin still wondered why Iris had ever climbed that tree. It had been too early for apples. He should have asked her at the time.

For lack of a better way to sort things out Elgin called the discovery of Iris in the tree Surprise One. Setting his memory in gear, he called the business at the river the following summer Surprise Two. The problem about the horse was number three. No, the horse came later. The rabbit was three. The business with the horse happened long after that, in London. Damn lucky, that horse.

The numbering went on.

And Elgin wondered how Iris's escapades could have gone undetected by her family. Perhaps it was because there were so many chicks in the nest that any of them could toddle off for a while without being missed. There might have been an overburdened accounting system, or a shortage of governesses, yet it was beyond him to understand why someone wouldn't have noticed Iris's many absences. When his thoughts included Iris's brothers, he wondered if disruptive habits were hereditary. And he wondered what Iris was going to do with the dead cat in her pocket.

Then Elgin reminded himself that all those things were behind him and he meant to keep them there. Starting today he really would mind his own business. Adjusting his bowler with a firm tug to the brim, he took a deep invigorating breath and exhaled his frustrations. Picking up the pace of the flagging horse, he trotted off into a rosy future free of ridiculous interruptions. He felt as though his entire world had just taken a new and better turn. Life would be carefree and truly enjoyable again. He whistled a lively tune. He had everything under control. No more surprises.

It started to rain and he didn't have an umbrella.

It was still raining when Elgin came rolling into the yard at Westbourne Hall. Tom, the head groom, was standing at the open barn door. Elgin jumped down from the trap, though he wasn't in any particular hurry, being soaked through. The grim expression he wore might be blamed on his soggy condition. Tom left the shelter of the big building, and together the two old friends walked the wet horse inside. After unharnessing the animal, they began to rub it down with towels.

Elgin said, "How is your father? I heard you've been to Nailsworth because he had taken ill."

"Nothing to fear now the fever's passed," replied Tom. Then he grinned and said, "I heard you went calling on Miss Huntington today. It be safe enough to talk—no one be here but us."

"It was merely a polite call on the family," insisted Elgin, taking more interest than ever in drying his side of the horse.

"And how be the family?"

"Miss Huntington and her aunt are well. The squire was nowhere about, though I caught a glimpse of Chumbly when I approached the house. The old sot looked like he'd slept in his clothes, with his belly hanging over his belt at a rakish angle. It's a wonder the squire doesn't send him packing."

"You know how it be with family, though I doubt the squire cares to have such for a brother-in-law."

The horse flicked its ears, and Elgin stopped to slide his hand over the place he had just rubbed. Deciding that there was nothing amiss, he went on to say, "Chumbly has taken on a rather yellowish tint. Drink is killing his liver, I should think."

Tom said, "I heard Miss Huntington's father brought her to the Manor and left her there like a sack of corn. Heard he was angry. Heard she was as smug as the creamery cat."

"You hear a lot."

"Didn't hear enough. Did the lady's arrival have anything to do with you?"

"Why in hell should it have anything to do with me?"

Tom grinned. "Because sooner or later, when no one else be near to hear, I know you'll ask what be happening over at the Manor. Some roundabout mention of Miss Huntington always creeps up. When are you going to be courting her proper?"

"I hardly know Iris."

"Oh ho! Now it be Iris, not Miss Huntington," said Tom, leaning against the horse's rump. "I know the look of a man after a maid. He's like a cow what stepped on its own teat. Had the look myself when I was sweethearting my Bess."

"This," snapped Elgin, cocking a thumb at his own face, "is not the look of a besotted fool! This," he repeated more insistently, "is the face of a man who, in less than an hour, has been driven to the brink of madness by the most provoking female that has ever been born!"

From the other side of the horse Tom laughed and said, "Felt the same way till I talked Bess 'round to meeting me in the hayloft for a little canoodling."

Elgin gave a snort of disgust, slammed the towel into the trap, and stalked off through the rain and mud toward the house.

Evening meals at Westbourne Hall were usually a quiet affair. Unlike most evenings, Elgin now stuffed himself with porcine enthusiasm. Uncle Neville—that is, Maxwell's Uncle Neville, sixth Duke of Westbourne and breeder of dogs—sipped his asparagus soup with proper regard to form. Elgin all but inhaled his own soup. Then brill with lobster sauce was shoveled in by the forkload. One might have suspected that the fear of famine had driven Elgin to become a determined trencherman.

The truth was that such ravenous behavior rendered him exempt from conversation. When his mouth was full of brill, or the lamb cutlets that followed, he couldn't very well be expected to say anything, and he really didn't want to say anything more about his visit to Huntington Manor. He had already said that he paid his respects to both Mrs. Chumbly and Miss Huntington, found them in agreeable health, and departed soon after. One would have supposed that such an accounting would have been sufficient for anyone.

Yet Glori would insist upon knowing more. Coming directly to the point, she turned to Elgin and said, "Why, when you were *invited* for tea at the Manor, didn't you *stay* for tea at the Manor?"

"Because I didn't want to be caught in the rain," replied Elgin. "As it was I didn't leave soon enough. Got wet on the way back, and a chilly business it was, I can tell you that."

"Is that all? You left because you didn't want to get wet?"

"That's the whole of it," Elgin assured her. He thought it sounded like a good enough reason. What fault could anyone possibly find in wanting to stay dry? He took a serving of boiled capon and set upon it with remarkable concentration.

"I'm so pleased to know that the weather was your only motive for such an abrupt departure," said Glori. "That being the case, you'll surely go with me tomorrow when I call on Iris. Prudence Chumbly hopes you'll give us all the news from London."

Elgin said, "Be a dear and extend my regrets, won't you? You see, I really don't know what's going on in London just now." He glanced at the place where his friend Max would have been sitting had he been home. Max would have helped him out of this social bind without offending. They had always helped each other, but Max was away on business. Elgin looked hopefully to Max's aunt for a means of escape.

The lady only shook her head and said, "Pups." It had taken but one word to explain that she would be spending her time in the barn with the new litter of sheepdogs. "Ah, yes, the pups," said Elgin, scrambling for a new topic. "Jolly little things, what? Perhaps I should have another look at them myself. I have a way with dogs, you know. In fact I'll help you with them tomorrow." The aunt lifted one quizzical eyebrow before returning to her meal. Even the uncle paused with glass in hand. The dinner chitchat went on without Elgin. To make sure it stayed that way, he kept his mouth busy with roast duckling.

The pang of guilt struck between the duckling and the gooseberry tart, when Elgin realized that he would be letting his best friend down. His old chum Max rarely asked favors, but before leaving for Scotland, he had asked that Elgin stay on at the Hall for a while to keep an eye on Glori. Make certain she wasn't lonely and all that. But now, when an opportunity presented itself for the girl to become better acquainted with a neighbor of her own age, Elgin hadn't felt inclined to escort her there.

Then it occurred to Elgin that if Iris spent her idle hours with Glori, there wouldn't be any more problems. Together the two of them would entertain themselves with the sorts of things that proper young ladies do. It was all so simple! Elgin brightened, for it was plain to see that everything would fall into place after all.

Using his fork to run a bit of pastry around the plate for a few laps, Elgin said, "Glori, perhaps I could take you to the Manor tomorrow. Max wanted you to become acquainted in the neighborhood, and befriending Miss Huntington would be just what he had hoped for."

Glori looked pleased and said, "Thank you. The day will be much nicer for your company."

Elgin smiled back. At least he hoped it was a smile. He went to work on his pudding.

Glori studied him, plagued by the same niggling thoughts she'd had the day before. Odd as it was she was certain that there had been *something* going on between Elgin and Iris that she didn't quite understand. It was like a current in the air. Or perhaps it was the way they tried not to get caught looking at each other. The newness of their association meant nothing to Glori. She was certain that whatever it was should be allowed, nay, encouraged, to develop into whatever it would.

That night Elgin stood at the window at the west end of the passage that overlooked Huntington Manor. He told himself that he just wanted to look outside. It was a good thing there was no one around to ask him what he expected to see. It was awfully dark. Even so he could distinguish the outline of trees against a midnight sky, along with part of the roof and a few chimneys of the Manor. Chimneys were solid, dependable things. Tomorrow beneath those very dependable chimneys he would see that Iris and Glori got better acquainted over tea and cakes. Then he would take himself off before anyone else besides Tom got strange ideas about him courting Iris.

Tom had got it all wrong. Elgin was certain that he hadn't asked *that* many questions about Iris. He admitted that he might have asked Tom *something* about her now and then, but surely not often enough to give anyone the impression that he had a particular interest in her. At least not in the way Tom thought of it. Elgin had never entertained the least notion of enticing Iris into a hayloft for a bit of canoodling. Furthermore, he would do great bodily harm to anyone who suggested such a thing to her.

Then Elgin wondered if Max thought he had ever displayed any particular interest in Iris. He didn't think so. Max never would have let it rest had he suspected anything. Besides, Max knew exactly how he felt about the wedded state. Max had been a guest at his home when they were boys. That visit had gone nicely until the third day, when his parents got into a battle during breakfast. His sisters hurriedly excused themselves and left the table. The footman walked quietly from the room taking a Sevres urn with him for safekeeping. A maid followed with a fine crystal vase filled with flowers.

Elgin hadn't wasted time on a polite departure. He took hold of Maxwell's sleeve and pulled him outside. The boys ran until they flopped down on the straw in the back stall of the stable. When he'd caught his breath, Elgin had said, "I'm awfully sorry this happened when you were here. My parents are usually better behaved when we have company."

"Do they do this sort of thing very often?" Maxwell had asked.

"I'm afraid so. Rather frightening, isn't it."

"Yes," said Maxwell. Then he added, "I know they must make you feel like a fool, but you mustn't get yourself in a pother over it. I expect I shall have to explain one of my cousins to you one day. He's growing into a rather nasty little boy, but I can't cuff him because he's smaller than I am, so I'm afraid that he'll get worse and worse. Between your parents and my cousin, I should think we're about even."

"How awful."

"How true."

After a long talk about cousins in general, the two boys left the stable for the kitchen. From long experience Cook knew to have another breakfast waiting for the children when they finally came out of hiding. Even now, so many years later, the memory of that day sent a shudder through Elgin.

The more he remembered caused him to remember even more, and he was glad that Maxwell hadn't been there on another morning when his parents had been trading insults. His father had turned to him and said, "Elgin, if you would be a happy man, take a mistress instead of a wife. You can just pay her off and get rid of her when she gets to be a pain in the arse." The remark was followed by a well-aimed plate of eggs from his mother's end of the table. Elgin and his sisters fled the room in their usual style.

At the time Elgin hadn't known what a mistress was. Now that he knew he still couldn't imagine what sort he would want if he ever went about getting one. Setting up a woman in a flat somewhere had never really appealed to him. He certainly couldn't imagine anyone like Iris as his mistress, but that was another matter entirely. A mistress would be much different than Iris. More alluring. More fashionable. And she wouldn't keep dead cats in her pockets.

Prior to this jaunt into the Cotswolds, it had been months since Elgin had seen Iris. Peaceful months. Months in which he had lived the life of a gentleman farmer, tending his land and livestock. But such unadulterated contentment was good for only so long and he had taken himself to London. That's when he met Iris again under rather maddening circumstances.

He'd been in his lodgings for only a few days when the urchin arrived at his door. He looked like Oliver Twist, holing up a screw of paper in a grubby hand. It was a penciled message on the back of an illegible shopping list. It read:

> EF,
> Please come at once to the library with the lion out front. I'll be inside.

There hadn't been a signature to identify the sender, but Elgin expected it would be Iris. It filled him with a curious dread, for he didn't want to get tangled up in whatever she was doing. Yet he couldn't ignore her call for assistance in the event that it might be something of a serious nature. Unfortunately he didn't know where to find the library with the lion that had Iris inside it. Problems. Fortunately the ragged child had stayed around in hopes of earning another coin by carrying the answering message. Elgin hired him as a guide. Before they reached their destination, however, Elgin's curious dread had become grim concern. Grim concern turned into anger. The things that could befall a naive, unattended female adrift in a public place were terrible to contemplate. Among other things it wasn't unheard of for white slavers to lure young women away and sell them into brothels—domestic or foreign.

When the cab made its final stop, Elgin's scruffy young guide hopped off the back step and opened the door—the driver hadn't allowed him to ride inside lest he leave any vermin behind. After a flourishing bow in Elgin's direction, the boy crinkled his face into a conspiratorial wink and nodded toward what could be a marble lion. Elgin had seen the statue before, but he'd always thought it was a dog.

A diminutive female was beside the beast, not inside it, whatever it was. She wore a dark mackintosh for protection from the cold and a scarf that shielded her face from wind and recognition. With the child at his heels Elgin went up the steps two at a time and boldly approached the bundled form. He tapped his walking stick on the stones, and the bundle turned around. It was indeed Iris.

Elgin paid off the child and sent him away. Then he tipped his hat and said, "Good day, *Miss Smith*. It is *Miss Smith*, is it not?" Iris wisely said that it was. He said, "Right this way, *Miss Smith*," and hustled her down the steps and into another cab. After telling the driver to take a turn around the park, Elgin climbed in and pushed aside the hooped skirt that crowded him. The door threatened to destruct when he slammed it. With the same consideration he yanked the shades closed. When he leaned back in the seat Iris's skirt bounced up and all but covered them both. She could hardly be seen behind the thing. Rising above it all, Elgin stared straight at the hair oil stains on the opposite wall and said, "Kindly tell me what in hell you're up to this time, *Miss Smith!*"

From behind the mountain of spring steel and fabric, Iris said, "I only wanted to spend a few hours at the library, but the time just seemed to slip away. Before I knew it the afternoon quiet time at home was over."

"Why the devil should anyone care if you've been to the library?" said Elgin irritably. "And if you got there in a cab, you could jolly well get back home the same way, though it is too bad of you not to have your maid along. Not the thing at all, really. You must know that it would have been more expeditious to have taken a cab home than send that boy to look for me to take you home."

Slowly, sadly, Iris shook her head and fiddled with the tassel on her handbag. "I'm afraid it's not quite as simple as that. The wicked truth is that I've been going to the library whenever I can slip away to read from the Waverley Novels. Father has forbidden them. I shudder to think what will happen if he decides to inquire too closely into what I've been doing." Then she looked imploringly at Elgin and said, "I had hoped you would help me get back into the house without being found out. You see, everyone thinks I'm in my bedchamber to rest and read inspirationally uplifting good works."

There was a moment of charged silence. Elgin's expression remained inscrutable. Then, with the head of his walking stick, he rapped on the ceiling of the cab. A little hatch opened above his head. The cabby called down, "Wha'll it be, Guv?" and Elgin had said, "Back to the library!"

The cabby turned around, nosing the horse through traffic. Iris sat stiffly, with her hands clenched tightly. Elgin lifted the edge of the window shade, interested, it would seem, in the traffic. When they finally neared the library, he broke the uneasy silence to ask, "What is your cook's name?"

"Please?"

"Come now, *Miss Smith*, you must have a cook, she must have a name, and I should think you would know what it is."

Sounding every bit as bewildered as she looked, Iris hesitantly said, "Haggerty. Her name is Mrs. Haggerty."

Elgin nodded. Suddenly he ordered the cab to stop, and he jumped out, calling to a familiar ragged child. The meeting was brief. With her view restricted by the window shade, Iris lost sight of the boy. Elgin returned to the cab. Pushing his way past her hooped skirt to regain his seat, he muttered. "Have your latchkey ready."

Iris got her latchkey ready. Neither of her parents knew she had one.

When they reached the corner nearest the Huntington residence, Elgin wrapped his cane against the back wall of the vehicle. With the lightness of a cat the ragged boy dropped from his hindmost perch to the pavement. Making his way directly to an impressive Georgian house with the number eight over the door, he disappeared down the area stairs.

Moments later the cab pulled up at the same address. A great deal of shouting spewed from the stairwell into which the boy had descended. Elgin pushed the cab's door open and said, "Hurry!"

Iris stepped out as quickly as she could. Elgin squashed the bulk of her monstrous skirt through the narrow doorway, then leaned back into the shadows in hopes that he hadn't been seen. Iris hurried up the front steps, opened the door, and slipped from his sight.

Now, all these months later, Elgin still wondered what had happened when Iris got inside the house that day. It was something he might have asked her this afternoon if other things hadn't distracted him. He might ask her tomorrow. Now he needed bicarbonate of soda for his suffering stomach.

That same night dinner conversation had been uncomfortable for Iris. Her aunt would insist upon asking questions about Elgin's visit with her in the garden. Iris felt like a tightrope dancer doing a balancing act. She had to take care lest she say any more about Elgin than she could have reasonably learned during a stroll among the marigolds. She scrambled through her brain for something she could say. Some trite thing that strangers might talk about.

Prudence said, "Iris dear, surely there must be a little something you can say about a gentleman with whom you have visited so recently."

"Cats," said Iris dear. "We spoke of cats. I believe Mr. Farley has some fine specimens in Kent. That's where his home is."

Prudence smiled, for she was well disposed toward anyone who liked cats.

The squire looked up from his plate and said, "Cats? Did Farley say anything about *old* cats?"

"No, Grandfather. Nothing."

He said, "A likely story."

Iris didn't think the comment required a reply. The squire was thinking of the mummified cat that lay in one of the crates in the Egyptian Room. He was certain that Elgin would never have talked about cats in the first place if he hadn't known there was a really old one nearby in a crate. As soon as the meal was over, the squire went on an inspection tour, paying special attention to the crates containing mummies. More precisely, the crate containing the mummy of a cat.

It was well after ten o'clock when Iris finally climbed into bed with a hodgepodge of thoughts to keep her company. She hadn't expected Elgin to refuse when she asked him to save her from the threat of marriage. It had left her rather numb. Random recollections of the man continued to rattle at the windows and blow down the chimney, but she fell asleep anyway.

· Three ·

It was the perfect morning for Iris to continue the work on her grandfather's accumulation of artifacts. Being helpful, however, wasn't the only thing on her mind. She hoped that by staying busy she could keep from thinking about the unfortunate circumstances under which she and Elgin had parted company the day before.

Assisting her grandfather with his treasures was a task Iris had performed since she had been able to pen an accurate line. For as long as she could remember she'd been fascinated by his stories of ancient civilizations. She acquired even more knowledge on her own.

There had been hours spent at the British Museum. Hours with booklets in hand that explained about the objects she was looking at. She had lingered before a display of ancient glass until her legs ached, but she could now appreciate the similarities in pieces from ancient Greece and Mesopotamia. Of late she had been developing a means to identify glassware that had come from the same factories, though they were made by different workmen.

Iris was certain that if her grandfather had

been aware of the purpose of her museum excursions, he wouldn't have objected in the least. Her parents, however, were of a different mind. It would have been unwise to let them know that she had gone there for anything that suggested study, unless it was to look at watercolor paintings, or the more respectable works by the old masters.

Of course there actually were times when Iris did study such things, but not with any desire to imitate the strokes that produced restful pastoral scenes or the sense of life and movement in a painted hand. She was more interested in how a smooth flat piece of paper could show depth and texture. She wanted to see how pen and brush could best create an amphora, or embossed beads, and how highlights, shading, and shadows could lift the objects she drew from the page. There were the correct mixes of pigments that could change the drawing of a pot from glass to gold to earthenware.

Yet care had to be taken to disguise these study trips, for a scholarly young woman was of no use whatsoever as far as most of society was concerned. It was fashionable to recognize a particular piece of artwork by title, know who the artist was, and perhaps even know its age and value. This was refined knowledge. But to pursue such knowledge in depth was considered rather vulgar for a female.

To avoid her parents' censure Iris decided to go to the museum during times of inclement weather. Not for study, of course not, but to take her exercise along the vast marble aisles protected from the elements. It was ideal. As the

maid she had chosen to accompany her was
happy to have a few hours on a bench to read
magazines—magazines with stories of romance
and intrigue to be continued in the next issue—
she wasn't likely to tell anyone what Iris had
been doing.

Now, however, the British Museum seemed
long ago and far away. Iris was seated at her
grandfather's worktable to take up her drawing
where she had left off a few days before. Unfortunately the object of immediate interest was nowhere to be seen. The monumental inkstand was
still there—Iris lifted the lid of the inkwell and
saw that there was still India ink inside. She got
some on her fingers.

The inkstand was an elaborate affair of cast
brass, having a small antlered stag's head as the
lid of the inkwell. One of the antlers was bent,
where a piece of it had broken off a long time
ago. Around the base of the stand were game
birds and rabbits laid in rows that formed ridges
to hold pens. There was only one pen there now,
the one Iris used the most. It had her tooth
marks on the end. More steel-tipped pens stood
in a cracked Wedgwood pot. She counted four.
There were four a few days ago, too. Her paper
appeared to be untouched. Only one thing was
missing.

Iris opened the big ledger to the last entry,
number 783-66. Beside the number her grandfather had written a detailed account of an unguent bottle of dark greenish-blue glass, with an
applied rim-disk around a narrow mouth. It
measured 14.2 centimeters in height and was
classified *alabastron*, telling one that it was

more or less cylindrical, with a rounded bottom that would have been set into a metal or wooden stand. Iris thought it looked a great deal like a pestle used to grind spice in a mortar. But unlike a pestle it was equipped with two applied handles just below the shoulder. There was a rough sketch at the bottom of the page that showed how small the handles were.

The piece had been core-formed in Rhodes during the sixth century B.C. Iris's grandfather had told her that core-forming was apparently accomplished by wrapping strands of molten glass around a core—perhaps a metal rod—then rolled until the glass was the right shape. However it was done, it was a common method of making glass vessels before glassblowing was developed. This particular unguent bottle was further described as well preserved, having some luster, slight pitting, and now Iris couldn't find the blasted thing to make the necessary drawing. How annoying!

During the ensuing search that Iris made through drawers and shelves, Maggie arrived—Maggie being the only maid allowed to clean any of the collection rooms and the things in them. She curtsied to Iris and quietly bent to her task. Iris smiled at her and quietly bent over some boxes on the floor to continue her search for the unguent bottle.

All too soon both women were distracted from their respective jobs by the arrival of Prudence's husband. It became obvious that Chumbly didn't know that Iris was crouching on the floor among the boxes. Otherwise he wouldn't have approached the maid as he did, creeping up from behind to grab her backside as she leaned over to brush some bits of packing material into a dustpan. Maggie gave a startled gasp and turned on Chumbly, whacking him several good ones with the weapon in hand. He backed out of range offering a colorful string of curses, which suggested that her parents had been unwed dogs. Then he promised to have her sacked.

That's when Chumbly noticed Iris standing there. She said, "Good afternoon, Uncle. Am I interrupting anything?"

"Of course not!" he snapped, forcing his sagging body to attention as he pushed back a few strands of thinning hair. "I simply mistook this *person* for my wife."

"I see," came Iris's dry reply.

Hand to his stinging forehead, Chumbly shot her a venomous look and left the room.

Maggie stared after him and said, "His eyes must be going weak. He mistook me for his wife twice before." Without issuing a single word of reproof, Iris went back to her boxes and crates. Maggie started her sweeping all over again.

Iris's thoughts turned to her Aunt Prudence, wondering how that gentle lady had been able to tolerate such a lecherous fool of a husband all these years. But she knew the answer. Prudence had no choice unless she went into hiding. A divorce was now available though the courts without having to petition Parliament, but they were difficult to come by.

Anyone who had read the newspapers during the past nine years knew that it was possible for a man to divorce his wife if she committed adultery. But adultery was not cause enough for a woman to divorce her husband. Men, after all, did that sort of thing. It was the nature of the beast.

A woman must show proof that her husband had committed bigamous adultery, or incestuous adultery, bestiality, sodomy, or an assortment of perversions that were jolly well impossible to prove with witnesses. Even ill use at the hands of her husband was not necessarily sufficient grounds for divorce. A man, after all, had every right to chastise his wife.

Iris looked up when Maggie left the room. The woman still had a firm grip on the long-handled brush she had used on Chumbly. Iris remembered when her grandfather had wanted to throw Chumbly out, but Chumbly said he would make Prudence go with him. He had the legal right to do it. As her grandfather didn't want his sister living in poverty with a drunk, Chumbly stayed. He gloated over the victory and drank even more.

Iris shifted about, a thoughtless gesture to shake off the unpleasant feeling that Chumbly invariably left behind. And she gave up the search for the bottle, assuming that her grandfather must have removed that elusive artifact and forgotten to tell her.

What Iris picked up next was a glass kohl bottle with a stopper. The stopper was a snug fit and needed a twist and tug to pull it out. Some of the black stuff was still inside. It had soot for the base of a cosmetic that had been used to outline the eyes of a long-forgotten woman. Iris rubbed a bit of it between her fingers. Powdery

slick, hard to get off. Some of it got on her
smock, but trying to brush it off only smeared it.

The case clock at the end of the hall struck one
resonant bong. Iris put her work aside, opened
the window, took a deep breath. Maggie brought
in lunch on a tray; Iris hurried through it. After
consulting the gold watch pinned to the bodice of
her dress, she walked about the room inspecting
the glass collection. She closed the window. She
rearranged the glass. She looked at her watch
again. It was time, or nearly almost time, and
that was close enough.

Impatient or not, it would be reasonable for
Iris to wait inside for the guests her Aunt Pru
said were coming. Inside is where the tea table
was. Inside it was dry. Inside the chairs were
soft. Iris went outside. Outside was the better
place to talk to Elgin if he should come. So once
again Iris was sitting on Aunt Prudence's stone
bench, getting colder by the minute. She'd been
watching a bird turn over dried leaves looking
for bugs. Finding nothing, it flew away. It was
the first time Iris had envied a bird.

Hearing voices, she looked up. Elgin, as elegant as ever, was there on the terrace. Tall and
lovely Glorianna Rutherford was at his side. Iris
thought Glori looked like someone from a face
cream advertisement and became uncomfortably
aware that her own cheeks must be apple red
with a matching nose. Though the smiles were
bright, the greetings held a thread of tension.
"So pleased to see you" and "Fine day" tripped
over "How good of you to come."

Iris could see that Elgin didn't look the least
bit pleased to be there. Before the situation be-

came too terribly clumsy, she said, "Shall we walk for a while? Aunt Pru will be happy to know that I've shown you how well her clematis is doing." Without waiting for a response, she took each of her friends by an arm and started them moving.

For Elgin, or any other man, such a walk was usually a threat to his shins, for each step sent the steel bands of a hooped skirt digging into his leg. But Elgin had walked with other ladies on other days and knew the risks. That's why, when dressing for this call, he had buttoned on leather shooting gaiters beneath his trousers. This precaution made it possible for him to encourage a friendship between these two females without endangering his person. It was exactly what he had been hoping for, the reason he had come. If he did it properly, he would no longer need to be Iris Huntington's keeper.

With Glori for company Iris really would be too busy to get into trouble. And though he thought her more daring than wise, Iris was good-natured and bright, with cheeks like roses. She was delightful, actually, now that she was as good as someone else's problem.

Elgin believed that all he had to do today was look at a few flowers. He'd say something about how striking they were and what fine color they had, then return to Westbourne Hall while the ladies had their tea. They stopped walking. Elgin gazed dutifully at the garden before him. There was an area of freshly turned earth, and he thought of the dead cat that Iris had put in her pocket the day before. But she hadn't mentioned it, so he wouldn't mention it, either. He respectfully removed his hat and said, "I say, these clematis are quite striking and have fine color."

"Those are dandelions."

"Oh, so they are. Amazing little things." Then he looked around and asked, "What's become of Glori?"

"She's gone back to the house to see Aunt Pru about a treatment for dandruff on sheepdogs. I told her that she would have to hurry or Pru would be in for her afternoon rest. Can it be that you truly didn't notice when she left?"

"Ahh, not actually, no. I was thinking about the garden and all that." Elgin's voice held a touch of regret, for he knew that he was stuck where he was, having to do the polite for a while longer because he couldn't very well leave Iris so soon after Glori had.

Iris said, "Have you thought of any way to save me from the Marquis of Bumpsted?"

Elgin clapped his hat back on his head and said, "Iris, that's not why I came here today. I came because I promised Max that I'd see Glori situated in the neighborhood. Having the two of you become friends seemed like a good way to discharge the favor he asked of me." When he saw Iris's mouth pinch into a thin line, he became rather irritated himself. "Iris, you don't need to be saved from Bumpsted. He's a decent chap, actually. Well thought of. When you're married you'll have plenty of money to do whatever you want to do and a grand house to keep you busy. Then you wouldn't want to be saved."

"Aunt Pru says that when I have babies I'll be too busy to—"

"When you have *what*?"

"Babies. Tiny little people. Rather like kittens, only different."

"I know what they are," said Elgin. "I just wanted to know what makes you think you'll have any. Surely Bumpsted, after raising so many children, is ready for the quiet life."

"It would seem that he isn't planning any such thing. My father, who keeps his ear open for anything concerning that gentleman, has heard it said that he is looking forward to enlarging his family."

Elgin jammed his hands into his pockets and frowned. The very thought of Bumpsted doing anything with Iris to make a baby was beyond indecent. He had assumed that when Iris finally married the fellow, they would have separate bedrooms—given Bumpsted's age and all that. Iris would be like the old man's granddaughter, reading to him in the evenings by the fireside, fetching his slippers, his shawl. Perhaps he would pat her hand in a fatherly way before nodding off to sleep in his chair. But a baby! Surely they wouldn't do *that*!

Elgin was more than a little uncomfortable when he said, "Iris, do you want to have children when you marry?"

"Yes."

"Why?"

"Well, kittens soon grow up and all you have are cats. And cats are nice, of course, but—"

Elgin looked to heaven and said, "This business of producing tiny people is more complicated than you might think. There is a great

deal of participation involved. I don't think it's
something you should do."

"Don't you like babies?"

"They're capital things, I suppose, but not now.
That is, not for you and Bumpsted." Considering
how that must have sounded, he tried again.
"The thing is, I don't think you would take to it.
I don't think you know what you're about. Perhaps you should talk to someone before you . . .
well, *do* anything."

The violent clanging of the fire bell stopped
Elgin mid-thought and sent terrified birds ex-
ploding from the belfry windows. Elgin ran toward the open doors of the carriage house along
with a dozen other men, all shouting directions.
With much straining and puffing they rolled out
the fire engine on wheels that groaned from lack
of greasing. More men hurried to join them, and
as a body they moved the big wagon along, pulling it by the shaft, pushing it from behind. Some
of the women and older children ran for buckets,
others formed a line from the horse trough to the
fire engine. The abrasive squawking of the barn-
yard pump added to the din. Dogs barked. Little
children cried.

Huntington Manor looked as though rats were
leaving a sinking house. With cries of "Look out
below!" mattresses and rugs were shoved out
open windows. Servants threw out bedding and
clothing by the armload. Tapestries and silver
followed. Sofas and tables were carried out and
put on the lawn. The pot boy held the back hall
door open. Waving a cloth, the boot black led the
way, but he was running backward and tripped
into the shrubbery.

Before they reached the house the firefighters did a great deal of yelling and slipping about on the damp grass. When they got to the back door, the women began handing up bucket after bucket of water so that the men could fill the big tank of the fire engine. One team of men held on to the long pumping bars at the sides of the machine, waiting for the signal to send the water out. The other men took hold of the brass nozzle and greased leather hose as it came off the reel, then dashed inside the house with it.

The first ones in went tail over teakettle on the hall rug. More men piled on top of them, resulting in a loud and profane struggle to get free. Any trace of Elgin's Bond Street cologne was lost in the sweaty scramble. Swinging his arms in an embarrassingly vigorous manner, the butler directed the men to the main stairway. With shouts of "More hose! More hose!" they raced up to the second floor. The floor where the Egyptian treasures were kept. The ones that would burn so easily. When the leaders with the hose reached the landing, a whistle blast stopped them.

"Fifteen minutes and twenty-two seconds!" the squire called out from his position at the railing. "We'll do better next time. Tonight there will be beer for you all!" Giving them a dismissive nod, he turned away.

Still breathing hard, the men started down the stairs with the hose. Before the squire could get very far away, Elgin said, "What the devil was that about?"

The squire stopped, pinned Elgin with a

beetley eye, and said, "That was a fire drill. Didn't you learn anything in school?"

"Do you do this sort of thing very often?"

"I intend to!"

With an effort at dignity Squire Huntington hobbled into the nearest room and slammed the door on anything else Elgin Farley might have to say. As far as he was concerned, Elgin had once again proved himself a spy. A dangerous one. Because the squire had sent word to all the neighbors to tell them there would be a fire drill today, he was convinced that Elgin had only taken hold of the fire hose as a means of getting inside the house, upstairs, and into the Egyptian Room! And he had acted as though he hadn't even known about the fire drill. There came a crowing cackle from behind a door as the master of the house congratulated himself on the manner in which he had outsmarted the devious intruder.

Iris and Glori were trying to stay out of the way in the downstairs hall. The shouting and running had ceased, leaving only the slow shuffle of booted feet and the scrape and thump of the hose as it was dragged downstairs and out the door like some great exhausted reptile. Right behind the beast came Elgin. He was a remarkable sight even without the bruise on his cheekbone.

His coat had been split along the back seam and at one elbow. Hair that was once neatly combed now stuck up and hung down. No one knew what had become of his hat, and his kid gloves were ruined, his trousers stained green. Then there was the grease from the fire hose that stuck to everything, and everything stuck to

the grease. Yet without that substance rubbed
into it, the leather hose would crack. It was no
surprise that Elgin was dirt all over. So was the
hall and two flights of stairs. And the carpet on
the stairs.

Iris thought it was a shame about the carpet,
for it had come all the way from India, but she
thought Elgin looked particularly impressive.
There had been something poking at the back of
her brain that caused her to wonder if he might
be overly concerned with his clothes and appearance. She had hoped he wasn't the kind of man
her Aunt Prudence called a *dandy*. Today's
events proved that worry groundless. Elgin's response to an emergency had been to do whatever
must be done, his clothes be damned. And
damned they were. But fast on the heels of that
revelation came Iris's understanding of Elgin's
deplorable condition.

Overcome by remorse, hands tightly clasped,
she said, "I'm so terribly sorry about your
clothes, Mr. Farley. If you'll wait I'll have them
brushed and mended—or something."

Elgin looked into Iris's troubled face and saw
just how much she wanted to make things right.
He'd seen that expression once before, when she
was stuck in a tree, about to cry. She really was
a sweet little thing, but just being near her provided one with more excitement than one de-
served. In addition to everything else than had
gone amiss, the smell of burnt bread made its
way up from the kitchen. Elgin didn't laugh at
the chaos, though he smiled. He looked at his
clothes—they did need attention. Then he looked
at the stairway that led all the way up to the

second-floor room where Squire Huntington cackled behind a closed door.

Shaking his head, Elgin said, "I think not, Miss Huntington, though I do thank you for your kind thoughts. I think it best that I return to the Hall for massive repairs."

Seeing how upset Iris was, Glori took her hands and said, "Don't fret so! We'll return tomorrow, won't we, Elgin, and we'll continue the visit that was so dramatically interrupted today. We'll still have sunshine and flowers, and we can still have tea and cakes." Glori looked like the picture of innocence when she glanced up at Elgin. He would have looked like the greatest of brutes if he contradicted her. It was just as well. Glori had no intention of seeing her friends separated for any reason. She cast a coaxing smile Elgin's way, saying, "It will be perfectly lovely."

Elgin didn't think it sounded lovely. Returning tomorrow wasn't anything he cared to do. But he felt trapped both by Glori and the promise he'd made Max to see Glori settled in the neighborhood.

The trouble was that he didn't feel all that comfortable about Glori calling at an establishment where the master of the house was an odd sort of bird. He didn't even like the idea of Iris being here, but that was something else entirely, because the bird was her grandfather. Elgin supposed he'd have to come back to Huntington Manor just to determine what the situation actually was.

Squire Huntington spent the rest of the day reveling in his triumph over the spy, an encounter that became more deftly executed and bravely met the longer he thought about it. He felt like a military genius by the time he blew out his bedside candle.

It was at bedtime that Iris began to have serious misgivings about what her life would actually be like if she ever married the Marquis of Bumpsted. She had six married sisters and had overheard the tear-choked description one of them had given another of her wedding night. If it hadn't been her sister telling it, Iris wouldn't have believed it. The ordeal gave Iris some serious doubts about the joys of matrimony—unless, of course, one had a husband like Elgin Farley. Elgin was her friend. Surely a friend wouldn't be unpleasant about that sort of thing. But Bumpsted wasn't her friend, and that thought covered her with gooseflesh. Iris stuffed her head under the pillow and stayed there as long as she could.

Across the park the inmates of Westbourne Hall were now resting peacefully, except for Elgin, who had become rather sullen. This lowering of an otherwise lively disposition had nothing to do with the ruination of his clothes during the fire drill. It had everything to do with the ruination of Iris if she should actually marry Bumpsted—that dirty old man. When sleep finally came, it brought visions of Iris crying softly in the dark. Heart pounding, bells clanging, drenched in sweat, Elgin tried frantically but unsuccessfully to reach her.

· *Four* ·

Blackthorn Manor dated from the time of Henry VIII, a sprawling pile of warm Cotswold brick that sprouted additions for generations after the main house was built. Rooms and wings, which hid children and their children's children for games of hide-and-seek, went off at odd angles and different elevations. Massive oak doors swung wide on hammered iron hinges and clanked shut with iron locks. Tall mullioned windows let in the sunshine, kept out the rain, and rattled in the wind. The roofs were covered in Welsh slate. And the seasons changed and the wind blew and the place slumbered, swathed in ivy that rustled with nesting birds.

In 1734, Piedmont Huntington replaced the Blackthorn family. Being a man of modest origins and immodest pride, he changed the name of the place to Huntington Manor. Then he had a stained glass crest set into the largest of the library windows: a shield with a card beside a hart triumphant on a field of green. Above the card (the three of diamonds) and hart (with a star between its antlers) was a banner with no motto, nothing on it.

With the house had come the means to support it in the form of hundreds of acres and thousands of sheep. Succeeding Huntingtons invested the profits from those sheep in railways. And sugar plantations. Coal mines. Gold.

They became disgustingly yet tastefully rich.

In addition to the usual comforts of life that revenue from those varied interests afforded, the money also provided generous loans to a select few among the titled folk who found themselves up the River Tic. Because of these financial considerations the Huntingtons were brought to the very brink of the glittering aristocratic world to which they aspired. Yet wealth could take them only so far.

It was said that Piedmont Huntington had acquired the Cotswold property through deceit. More precisely by deceitfully marked cards. Others insisted that it hadn't happened that way at all, that it had been plain good luck for Piedy— his friends had called him Piedy—and no luck at all for Blackthorn, who was known to be a poor player and a bad sport. This was still held to be the truth by those who had ancestors that witnessed the event.

However it happened the real damage was done by persistent gossip. Successive generations of Huntingtons did good deeds by the cartload in an effort to live down the notoriety of that card game. It proved useless. Over the years the desire to be accepted by Society became more than a family passion. It was a Grand Obsession.

Prudence had once said, "If the fortuitous Piedmont had been gaming with a shipbuilder instead of an earl, the whole thing would have blown itself out long ago."

In all probability she was right. Yet Blackthorn of Blackthorn Manor had been an earl, and his descendants were still being unpleasant about the incident. That unpleasantness kept any Huntington from being accepted by the people who mattered at the top of the social ladder. They were invited to those formal receptions at court that were awarded to the generously wealthy, but access to that inner circle eluded them. In desperation Iris's parents finally decided that the only way to overcome the problem was to have a Huntington marry into that charmed circle.

That's why Iris was sitting on the gold damask sofa in the ladies' parlor at Huntington Manor in disgrace. She hadn't been inclined to marry according to plan, which showed a shocking disregard for the good of her family. While her mother doggedly insisted, "We shall come down Society's chimney if we must!" Iris was saying, "What twaddle!"

None of it, however, was the concern of the moment. Just now the most important thing to Iris was keeping out of the way of the staff that was trying to clean the house. Next she wanted to get the India ink off her fingers before Elgin and Glori arrived, though she knew that Elgin might not arrive at all. He hadn't really wanted to come yesterday, and yesterday had turned into a disaster. She wanted everything to proceed more calmly today.

With calm in mind, tea would be served at the farthest end of the garden, far away from the house and carriage house, just in case the fire bell rang again. In such a private, undisturbed setting she could tell Elgin that she had figured out how she could keep from becoming engaged and subsequently married to the Marquis of Bumpsted. The idea had come to her that morning with her coddled egg, but after the toast and jam.

"Iris dear, your friends have arrived." It was Prudence. She had a small jar of something in her hand.

Iris said, "Thank you" and discarded the piece of cotton wool she had been using with no success on her inky fingers. Both hands now smelled of witch hazel.

Prudence said, "Maggie has put them in the drawing room. I said you'd all be going outside again, so they still have their wraps on. Glorianna has a scarf tied under her chin like a peasant, though a most charming peasant, I assure you. It's a silk scarf. *Quite* nice. Mauve, I believe. Mauve silk." Then she frowned and added, "Mr. Farley, that *dear* man, doesn't appear to be at his best today. He is, I believe, distressed about something, though I don't know what would worry him so. Indeed I don't. I must send out a dish of arrowroot, or perhaps hollyhock biscuits for his tea. Soothing to the digestion, you know."

"Won't you be joining us?" asked Iris, for there was always someone nearby these days, watching.

When Prudence shook her head, her lace cap went a bit cockeyed. "I'm on my way to make up a poultice for your grandfather's gout. The juice

of the cuckoo-pint plant"—she held up the jar—
"must be mixed with ox dung while it's still
warm. I've sent a boy into the pasture to wait for
it. Your grandfather is having a bad day, I'm
afraid. Cook is preparing something special to
help keep his mind off the pain."

Prudence then smiled reassuringly and added,
"Now, Iris, you mustn't fret about my absence.
Glorianna is, after all, a married lady and quite
respectable, even though her husband is away.
Business in Scotland, I understand, something
to do with an ironworks, so it must be terribly
dirty. My goodness, all that smoke and soot, but
she's all you'll need to maintain propriety."

When Iris entered the drawing room, Elgin appeared to be the most eager to get outside,
though when they got there his conversational
skills appeared to have atrophied. On the other
hand Iris and Glori talked about the fire drill of
the day before, the mess in the house, and the
sad condition of the carpets that wouldn't come
clean. The occasional gust of wind sent hooped
skirts swinging, hobbling Elgin with the mass of
fabric that bunched around his legs. The same
wind sent rude drafts under wide skirts and
chilled the nether regions of ladies wearing insufficient flannels.

Though the place was a bit of a hike from the
house, the tea things were laid out in the Ha-ha.
It had been built into a steep bank above the
river, using stone plundered from old Roman
roads to construct a retaining wall and a small
terrace floor. A thick planting of lilacs softened
the landscape. New foliage turned the wood into
a lacy green tent. Wildflowers poked up through

a blanket of dried leaves to yawn and stretch. The earth smelled of damp and moss and spring and miraculous beginnings.

Looking around the Ha-ha, Glori said nice things about the cozy setting, the picturesque view, the elegant little table. Once seated everyone smiled nicely and Elgin said it was a nice day and Iris agreed that it was nice, awfully nice, though it could be warmer for May, and realized how much she was beginning to sound like an aunt she knew and loved. As they were out of the wind, hats and wraps were put on the one vacant chair. Elgin eyed Iris's monstrous chapeau, then the river, thinking that one good spin would land it about halfway across. It would float away, never to be seen again.

"It's Aunt Pru's hat," warned Iris. Elgin looked disappointed.

Waiting for them in the Ha-ha had been one of the younger maids. She set out tiny sandwiches that soon developed dried tops. She poured tea that couldn't be kept hot enough, even though the pot had been kept in a straw-lined box. Iris pronounced everything nice and sent the girl back to the house lest she take a chill. Besides, one less person underfoot made the hope of private conversation with Elgin that much more likely. But when the girl was gone, all Iris did was stir her tea and stir it more.

Elgin, who looked as if he hadn't slept too well, had intended to demand that Iris tell him what in hell she was going to do about the Marquis of Bumpsted, that cad! He began, "Miss Huntington," then remembered that Glori was sitting

there, too, and said, "the . . . umm, the sandwiches are . . . quite nice."

Another silence fell on them like a brick.

It took considerable effort for Glori to conceal
an expression of marked amusement as she observed this bizarre behavior of her friends. She
decided that the best thing to do was let them
sort it all out by themselves. The unshakable Mr.
Farley was clearly shaken. It was no less interesting to find Iris so acutely tuned to that gentleman's irregular behavior.

When Iris eventually said, "Yes, quite nice, I
mean the sandwiches," Glori thought she'd go
mad from listening to such inanity.

It was obvious that these two had a great deal
to say to each other, but Glori knew she couldn't
simply leave them so that they could get on with
it. It wouldn't be proper. She was, after all, the
chaperon. A thought later she pushed her cup
aside, set her napkin on the table, and said,
"Shall we walk along the river? I can't think of
anything more pleasing on a day such as this."

"What a nice idea," replied Iris, removing herself from the table as quickly as her hoops would
allow.

Thus it was that the three of them set off
again, strolling along the river path. The flora
received considerable attention from Iris, who
gave an account of the medicinal properties some
of the plants possessed. Things she had learned
from her Aunt Prudence over the years.

This went on until Glori stopped and said,
"Oh, dear! My shoes simply aren't up to this
damp ground. Would you mind awfully if I went

back to the table? I have a perfectly lovely book of poetry in my pocket to keep me company."

Without waiting for a reply, Glori gave her friends a smile and turned back toward the Ha-ha. She was outrageously pleased with herself, yet some of the fun of it faded when she thought about how much she would like to be walking along that path with her husband. That thought only served to strengthen her resolve that nothing would keep Iris and Elgin from pursuing their own destiny, wherever it might lead them. At the moment it led them through the wood beside the river.

There had been a few occasions when Glori had teased Elgin about his interest in Iris. At first he denied it. After that he simply teased back, sometimes agreeing that he loved Iris madly, the way he loved apple pie and his dog back home. Each time he went to such extremes that he made the whole thing sound monstrously silly. Confident that she had done all she could do for the time being, Glori set upon her poetry book.

In the wood by the river Iris was trying to keep up with Elgin. She had half walked, half trotted for much too long before either spoke. Then it was Elgin who said, "Well?" and Iris who said, "Well, *what*?"

"What are you going to do about Bumpsted?"

"I've been simply longing to tell you! I've decided that if I become engaged to someone else I can't very well become engaged to the Marquis of Bumpsted. It's a wonder I hadn't thought of it before."

"First off," said Elgin, "I'm not convinced that

it will work. Secondly, I wasn't aware that there was another title up for consideration."

"There isn't; however, if rumor of a pledge just slips out somehow, and people believe there's an understanding between myself and another gentleman, then my parents will surely have to halt their matchmaking whether they like it or not. If they don't it will inspire considerably more talk among the people that matter."

Elgin still wasn't convinced. It was curiosity that made him ask, "Is there anyone in particular that you have in mind for the position of your intended?"

Iris smiled at him angelically, fluttering her eyelashes.

"Me?"

"You are too kind. I accept."

"Oh, no! I wouldn't touch it with a coal shovel. Dismiss that thought from your mind at once, my girl. *At once!* We are the best of friends. Don't mess about and spoil it with some rumor of an attachment."

"I suppose there's always one or another of my brother's friends who—"

"That's absolutely out of the question. Your brothers and their friends haven't a decent notion between them in church on Sunday."

"Then Sidney Morton might do. I know his sister, and she speaks quite fondly of him."

Hands jammed into his pockets, Elgin said, "Not Morton, either."

"Why not?"

How could he explain that Morton's fond sister couldn't know that her brother had screwed everything from a hot stove to an old horse collar and bragged about it in public places? He had also developed a most peculiar rash.

"Morton won't do," was all Elgin would say, and he said it like he meant it.

"For heaven's sake! There must be *someone* you can recommend."

But Elgin could think of no one he would trust with the care and keeping of such a creature as Iris. He didn't think any of the fellows he knew would keep their hands off her, either. But then keeping one's hands to one's self wasn't what marriage—or even a discreetly conducted engagement—was about. And they might forget that it would be only a mock engagement.

"Calvin Wallace," said Iris.

"Please?"

"Perhaps Calvin Wallace would do. You must know him."

Of course Elgin knew him. Everyone who knew Wallace liked him. A sterling fellow. Also to be considered was his fine town house, country estate, and financial solvency. Though he lacked a title, he was a charming fellow. A handsome devil, actually. Plenty of teeth. He had been known to sing Italian love songs when the urge overtook him. He had been Elgin's choice of a husband for his favorite sister, though his father had picked someone else.

He said, "Wallace is far too old for you."

"He can't be *that* old."

"Well, he is. And you don't even understand Italian."

"Why should that matter?"

"It just does."

"Then we're back to *you*."

"The devil we are!"

"You have to marry sometime."

"No, I don't. It's not as though I need an heir to ensure a title, or anything like that."

"Elgin, who will inherit your property when you pass through the pearly gates?"

"As it now stands it will be divided among my five sisters and consequently their husbands and children." Giving the arrangement some additional thought, he said, "You know, I hate to think of Cassy's husband getting any of it. Can't abide the man. Has something of the lizard about him. He's even thinner in the winter when there aren't any flies."

"How frustrating that must be for him," said Iris. "Have your family been vigorous in their efforts to see you married?"

"Vigorous! The last time I visited Cove House and its inmates my mother just happened to have two females there. Distant cousins—quite pretty, actually, but that's beside the point. You see, the purpose of it became apparent when one constantly found one's self alone with one or the other of the young ladies. The rest of the time I was regaled with their accomplishments. I felt like a clay pigeon at a trap shoot."

"There you have it," said Iris. "An engagement is the only answer I can see for either one of us."

"Wouldn't that be like killing the dog to stop the fleas?"

"Then we're right back to me and the Marquis of Bumpsted," sighed Iris.

Elgin trod on in grim silence, for thoughts of Iris being mauled by Bumpsted were beyond bearing. Visions of Morton drooling over her supine form made him want to strike the fellow. Iris swooning over Calvin Wallace's stupid songs was almost as bad. Feeling as though he had a pack of hounds nipping at his heels, Elgin quickened his naturally long-legged pace so that Iris was almost running to keep up with him until she cried, "Elgin, stop!"

He stopped. "So sorry. Didn't mean to race you about." He began again at more reasonable pace. And thought more reasonable thoughts. After all, this engagement Iris was talking about was just that. An engagement. Engaged was not married. The more he thought about it, the more he came to realize that there really was an element of safety in an engagement. A lengthy engagement would eventually dribble away to nothing at all. He'd heard of people who had been engaged for ten or fifteen years and nothing had ever come of it.

He said, "Iris, if we did take a go at this betrothal business, might we make it a long one, without setting an actual date?"

"If you like," said Iris with annoying good cheer. "I'm told that the appearance of unseemly haste is to be avoided where matrimonials are concerned. Impetuosity inspires another sort of talk."

"Then it's settled. If your parents are going to announce an engagement you don't fancy, word will be put about that you and I have a long-standing agreement, one of which your parents first approved, then changed their minds about because they'd rather have a son-in-law with a title. If it goes that far I expect they'll be mad as hatters, but that ought to do the job. Whenever one tells a lie, it should contain as much truth as possible to make it believable. As for circulation, I know just the fellow for the job, if we should ever need him. He'll think it's a grand lark. Just remember, your family won't be happy about this."

Iris waved a flippant hand, ignoring all the *ifs*. "I still have two unmarried sisters. Perhaps one of them will manage something." Then she hugged Elgin's arm and said, "The sooner the gossip starts the happier I'll be."

"Iris, do you really want to go through with this? Keep in mind that this sort of thing can be extremely destructive to your reputation."

"It can't be as bad as being married to the Marquis of Bumpsted."

"Your parents will vigorously deny whatever is said. They'll look like such upstarts."

"Which might make it sound that much more convincing. Especially if you simply refuse to discuss it when anyone asks. That should do wonders to push it along, don't you think?" Iris jiggled Elgin's arm. "Are you listening?"

He said, "I was just thinking about the possible ramifications of all this," and she said, "I believe you're supposed to kiss me now that we're betrothed."

Elgin looked at her as though she'd gone a bit off.

"It's tradition," she insisted, stepping closer.

He was all too aware of the faint trace of honeysuckle perfume, the same sweet flowering vine that grew beneath his bedroom window at home. She tilted her face up. He felt something like panic and stepped back into the ferns. There was a fine film of perspiration on his brow. Kissing wasn't part of the plan. Not *his* plan. A gentleman didn't go about kissing young ladies like Iris without honorable intentions, and his intentions weren't quite honorable. That is, he didn't intend to marry her, kissing or not, so he knew he'd better not. Kissing turned friends into husbands and wives and ruined everything. His parents had proved it.

"Elgin?" she said, stepping toward him.

He shook his head and said, "No kissing. We'll become engaged, if we must, because I can't bear to think of anyone . . ." Shaking his head, he looked off across the river instead of at Iris. Shuffling his thoughts, he tried again. "Iris, you must stay away from Morton. You see, he's a bit of a cad with a hint of malicious villainy."

"Are you aware that you sound a trifle demented?"

Still gazing at the trees across the river, he said, "I wouldn't doubt it."

Then Elgin took Iris by the hand and waded through the sea of ferns to the path. She was so quiet that he found it unnerving. He said, "I'll have to leave in a few days for my youngest sister's coming out and all that. Parents tried to pop her off last winter, but she'd taken up with bad tonsils and almost missed being presented to the queen." His thoughts scattered and collected again. "I'll return to the Hall as soon as I can. The duke and duchess let me come and go like a long-lost cousin." After that they walked on in silence.

Glori was feeding bread crumbs to the birds when they returned to the Ha-ha. She smiled and Iris smiled and Elgin looked preoccupied. Iris went to the table and declared that the tea was cold. When Glori suggested that they should be going anyway, Elgin smiled and Iris looked preoccupied.

After the good-byes were said on the steps of Huntington Manor, Iris remained on the porch. She was trying to think of a way to bring her grandfather to view Elgin with less hostility than he had the day before. As she and Elgin were going to be engaged, she thought it would be awfully nice if they could all be friends, or at least friendly. If her grandfather's behavior persisted, Elgin might not come to call anymore. Hardly an auspicious beginning. She decided that she would arrange to have her grandfather and Elgin meet under less distressing circumstances than a fire drill. She was certain that if they could meet in an atmosphere more suited to conviviality, then they would surely become more convivial. How simple. How logical. How mistaken could anyone be.

When Iris entered the house, she saw Maggie on her way up the stairs with a tray. "Might that be for my grandfather?"

Maggie stopped. 'Yes, miss. Steak-and-kidney pie. Cook made it up special to tempt his appetite. He does enjoy a well-put-together pie."

"I'll follow you up and take it in to him. Where is he, please?"

"In the Egyptian Room, miss."

"Splendid. I shall be there directly I've put off my wraps," said Iris. Maggie dutifully took the tray upstairs and waited.

There was a moment of indecision when Iris finally entered her grandfather's sanctuary, for every place that might support a tray was covered with papers, books, or yet to be cataloged objects.

The squire looked up at Iris and smiled fondly. Pointing at a packing crate, he said, "Put the tray over there, if you please. Canopic jars inside. Eleven of them and in rather splendid condition, if the list is correct." Once again he consulted the paper he held and recited, "One man, four baboons, three falcons, three jackals, intact, some cracks. It doesn't say if any of them are sets." His voice fairly crackled with excitement when he said, "How I wish I could have been there to find them! To have been the first to touch those jars in three thousand years! Just imagine it!"

While her grandfather expounded upon the glories of ancient times, Iris found another smaller box to use as a table. She set it beside his chair taking care not to bump his foot. The table where the tray was usually placed held clay miniatures of everyday life in ancient Egypt. There were figures of bakers and brewers, weavers and cattle. Little fishermen with tiny fish.

When a pause occurred in her grandfather's accounts of the old days, Iris said, "Wouldn't it be more interesting if you had someone else to talk with about the beautiful things you have? Someone, a man, perhaps, who could appreciate your interests."

With those words ancient Egypt faded away and the squire was all attention to the present.

"This man," he said ominously. "Might he be someone we already know?"

"Yes!" Iris was delighted to say. "As a matter of fact it's Elgin Farley. I think he would like to see your wonderful things."

"Oh, he would, would he? And why would he like to see my wonderful things?"

"To be friendly, I should think. He does enjoy conversation with interesting people. He might be interested in all this." Iris gave the room an inclusive sweep of the arm.

The squire's barking laugh kept Iris from saying anything else, though he could see that she didn't understand why he found her suggestion ridiculous. It was obvious that Iris didn't know that Elgin Farley was there to spy on his antiquities. He wasn't going to tell her, either. He didn't want Farley to find out that he knew.

Composing his words with care, the squire said, "Iris, you may tell Mr. Farley that I'm not ready for his visit, but when I am I will see that he is informed accordingly."

"But, Grandfather, there is a private matter that I think he—"

"Iris, you don't need to think and he will have to wait!"

"But, Grandfather, I'm of the opinion that—"

"Women have no need of opinions. And whatever Mr. Farley wants is of little importance to me. Have I made myself understood?"

"Yes, Grandfather."

"Now I have some reading to do, so you may as well run along."

"Yes, Grandfather."

She left the room promptly, closed the door quietly, and said a frightfully bad word.

Too restless to light anywhere for long, Iris played with the cat. She watched Cook simmering mint for mint jelly. Helped Prudence sort through the dried red clover blossoms that would be used in yet another infusion for treating gout. After an inspection of the ladies' parlor she determined that there wasn't a magazine she hadn't seen. Yet she needed to do something, and she wasn't in the mood for needlework, so she decided to clean her brush and combs because she was still trying to get the ink off her fingers anyway.

A solution of hot water and washing soda, not soap, made a dip for the hog hair bristles of the brush. The bone handle was kept dry so it wouldn't split. When it was clean the brush was put bristles down on a towel in the sun to dry.

There was a specially made, stiff little brush that Iris used to clean combs. The combs—one of horn, two of tortoiseshell—were brushed clean, then wiped and laid back in the drawer.

During this time Iris didn't have even one small distracting thought about Elgin and her grandfather. Her thoughts were fixed on Elgin and the color of his eyes, the timbre of his voice, the warmth of his hand as they walked through the ferns, the touch of that hand low on her back as he guided her around a branch on the path. It wasn't at all proper to be thinking about his hand on her back, which made her wonder if propriety might be valued beyond its worth.

While considering virtue in general, Iris wandered into the kitchen where there were jars of

mint jelly lined up in a neat row. Brown paper
had been tied over the tops to keep the wax seals
clean. She played with the cat again. Arranged
some flowers. Eventually she went upstairs to
read a book—a book she kept way under her
mattress.

When Elgin and Glori stopped at the front
door of Westbourne Hall, Elgin let Glori down,
then drove around to the barn. He could have
left the gig at the house and a groom would have
taken it from there, but that's not what Elgin
wanted. Sympathetic male company is what
Elgin wanted. Tom came out of the shadowed
barn, took a look at Elgin, and the two men
walked toward the paddock. Elbows on the top
rail, booted foot on the bottom rail, each of them
studied the horses. One by one the big animals
ambled over to push soft velvety noses into
warm hands.

Tom said, "Might the housekeeping be slipping
at the Manor? You look like you found a bug in
the cream pot."

"That's because I found a bug in the cream
pot."

"Did it have fine blue eyes and dark curling
hair?"

Elgin gave his friend a tired smile and returned his attention to the horses.

"What be the problem?"

"Iris and I have an understanding."

"When be the wedding?"

"It's not that kind of an understanding."

"What other kind be there with a girl like
that? You can't mean to set her up someplace."

"No," sighed Elgin. "Nothing like that."

"What then?"

"I'm just trying to protect her from some bad things."

"You've gone weak in the head."

"Iris said something of the same nature. I agreed with her."

"Be that so?"

"The thing is, we've become sort of . . . engaged. It's something else that's hard to explain."

"Try."

"Tom, there are things that can't go past this fence. For instance, the family wants Iris to marry a title."

"Oh, we all know that. My cousin works for the squire in the creamery, and she hears this and that. She heard that."

"Is there anything else I'd like to know?"

"No. Just take the lady to Scotland and be done with it. Married over the anvil be married still, even if the family won't like it."

"That's not how it is. You see, Iris and I are almost engaged, but that's all there is to it. This way she won't be shackled to someone she doesn't want to marry. We've never even discussed marriage."

"Be that enough for the rest of your life?"

"This isn't about the rest of my life. This is about Iris being pushed into a marriage she doesn't want and how to keep her out of it."

"Tell me," said Tom with a twinkle in his eye. "What would you do if you had but a week before the end of the world?"

"I haven't thought about it."

"Me, I'd cuddle up in front of the fire with my Bess and Little Tom and watch the baby sleep. A sleeping colicky baby be a rare and wonderful thing."

"That's all?"

"Maybe I'd scratch the dog with my foot."

"For an entire week?"

"For part of it." Tom grinned. "The rest of it be private."

"Is life really that good? I mean with you and Bess?"

"It be that good. I suggest you do better with what you have. Even Methuselah didn't live forever." Tom gave a tug to the brim of his hat and left Elgin at the fence.

It wasn't until Tom was gone that Elgin wondered what he might do if there really was only a week until the end of the world. Or if there was only a week before the end of *his* world. What if he got run down by a brewery wagon when he went to London? What if he got cholera? In a few horrible hours after the first symptoms appeared, he'd be a thing of the past. Then Cassy's lizard husband would get his best shirts and gold watch.

And Iris would end up married to Bumpsted. Damn!

Sore elbows made it necessary for Elgin to find a more comfortable place at the fence, where he gave further consideration to the understanding he and Iris had. He supposed it might go on for four or five years before they gave it up. By then Bumpsted would surely have found someone else.

Too bad Elgin didn't know that Iris considered

their understanding to be a real engagement. A long engagement of four or five months, when the usual thing would happen. After all, Elgin had never actually said that he expected the whole thing to fizzle out.

· Five ·

Because of Glori's efforts Iris and Elgin had time together beyond the confines of Huntington Manor. Sketching expeditions were arranged for the two young ladies, with Elgin to drive them about the countryside. With a well-stocked picnic basket they visited a stone ruin that was well off the traveled path. They spent a peaceful day on a riverbank near a picturesque old mill. There had been a birthday party for Glori.

Nothing happened to disturb the daydream they were enjoying. The subject of Bumpsted hadn't come up; neither had there been an opportunity for Iris to get Elgin and her grandfather together. For the time being the sun was in its heaven and all was right with the world and Elgin wasn't eager to mess about with it. The days were wonderful. Occasional fantasies of Iris disturbed the nights, but the days really were quite wonderful.

"This be a fool's paradise," warned Tom after one of the sketching expeditions.

"Whatever it is, it's fine for now," replied Elgin.

"In the past you gave some good advice to other people."

"I've noticed that it's much easier to give good advice when it isn't my problem."

Having exhausted the subject, the two men went off to the pub in Little Woolton for a beer. The next morning Elgin was on his way to London for his sister's coming out.

Though Iris had been banished to the Cotswolds, she had all but forgotten that she was supposed to be in disgrace. If it hadn't been for missing Elgin so much, she would have been having a fine time of it. She made a point of not thinking about how his eyes wrinkled at the corners when he laughed, or the way he stuffed his hands into his pockets. Or the way he'd watch her when he didn't know she was aware of it.

There were other things Iris could think about. Like the afternoon the gypsy called on her Aunt Prudence. The woman's name was Sofia, and she always came by when her people were camped near Huntington Manor. She and Prudence exchanged herbal remedies. On one such afternoon Prudence invited Iris to join them under the shade tree beyond the kitchen garden. Iris did so, finding Sofia herself as fascinating as the stories she told of her life and travels. She had seen so much of the world from the seat of her gaily painted caravan.

When the old woman concluded one of her tales, she squinted at Iris and whispered, "Show me your palm, and I'll tell you of the dark stranger in your future."

Iris declined, saying, "No, thank you. Not today." She couldn't help but smile after that, for Elgin was neither dark nor a stranger.

At supper that night Iris retold the gypsy's stories, taking special delight in the tales about the old woman's clever grandson and the assortment of animals he had trained. Best of all had been the horse he taught to count. The squire enjoyed it all. Iris was glad of it, for she hoped to put him in a good enough mood to talk about something else she had on her mind. That something else was Elgin. But tonight, when Iris might have spoken of him, the squire became so fixed on the travel stories of his youth that no other subject would do.

That's why Iris had to wait for a more favorable time to introduce the subject she wished to pursue, having faith in Elgin's ability to charm her grandfather when they met under those yet to be realized favorable conditions. If Iris's faith wavered in the dark of the night, she had only to remember Elgin's heroic rescue of her from the apple tree to know that he could do anything.

Because of her steadfast belief that things would all come about, Iris remained cheerful and agreeable. So agreeable that her grandfather decided that it was the right time to make her better acquainted with the Marquis of Bumpsted. Not in London, however, for there could be no certainty of the man's undivided attention. He thought it would be best to get him here, to the Manor.

When explaining the plan to Prudence, he said, "The trouble is that I can't ask the fellow to pop in to look over my granddaughter with an eye to conjugal bliss. It simply won't do. Such an approach wouldn't be productive."

The rhythmic tap-tapping of thin fingers on the arm of his chair marked a long moment of deep thought for the squire. Eventually he said, "There must be something the marquis won't be able to resist. Unfortunately I don't keep hounds or hunters. It isn't bird season, either, and the fishing hasn't been much to speak of."

Prudence said, "In the library there is a nicely bound book of parlor games and simulated magical deeds, but they all seem to be disruptive. Too disruptive, actually. Shooting corks from bottles so much of the time. Good heavens. Valuable things might be broken. Of course there are the trickeries where things are balanced on strings to present an amazing illusion to mystify and amuse one's friends. The book says that such things are accomplished by changing the center of gravity of an object, perhaps a cork—those *poor* corks—by putting two dinner forks into them like this." Prudence pressed her index fingertips together to form a little steeple where one of those poor corks might be impaled. Then she wiggled her thumbs below that point to show where the new center of gravity would be when the cork was resting on a tightly drawn wire or string. She said, "Of course we would have to have things to hold up the string, when a magical deed called for balancing something on a string, and that might mean nails, but I don't think—"

"Mummies!" the squire cried into the practically empty room. The squire did his best thinking in an empty room. Even when Prudence was there, he still thought of it as an empty room. As though to himself, he said, "You must send invitations for a house party, saying that there will be an edifying entertainment, namely the unrolling of an ancient Egyptian mummy!" Leaning toward Pru, he said, "I'll use the one that has the outer layer of bandages that are in rather poor condition. You know, the mummy that doesn't have any feet. I still wonder whatever happened to them." After more thoughtful finger tapping, he added, "I could unroll the mummified crocodile, of course, but there doesn't seem to be a suitable appreciation of them. Besides, the wrapping is much too beautifully done to cut it up, and I am rather fond of it. You know the one. It has the top layer of bandages that are woven into a diamond pattern, with brass studs in the centers of the diamonds." The squire became so absorbed in thoughts of mummies that Prudence left the room and he didn't even notice.

Later that day Prudence told Iris about the forthcoming mummy unrolling. Iris said, "How absolutely grand!"

Having done several drawings of that particular mummy, Iris was quite curious about it. When she found out the unrolling would take place before Elgin returned from Town, she was less excited. She would have liked him to be there. Even so she wrote the invitations in a fine hand, helped with the menus, sorted out rooms for fifteen guests. Those numbers would include her parents. She wasn't aware that one name had been left off the list she had been given, that name being the Marquis of Bumpsted. The family had agreed that there would be less trouble with Iris if she didn't worry herself about Bumpsted ahead of time.

It was while they were preparing for the house party that the package arrived from London. It had been sent on ahead to Prudence, not directly to Iris, which ensured its survival. Prudence removed it from the wrappings and suspended it rather distastefully between her fingers and thumbs. It looked strange indeed. The next morning she took it in to Iris while she was doing her exercises. Prudence cleared her throat.

Iris stopped swaying from side to side to study the shriveled mass in her aunt's grasp. Unable to puzzle it out, she finally said, "What *is* that?"

"According to the letter from your mother, this is your Genuine Patented Inflatable Undulating Bosom. My goodness. It is, I believe, made of rubber. Your mother has sent it to you. It was necessary to inform her that the breast enlarging cream doesn't seem to be working, not in the least, though it smells of coconuts. She has sent this instead. Deary me."

Iris was speechless. Prudence wasn't. She said. "The instructions say that it is to be inflated and worn next to the skin, though it seems to me that the entire arrangement would be rather unpleasant." From her expression one could tell that Prudence didn't approve of undulating rubber bosoms.

Iris took the curious thing from her aunt. Following the directions, she blew it up and fastened the little plug into the end of the inflating tube. Much amused, she stood before the mirror and held it in front of her. It looked like a double-bulbed, wedge-shaped pillow. The tapered

edge was designed to fit just below one's collar-
bone. The bulbous portions hung over those
areas of one's self in want of enhancement.
Though Iris wasn't quite sure if the thing undu-
lated, the right side did bulge out when she
pushed the left side in. She did her best to appear unaffected by either the bulging or her
aunt's look of dismay. It finally proved impossible, and she gave way to a fit of giggles.

That's when Maggie arrived with fresh linens.
It was Prudence who explained the purpose of
the thing Iris was holding, saying that it had to
go inside Iris's corset. It was to Maggie's credit
that she didn't laugh, at least not out loud. Perhaps it was because she'd had long experience
with the upper classes and knew the peculiar
things they did. Even so she didn't look as
though she had much confidence in rubber
bosoms, either.

The dressing process went from silly to ridiculous, especially when one considered how difficult it was to keep the new bosoms level, for one
side did tend to creep up with every breath Iris
took. To no one's surprise her dress couldn't accommodate her new figure. Letting some air out
of the inflatable helped, but not a great deal. Iris
still looked stuffed because she was.

Prudence said, "My *goodness*," and seriously
cautioned Iris to avoid stoves, lamps, candles,
cheroots, and anything sharp.

When the jest of it all had worn thin, Iris said,
"Aunt Pru, I must thank you for an amusing
morning, but I fear that this device will not
serve. You can see for yourself that I look ridiculous."

Prudence sent Maggie from the room. When they were alone, she said, "Iris, dear, I'm afraid it's not that simple. It isn't that I don't understand what you're saying, for I share your sentiments. Indeed I do. Your mother, however, has decided that this is what you must wear. If you don't wear it now, I expect she will come here to make certain that her instructions are carried out. Or she may insist that you return to London, though perhaps she should come and see this bosom for herself. Then she might decide that it really isn't such a good idea after all. Not at all."

Iris sank onto the edge of the bed, her expression bleak. Ever so softly, Prudence said, "I am sorry, dear."

Iris was sorry, too. The last thing she wanted was to have her mother here at Huntington Manor. The next to last thing she wanted was to return to London, because she'd never be allowed to have Elgin's company there. "I understand," she said with a defeated sigh.

Consulting her watch, Prudence reminded Iris that breakfast was waiting, relieved that the girl hadn't asked exactly why she had been fitted with such a ridiculous device. If a direct question had been asked, Prudence would have had to say that the Marquis of Bumpsted was known to admire buxom women. It was intended that the marquis should admire Iris, too. Prudence couldn't have lied about it. She couldn't lie about anything.

When Prudence left the room, she sent Maggie back in to dress Iris, but the situation wasn't funny anymore. Neither was there the least

trace of amusement about Iris when she finally
left her room. While dressing she'd felt cold. Now
she had a sweaty, sicky feeling and her stomach
rolled. But she lifted her chin, looked straight
ahead, and made her way downstairs to the
breakfast room. Even so she couldn't miss the
odd looks the servants gave her, or ignore the el-
bowing one of them gave another.

Upon entering the breakfast room, Iris said,
"Good morning, Grandfather."

Her grandfather looked up and choked on his
toast. He didn't actually *say* anything, but he
had to avoid looking at Iris and the chest that
made her look like a melon smuggler. Iris felt
her face turn hot and red and wanted to climb
under the table. She had to blink back the tears.
Conversation was unavoidably awkward no matter what Prudence did to help it along. On the
pretext that the room had a draft, Iris sent a
maid to fetch her spencer. Hiding inside its knit-
ted bulk was the best she could do to cover herself.

By the time Iris finished her morning meal,
the entire household had heard about her al-
tered appearance. A handful of the staff managed to find tasks that could be performed with
a view of the breakfast room door. The housekeeper routed the lot of them before Iris
emerged.

Iris kept to her room for the rest of the day.
She sent her regrets for lunch and supper, saying that she had the headache. No one doubted
it. Trays were sent up to the bedchamber where
that poor Miss Huntington still wore the much
detested rubber bosom. Prudence said she would

simply have to get used to it before the house party, though she did suggest that she might be more comfortable if she had a pretty shawl draped around her shoulders. Iris no longer cared to have Elgin among them to see the mummy unrolled, though that wasn't quite the right of it. Iris no longer cared to have Elgin about to see her looking foolish.

When the big day came, Huntington Manor fairly buzzed with activity. Iris and Prudence were on hand to greet the guests, though Iris was puzzled by her aunt's fidgeting at the appearance of each coach, and her noticeable relief as whoever it was came up the steps.

Iris understood those fidgets when the Marquis of Bumpsted emerged from the stark black coach with the crest on the door. Judging from the guilty expression on Prudence's face, she had known the man was coming and had been forbidden to volunteer that information. Iris then reasoned that the rest of the family must have known, too. After that came the suspicion that this entire event had been staged to entice the marquis to the Manor to become better acquainted with herself. The mummy had simply been the bait. And she supposed her new bosom was also intended to make a big impression on the same man.

Near to tears from a horrible sense of betrayal, Iris clutched her shawl tightly and smiled stiffly. A discomfited Aunt Prudence introduced her to the marquis, reminding him that they had met once before.

He graciously replied, "Yes, it was in Hyde Park, I believe."

Iris said yes, it was Hyde Park, that dinner would be served at eight, and had the footmen gather up his luggage to escort him upstairs.

Prudence had arranged the seating at table that night so that Iris would be next to a gentleman who collected stuffed South American birds. Iris's mother followed right behind Prudence and rearranged the cards so that Iris would be sitting next to the marquis. Prudence would sit next to the stuffed bird man.

Iris was exceptionally quiet throughout dinner. Her parents were exceptionally annoyed.

The next day was the first full day of a house party that was scheduled to last for an entire week. A jolly collection of people made their way through the library and into the glass enclosed conservatory. The lighting there was exceptionally good. A library table had been placed in the middle of the room. The linen-wrapped mummy lay there on one sheet, covered by another upon which the Huntington crest had been embroidered. The mummy now appeared to have feet, for a box had been placed on end under the sheet, where the feet should have been, to create that comforting illusion.

Lord and Lady Westbourne were there. Glorianna came with them. They had driven over from Westbourne Hall especially for the unrolling. Also present for the day were the minister and his sister, who kept house for him. The doctor from Chipping Campden was there as well as the Huntington butler, for he had shown a pronounced interest in mummies.

There was one footman to assist with sawing. A second footman was standing by with a pan and tweezers to collect the oddments that were invariably revealed as the layers of cloth came away. Two more footmen took their places at either end of the table as soon as they entered the room. The ladies found seats in two rows of chairs that faced the table. The gentlemen stood behind the ladies.

Like an orchestra conductor, Squire Huntington was the last to enter the room, dramatically taking his position on the far side of the mummy and facing his audience. Unlike an orchestra conductor, he was assisted out of his frock coat by one of the footmen. In dignified silence he held out his arms to allow a canvas apron to be tied about him as a surgeon might wear it. It was a surgeon who often performed mummy unrollings due to his knowledge of anatomy.

The instruments of dissection had been laid out on a conveniently positioned side table. Squire Huntington first inspected the scissors. Then he looked closely at the saw, for much of the resin-coated cloth would be as hard as wood and difficult to cut through any other way. Brushes were lined up according to size. Tweezers and pliers. A hand lens. Hammer and chisel were there for the same reason as the saw. A box lined with cotton wool had been prepared to receive jewelry and amulets. On the floor was a tin tub into which the linen bandages would be placed as they were removed from the mummy.

When the squire finally faced his audience, the shuffling of feet ceased. Murmuring faded. Someone coughed. A chair creaked. The squire lifted his voice and said, "Ladies and gentlemen . . ." the words echoed around the vaulted room. "Before you lie the remains of a nameless being who breathed his last breath long before the birth of Christ. He was a thousand years in his windings before William would conquer England. Another thousand years before Napoleon would come and go." The squire paused to let the vast amount of time sink in. "When this man lived he'd walked the streets of ancient Egypt in fine shoes and elegant clothing. We know this because of the elaborate manner in which his body was prepared. Only a wealthy family could have afforded it."

Huntington leaned his hands on the edge of the table to study the sheet-draped form, then returned his attention to his guests, saying, "It took the embalmers and priests some seventy days to prepare the deceased for his coffin, often preserving select organs in canopic jars. The heart, however, was supposed to be the seat of all thought, emotion, and wisdom, so it was usually left in place." Out of consideration for the delicate sensibilities of the ladies present, the squire didn't explain that other internal organs were removed through an incision on the side of the abdomen, or that the brains were taken out through the nose.

"The first nineteen or twenty days of the mummification process were taken up with the salting of the remains," continued the squire. He shifted his weight in an effort to ease the throbbing in the gouty toe, which objected to being confined in a shoe. "Fifteen or sixteen days were used for cleansing. Spicing and bandaging required another thirty-four to thirty-five days, which included rituals and prayers. Then there were the amulets—you might call them charms—that were inserted among the strips of linen during the bandaging process of some mummies. There were amulets shaped like people, others like animals or particular objects. They might be made of gold, glazed pottery, or semiprecious stones. Jewelry was also included."

All eyes had shifted from the squire to the mummy itself, with everyone wondering what fantastic things might be wrapped in the linen.

"A mummy might have as many as twenty layers of wrapping," the squire explained in tones of wonder. "Great folded pads of cloth were used to fill out the form and produce the familiar, cylindrical shape we now recognize as that of a mummy. Over a thousand yards of bandages have been removed from some examples of the embalmer's art." By now everyone was so interested in the mummy that no one thought it strange that Chumbly was inching closer to it.

The squire said, "When the unrolling is completed you will see that the end of each finger has been provided with a gold nail sheath before the individual digit was wrapped in linen strips. After that the arms and the rest of the body were wrapped." The squire was careful not to say anything vulgar such as each *leg* was also wrapped separately after the toes were wrapped. One must simply assume that it was so, for no decent person would say so before a refined audience of both sexes.

The squire's voice dropped dramatically when he said, "Now, my friends, we shall look upon the face of time, a face that the sun has not touched in *over two thousand years!*"

Taking the sheet by the top edge, he slowly drew it down over the mummy. The audience gave a soft gasp as the ancient form was revealed. The squire gave a louder gasp, for the bandages were in greater disarray than they had been a few hours before. It was obvious that someone had been messing about with the wrappings. He dropped the sheet on the mummy's legs. A muscle jumped along his jaw, though he said nothing. Iris wouldn't have been surprised if a dark cloud suddenly blotted out the sun and a rumble of thunder shook the house. She could see that the cartoonage, a sort of papier-mâché mask that covered the head and shoulders of the mummy, had been completely exposed. The painted face was still brightly colored.

Taking up the scissors, the squire carefully snipped away at the frayed and discolored strips of cloth. As the wrappings were handled a musty dusty smell like old clothes from the attic overwhelmed the floral scents the ladies wore.

Without taking his eyes from his work, the squire said, "The mask is made of papyrus and plaster over cloth. It was artfully molded and painted to portray a handsome young man, though the individual it represents may have been neither handsome nor young when he departed this world." Putting aside the scissors, the squire placed a handful of crumbling linen in the tub. Taking up the scissors again, he said, "The face we see here is supposed to be one that the man's spirit, his Ka, would have recognized. Without such recognition the Ka wouldn't have been able to return to the correct body in the evening after being out and about in the living world during the day."

As the squire continued to snip away, something fell from between the bandages. Chumbly had hold of it as soon as it hit the floor. The gasp from the onlookers was one of horror, not wonder. The squire said nothing, but raised an eyebrow menacingly as he extended his hand to Chumbly.

That unfortunate individual glanced about furtively, unable to miss the hostility directed at him from others in the room. Fearing that the men might rise up and painfully force him to relinquish what he had so nimbly claimed for his own, Chumbly grudgingly dropped the small object into the outstretched palm of his much detested brother-in-law.

Looking intently at the object that had been returned to him, the squire rolled it over, then resorted to the hand lens to be certain it was what he thought it was. Yes. A beetle. An ancient dead bug, not an amulet, over which Chumbly had made such a greedy ass of himself.

The squire had heard of other debris being found in mummy wrappings. The list included various insects, bits of reed off the floor, even resin swabs that had been used in the preparation of the mummy. He'd also read the description of stuff that sounded like floor sweepings. And a dried mouse. As there were no records of swabs or mice being deliberately included in the wrappings, the squire attributed it to careless handling during preparation. The humble insect that Chumbly had tried to take was the first thing to be placed in the pan held by one of the footmen. Curious whisperings hissed through the room.

While the audience strained to see the small object in the pan, Iris's father snatched away the shawl that she had draped so modestly about herself. With that one move she felt as though she had been assaulted and left exposed to the snickering world. Without the shawl everyone could see the absurd degree to which her figure had been padded. Her heart cramped painfully. She wanted to hide. But no one was looking at Iris. They were all watching Chumbly, not wanting to miss a second of it when the mummy's curse struck him down for what he'd done.

Few if any noticed when Iris slipped from her endmost chair and fled upstairs. No one suspected that anything was wrong until they smelled the smoke and heard a deep voice that boomed:

"Fire!"

The servants ran to the appointed stations and assumed their duties. Having no thought as to what he would find, Hubert Huntington dashed upstairs to the room with the smoke billowing out the door. It was Iris's room. Inside he found his daughter, coughing and choking, blinded by the smoke. He pushed open a window and leaned her out into the fresh air. The fire bell began to clang. Dogs howled. Men shouted.

As soon as he could, Hubert steered the curious away from the room, saying, "There's been a slight problem with a blocked chimney, nothing serious I assure you, ha-ha." He tugged at his constricting necktie and added, "It might be a jolly good idea if you gentlemen would escort the ladies back to the conservatory and the mummy so that their lovely dresses won't become smoked."

"Egad, the mummy!" cried the squire, fearing that someone might have made off with his treasure while they were all distracted by the smoking fireplace.

Hobbling back to the sheet-draped table he was much relieved to find that the Ancient One was still there, just as he'd left it. Someone else noticed that the old bug, the supposed amulet, was no longer in the pan.

Another hiss of whispers said, "Chumbly's cursed, poor devil—the old boy's done for—serves him right, the blackguard!" The last remark was issued by a gentleman who, on another occasion, had taken exception to an inebriated Chumbly fumbling about under the dinner table in search of his wife's knee.

That's when the back door crashed open and the pounding of booted feet announced the arrival of the fire brigade with the greased hose. Charging up the hall stairs the burly men shouted, "Hold on! We be comin' for you, miss!" for they had seen Iris leaning out her smoking window.

Waving his arms frantically, the squire half hopped, half ran from the conservatory, through the library, and into the hall shouting, "No water! For God's sake, *no water!*"

Outside the cry was taken up as "More water! More water!"

The water came just as fast as the men on the fire engine could pump it out, for they were set

on saving Miss Iris. Walls, ceilings, floors, the
squire, everything got sprayed.

Never had guests at Huntington Manor been
so entertained, though they might not have
found it quite so amusing had they known that
upstairs the servants were throwing mattresses,
rugs, and things, *their* things, out the windows
to save them from the threat of fire.

It would seem that humor consists largely of
disagreeable things happening to someone else.

When the squire finally made himself understood, the pumping stopped and the firefighters
sloshed out with the defeated hose. It took hours
to get everything back inside the house. Drying
up the hall didn't progress much faster, for the
greasy wet carpet had to be taken up from the
stairs. The housekeeper was in despair. The butler was in the pantry with a bottle of scotch. The
lingering smoke from the fire Iris had set left
the house smelling suspiciously of burnt rubber.

Those who had come for the day to see the
mummy unrolled left immediately. A few more of
the guests were gone by dinnertime as the train
schedule allowed. The rest of the company departed the next morning, right after breakfast.
Bumpsted was among that group. The family
kept to their rooms and out of sight.

After the last of the house party had gone from
their midst, the Huntingtons gathered privately.
That is to say they gathered without Iris. Iris,
after all, was the problem that prompted their
gathering.

"She really is quite mad," her father said
sadly. "I don't think she would hurt anyone, but

she is quite mad, nonetheless." Everyone agreed, except Prudence, who wept copiously.

Hubert said that he and his wife would leave immediately to consult some doctors, specialists in London. No one cared for the thought of locking Iris away in a lunatic asylum, or even confining her to a few rooms in a remote country house, but what else was there to do if they couldn't make her behave?

· Six ·

Things were frightfully quiet at Huntington Manor. It had been almost a week since the smoking-out, and windows were still open to air the house. There were those who thought the place would always have a peculiar burnt rubber smell no matter how many bowls of potpourri Prudence set about. Her eyes were perpetually red, though not from the lingering sting of smoke. She was worried about what would happen to Iris. Tear-dampened handkerchiefs were twisted to shreds in her plump hands as a testament to that concern. The squire spent most of his time alone in his chamber, having first locked the doors of his collection rooms. Chumbly came and went in a fog as he had for years.

Only Iris walked about in the gardens, though much subdued, and with a slight cough from breathing so much smoke. At night her aunt treated her with a hot chest plaster made of onions, rye meal, and vinegar to keep that cough from becoming something deadly.

After Glori sent a note around asking if she might call on Iris, the two young women roamed the garden paths together. Glori appeared quite fetching in an older dress that had been remodeled into something more stylish, thanks to the illustrations in a French fashion magazine. The fabric was an especially fine merino wool and too good to waste.

Iris, on the other hand, was content enough in a dress that would have been retired long ago by a lady of fashion. Her hat wouldn't be mentioned in fashionable company, for the straw had been rained on and dried without benefit of blocking. Her parasol had two slightly bent ribs, though it appeared reasonable enough in the hands of someone who was describing her inflatable bosom and why she had set it on fire.

"It's all been *too* annoying," said Iris. "And I do miss Elgin so. Who could have known that cholera would strike London again and send him and his family dashing for the country? Who could have supposed that there would have been such a ferocious storm after he got there?"

"Who indeed?" said Glori, adding something about the weather being like that.

"The atmospheric conditions haven't been too nice here, either," continued Iris. "It's because of the smoke and all, though it came from such a small fire. You know what a small fire it was. There's been such a big fuss about such a small fire that perhaps it's just as well that Elgin isn't here."

Glori had picked a zinnia, pulled off a petal, and paused, saying, "I'm afraid I've missed the connection between the dreadful inflatable fire and Elgin's return."

Iris gave a long-suffering sigh. "Grandfather is still badly out of humor with me because I smoked out the mummy unrolling. For that reason I'm truly afraid that if Elgin should attempt to see Grandfather now he would be treated quite badly."

"Yes, I see what you mean," said Glori, dropping the first petal, then a second. He loves me, he loves me not.

"Glori, when you and the duchess write to Elgin, would you please tell him that he's likely to be regarded in a very poor light if he should return too soon?"

"Yes, if you like." The petals continued to fall.

"Now, tell me about Elgin's letter again, just in case you missed something the first time around."

Glori smiled indulgently and pulled the letter from her memory. "Elgin said that he is still at his home in Kent, with no immediate plans to leave. He has been kept quite busy arranging for repairs to some outbuildings since the storm, and they needed a new chicken house, anyway. The storm also ruined some crops."

"And?" said Iris anxiously.

Glori studied the flower she held, unable to remember if she'd left off with being loved or not loved.

"Well?" prodded Iris.

Glori still stared at the flower and said, "The roof of the dovecote is being repaired, having been put on in seventeen something."

"Didn't he have anything to say about me?"

"Good heavens, the man's no fool. He's taken every care not to compromise you in ink. I doubt that your family would approve of your name being mentioned. His letter wasn't even addressed to me, but to the duke and duchess as he has always sent them. It was the duchess who passed the letter on to me after reading it at breakfast."

"Oh, bother!"

"Iris, are your parents still angry with you for the hasty departure of the Marquis of Bumpsted?"

"Any correspondence I have had from them has been brief and to some other point, so I'm truly unable to describe their sentiments. More than anything else I'm aware that Grandfather is still frightfully upset about the house party. He had been looking forward to telling everyone so many things about mummies. Of particular interest to him was the pile of bandages from another mummy that appeared to be out of the ordinary."

"Umm," said Glori. The petals fell, loves me, loves me not.

"When the suspicious strips of cloth were laid out and matched up they weren't the remains of well-used household linen, as would be expected. There assembled on the floor was the sail of a small boat! Isn't that extraordinary? Well, I promise you it is. One might wonder if the individual who had been wrapped up in it had been a sailor, though I suppose cloth might have been purchased from other sources if the usual supply of collected household linen proved insufficient."

Glori said, "Do you mean to say that the Pharaohs were wrapped up in old sheets and table-cloths from the royal palaces?"

"Goodness, no. Royal mummies had linen strips specially woven for that purpose. Did you know that not too many years ago loads of wrappings from mummies were sold as rags and shipped to a firm in America for the manufacture of paper? Yes, it's true, though they could produce only brown paper because the stain from the resin couldn't be removed from the linen, but Grandfather didn't have an opportunity to tell any of that, either."

Such conversation came to a halt when they went into the house for tea. Over a cup of Darjeeling, a plum tart, and the essence of burnt rubber, Glori spoke of what her husband was doing in Scotland. It was clear to Iris that her friend would rather have been in that north country than conducting their marriage by post from the Cotswolds. The two women had a sympathetic understanding of absent menfolk. When it came time to take her leave, Glori leaned toward Iris and whispered, "The duchess might write to Elgin this very afternoon and tell him how you are getting on. She is such a dear."

"I would far rather write to him myself," said Iris.

"You know very well that you can't," said Glori. "You're in enough trouble as it is." When she left she was glad that she could at least pass messages between Iris and Elgin.

Since the ill-fated house party Prudence had warned Iris that she must be on her very best behavior. Iris did the very best she could, immersing herself in more illustrations of more ancient glass. Some pieces had side views, back views, and even views from above and below, with enlargements of decorative trim in addition to the customary frontal representations.

Life assumed a predictable routine, and Iris

began to wonder when she would see Elgin again. She spent entirely too much time gazing out the window wondering how his arms would feel when he held her close and how his jacket would feel against her cheek. She was certain that she'd know the beat of his heart from all other hearts. And she spent too many nights wondering what it would be like to cuddle up and fall asleep with the man she loved. The thought left her with a faintly dreamy smile.

She then recalled an incident that occurred while she attended Miss Sparrow's Finishing School for Privileged Young Ladies. There had been an older student, one Lucinda Reading-Smythe, who suddenly left them to be just as suddenly married. Iris had thought it odd that Lucinda had been almost smiling when she left, even though she left in disgrace. The older girls spoke of it in shocked whispers.

Having a perfect fit over the incident was their dour instructress of deportment, a pious woman who had her ears and eyebrows pulled back into a tight bun along with her hair. She had said, "Mark my words, Lucinda is doomed to sin and privation! Lucinda will never experience the ecstasy of a higher calling!"

The effervescent little maid who swept and scrubbed the place had snickered and said, "How the devil would *she* know what ecstasy is?" The effervescent little maid was promptly dismissed.

Iris hadn't been able to comprehend the events at the time. Since then, however, she had begun to have an understanding of why Lucinda Reading-Smythe had been smiling.

Putting her school days from her mind, Iris

tried to concentrate on the work before her. It soon became apparent that she hadn't blended her watercolors to match the old Roman glass of which she had made extensive illustrations. Today she had idly mixed the blue-gray-greens of Elgin's eyes. Tints and shades that changed with the light. Changed with his mood. But such a diversion didn't last long because of the news that arrived from Westbourne Hall.

Someone had died.

Not someone who was actually in residence at the Hall, but someone who belonged there. The deceased was Randolph Rutherford, a disreputable young man who was the only child, son, and heir of the house. While in Paris he had taken a nasty fall under questionable circumstances. But the landing was worse than the fall, and that's what did him in. Beastly luck.

To make things even more distressing for the Rutherfords, their nephew Maxwell wasn't immediately reachable, being somewhere in the wilds of Scotland on a fishing trip. Beastly timing.

When Elgin heard the news, he returned to Westbourne Hall to offer his services to the bereaved parents. He was also rather desperate to see Iris again and fervently hoped that her grandfather wasn't still behaving like a beastly bore.

Huntington Manor had been thrown open to accommodate the overflow of funeral guests from the Hall. Even so, Iris and Elgin didn't see each other until the funeral, and then their meeting was quite public, equally formal, and frustratingly brief.

To make things even more maddening, Elgin had heard strange tales of a fire to which Iris had been a party. One version held that it hadn't been a chimney that was smoking but the lady herself. Another version made the event sound like the Great Fire of London. Through it all Elgin hadn't had an opportunity to ask Iris exactly what had happened. The duke and duchess had gone into seclusion or they might have told him something more, for he understood that they had been at the Manor when the fire occurred.

From behind her black silk fan Glori assured Elgin that "Iris emerged unscathed by the conflagration. Only the house and her family are still smoking."

It took conscious effort on Elgin's part to keep from staring in Iris's direction, following her movements through the flow of the crowd, listening for her voice through bits of conversation that said, "Surprised he lived this long—In a brothel you say?—I heard he owed—No trousers? Good heavens!"

Elgin was grateful when Maxwell finally arrived home during the funeral dinner. This allowed Elgin to slip unobtrusively into the background and have a word with Iris. It was then that they arranged to meet in the village two days hence.

It happened over warm buns at the bakery. Their conversation was, by necessity, vapid. When the man behind the counter seemed to be listening much too closely to what they were saying, it was obvious that they couldn't stand about much longer. While explaining her preference for cinnamon rolls over Danish pastries, Iris slipped in a whispered plea for another meeting.

Elgin said, "Perhaps you have more shopping to do, Miss Huntington." Miss Huntington replied that she might shop more on the following day. Before Elgin left he bought a loaf of bread as though it had been the reason he had entered the bakery in the first place. After feeding part of the loaf to his horse, he threw the rest of it in the road for the birds.

Meanwhile the squire, fearing that Iris's peculiar inclination to light fires might strike again when least expected, arranged for someone to follow her when she left the grounds of Huntington Manor. It was for her own good, of course. So it was that the pot boy had trailed Iris into the village the next day and crept around corners and peeked into shop windows to see what Iris might be doing. He watched when she went into the emporium. Watched as she purchased a length of ribbon and eight mother-of-pearl buttons. Watched as Elgin entered the establishment and held the door open for Iris when she was on her way out. She stopped, they talked, though briefly. Afraid of being seen, the boy scurried away. That's why he hadn't heard Iris whisper, "Meet me in the Ha-ha tomorrow. Twoish." Before Elgin could reply she was down the steps and beyond contradiction.

On returning to the Manor the pot boy told the squire that he had seen Miss Huntington buying things at the emporium. When asked if Mr. Farley happened to be about at the time, the boy said that gentleman was going in as Miss

Huntington was going out. The squire didn't think the meeting had been accidental. Not for a minute. He believed that the crafty Elgin Farley had followed Iris to the village to tease information from her about his collections of antiquities. There could be no other reason for it. Iris was, after all, quite strange in the head. A sweet little thing, in her way, but a fruitcake all the same. It was obvious to the squire that Elgin was after something other than Iris. It could only be more information about certain ancient treasures.

Later that day, when Iris was questioned about the meeting in the emporium, she said, "When Mr. Farley and I passed at the door, I initiated a conversation to ask after the health of Rutherford family since their bereavement," which was true enough. It would have been unseemly had she not inquired.

Iris then told her grandfather that Mr. Farley had informed her that the duke and duchess were planning to go away for a while and that Maxwell wouldn't be returning to Scotland. Elgin hoped that the Huntingtons hadn't been greatly inconvenienced by the invasion of funeral guests from the Hall. That, too, was true. Then Iris said, "I assured Mr. Farley that the guests hadn't really disturbed us, and that I even continued to make drawings of your glass collection the whole while."

"Ah-ha! I *knew* it!" exclaimed the squire. "I *knew* he was after something, that scoundrel. I have said exactly that to your Aunt Prudence."

"Who was a scoundrel?"

"Elgin Farley, *that's* who! I told your Aunt Pru the same thing."

"Whatever makes you think so?"

"Never mind. I know *exactly* what's going on."

Iris turned ghostly pale. Had her grandfather found out that she had a personal interest in Elgin? Did he know that Elgin intended to save her from the Marquis of Bumpsted? How could she be sure? She couldn't very well ask.

The squire said, "If Farley has any sense, he'll leave while he still has his kneecaps. You might tell him that I said so."

"Yes, Grandfather."

"Don't look so upset. This has nothing to do with you."

"It doesn't?"

"Of course not! You're the innocent dupe. You've also had quite enough polishing for mixed society, so you won't need Farley's company anymore."

Half an hour later a note was on the way to Westbourne Hall, written in a fine hand on fine paper, addressed to Mr. Elgin Farley, Esquire. Iris repeated her grandfather's pronouncement and begged Elgin to go away for a while. She explained that her grandfather was quite angry with him, though she wasn't certain what the cause might be, but took into consideration his gout and complications of ill temper brought on by the recent upset at the house party. Teardrops marked the page that ended with Iris's initial.

Elgin was furious when he read the note, though he didn't think it wise to confront the squire to demand an explanation. He was certain that such an act would only make things worse in the long run. A challenge would set the old boy's back up, and Iris might be sent away as a result. So Elgin unloaded his spleen on a placidly grinning, all-knowing Tom while they were on their way to the harness makers to have two saddles and a pile of tack repaired.

Tom, who was driving the wagon, found it a great joke. Beside him, practically foaming at the mouth, sat his old friend. The same old friend who had smugly sworn himself to the peaceful life of a bachelor when Tom had been married. But Elgin wasn't facing placid old age. Elgin was obviously beyond redemption over a female who could undoubtedly drive the angels out of heaven and the devil out of hell, all before lunch, by doing God only knew what. It was also of interest that Elgin appeared to be incapable of understanding his own condition.

When Tom heard for the second or third time what Elgin thought of the squire's heavy-handed way of treating Iris, he said, "Well now, what will you be doing about it?"

"Doing? I'll have to send a reply to the damned note! It will be an awfully polite thing, but not one I'm prepared to compose at this moment, I can tell you that! It will be sent to Mrs. Chumbly, knowing full well that the squire will read it as soon as it arrives." Elgin leaned back in the hard seat and propped a booted foot on the dashboard. Thumbs hooked in his pockets, he said, "My note will probably say that I must regrettably take my leave of the Hall because my presence is required at home, and that I'll be off as soon as the duke and duchess are no longer in need of my company, or something like that."

"Be you such a lapdog, then?"

"Lapdog, my foot! I also intend to say that I'll

be returning in a week or two, I don't know. At that time I shall call at the Manor to pay my respects to the family. Kindly remember that I'd only be leaving to let things cool down for Iris."

"Has your interest in Miss Huntington set the old man off?"

"I don't think he knows about us. There's some other stone in his shoe."

"And you won't see the lady for a senite or more? That be longer than I could have stayed away from my Bess when we were courting."

"Iris and I aren't courting. We're just friends. The business about the engagement is a ruse to keep her from being married off to another fellow she doesn't fancy. Even so, this order from the squire to quit the area is an insult. My intentions are honorable enough."

"Oh, yes." Tom grinned. "I remember how honorable my intentions were when I was courting my Bess."

The next day Elgin asked the duke if he might use some fishing equipment. He was told to take anything he liked, though there wasn't much to catch. The duke suspected clumsy poachers, as he'd found dead fish lying around. Elgin explained that it wasn't fish he was after, but the mastering of the technique of catching them that interested him just now. This made perfect sense to the duke, who considered fly fishing an art form. Elgin was provided with a rod, a winch with new linen line, and a selection of the duke's own hand-tied flies with which to dap the waters. Elgin hooked them to the band of his bowler hat.

The weather was warm, but not too warm, with plenty of shade and fresh air along the river. Spikes of purpley-pink flowers bloomed in the shallows, so striking against the shades of greens in the wood. Birds swooped through the trees and squirrels chattered from the branches. A water vole paddled for his home in the far bank.

Elgin slapped his cheek, muttering, "Damn vultures." The insects were particularly aggressive. He was convinced that someplace nearby was a field dotted with lifeless cows all shriveled up into Hereford prunes attesting to the efficiency of this new strain of vampire gnat. He swatted his neck and dispatched more of the winged fiends, the proof of which stuck to his palm. He swished his hand in the cold water and wiped it off on his tweed knickerbockers. For Elgin the venture had become an uncommon amount of suffering just to appear as though one was actually fishing. Yet he dearly wanted to see Iris, and this was the only way he could give a plausible reason for his being on Huntington property, especially since old Huntington had threatened his kneecaps.

He turned his collar up. His ears, however, were defenseless against the swarming, humming horde, and that was the end of anything that vaguely resembled the fishing game. Espying the Ha-ha in the distance, Elgin made for it. A cloud of gnats followed him until he encountered a breeze that blew them away. Glad to reach his destination, he scraped his boots as clean as he could and stepped onto the floor of the sheltered terrace.

Relieved to be without the halo of insects, Elgin unloaded his gear onto one of the benches to wait for Iris, for this was the day and place she'd asked him to meet her. If pressed to explain his presence to some overly inquisitive individual, he thought he might say that he wanted to sit it out while untangling his line. His line, however, was neatly wound.

To remedy this contradiction Elgin cast the fly, gave the long rod a jerk, then made no attempt to stop the winch from spinning. The move presented an impressive mess. After removing his bowler and unbuttoning his jacket, Elgin set about undoing the tangle. And he thought more about Iris because she was another tangle in his life.

In spite of the difficulties they had encountered over the years the old jokes they'd shared sprang to mind and he welcomed them like a warm stone on a cold night. And he thought about other warm things, like the way Iris smiled, and sometimes she giggled or even gave in to the kind of laugh that a lady should never unleash. An irreverent celebration of life. And she made him laugh. But he didn't want to think about how his gut tightened when she smiled at him. It wasn't conducive to being friends. That's when the barking dog sent his thoughts in another direction. A deep woofing, followed by the thumping of great furry feet. Elgin watched the destruction of small trees beneath the great furry body as it stumbled and skidded down the hill. An impressive splash followed. More woofing. More splashing.

"Good afternoon." The voice came softly, almost a whisper.

Elgin looked up. While he'd been watching the dog, Iris had stepped quietly onto the terrace holding a small willow basket. In it were a spade and a few plants wrapped in paper. She glanced over her shoulder.

Putting aside the fishing rod, Elgin stood. "Is anything wrong?"

"I don't think so, though I'm certain that I was followed yesterday when I went to the village. By the time I returned home Grandfather knew that we met there, so I wondered if anyone followed me today." She put the basket on the table, then removed her gardening gloves and put them in with the plants. "I wasn't sure if you would be here after the note I sent advising you to go away for a while."

Iris's face could hardly be seen under the big hat, the one Elgin didn't particularly like. He stepped in front of her and began to undo the ribbons that secured that hat, working long trim fingers into the knot. His voice was low but clear when he said, "I've thought angry thoughts about that note, and I probably should go, but I haven't said I would go." When his knuckles brushed her throat, he quickly stuffed his hands in his pockets and left the rest of the untying to Iris.

Pulling the ribbons free, she said, "Grandfather is in such a temper that you simply must go away for at least a little while . . . please?"

"One moment. You'll notice that I've just returned. I've been in and out of Westbourne Hall like a jack-in-the-box, and I'm not ready to leave again." Touching her cheek, he said, "Don't look so troubled, it will all come about." But their eyes held and his hand lingered beyond a simple gesture of reassurance. He was all too aware of shadowy-blue eyes. The scent of honeysuckle. His thumb touched her mouth. The hat slipped from her fingers. His gut tightened; he swallowed hard and whispered, "Iris, I don't want to leave you like this."

He saw such hope in her eyes. His hands went back into his pockets, and he looked off into the trees. A long moment later he said, "I suppose I could leave for a while, but only because I find it so very difficult to refuse you anything . . . I mean because we're such good friends and all that." Without looking at Iris again he went back to his fishing line to work at the mess it was in. Giving the snarl a yank, he said, "How long can you stay out here?"

"Not too long."

"Long enough to tell me about the fire?"

"The fire?"

"Was there more than one?"

"One seemed to be quite enough."

"Were you hurt?"

She shook her head.

"Did you light it?"

"If you're referring to a very little fire that involved a great deal of smoke, yes, I lit that fire."

"May I ask why you did it?"

"Well, I didn't do it with the intention of smoking out any of the house guests that were there at the time. That was serendipitous. I simply wanted to burn something."

"Burn something?"

It was a long uncomfortable moment before Iris could say, "My inflatable."

It was another long moment before Elgin asked, "Your inflatable *what*?"

Painfully embarrassed, Iris turned a delicate crimson and said, "My inflatable bosom."

His glance went to her chest.

She turned away and folded her arms over that part of herself. "I see that you don't understand, so I shall have to explain."

And she did explain, from the morning her Aunt Prudence delivered the bust enhancer to the afternoon it went up in flames and an impressive amount of smoke. And she told him that the smoke came about because she had used too much newspaper to get the fire going. Some of the paper got caught in the hot updraft and stuck in the chimney, effectively blocking it, which resulted in a smoke-filled house. Nor did she leave out the ringing of the fire bell, the thundering return of the fire brigade, or the drenching of the hall, or everyone's things getting tossed out the chamber windows. Iris concluded with "It truly was awful when it happened, though the result was rather nice, as the Marquis of Bumpsted went away."

Elgin looked quietly amazed until his guffaw shook the birds from the trees. Wiping his eyes, he said, "Do apprise me of any future event."

Hearing the noise, the dog galloped up from the river to see what he'd missed. Not one to arrive empty-handed—or empty-mouthed—he dropped a fish at the edge of the terrace. Pink tongue flapping, long fur dripping, the dog then bounded over to the only company he could find.

To make himself presentable he shook vigorously muddy water flying everywhere.

He could tell that these people were excited about his arrival, because she gave a squeaking shriek and he offered a profound comment. To make room for him they backed right up to the stone wall of the Ha-ha. The dog smiled and trotted after them on sloppy feet. To demonstrate his friendly intentions he laid his wet self down on the edge of her skirt. The garment offered this unusual opportunity as her skirt was dragging in front because the great hoop was being pushed up from behind against the wall.

Iris tugged at her skirt and said, "Get up this instant!" The dog only stretched out and gave a contented groan that ended in a sort of woofing *snort-snort*.

Elgin positioned himself in full view of the dog. He assumed that beneath the mop of fur on top of the beast's head and behind the black leathery nose were its beady eyes. Just in case the dog had gone to sleep, Elgin clapped his hands to attract its attention. Then he said, "Come on, old chum. Let's roll over this way, shall we? Come on!"

Nothing happened.

Elgin tried to move the dog. The dog tried to bite Elgin. This proved that the dog was not asleep, that Elgin had quick reflexes, and exposed Iris to a more colorful vocabulary than she had previously experienced. The outburst was immediately followed by an apology on Elgin's part. The dog gave no account of itself, which seemed rather rude, given the circumstances.

Stuffing his hands safely into his pockets,

Elgin said, "Your dog doesn't seem to like me."
When he saw the blank look on Iris's face, he
said, "It isn't your dog?"

"I've never even seen it before."

Elgin puckered in thought, then said, "We
could simply cut off the part of your skirt that
the beast thinks is his and be done with it."

Iris frowned and shook her head.

Elgin looked at the dog again, then his watch.
This wasn't what he'd had in mind for a clandestine rendezvous for which they had so little time.
He thought they would talk, but not about this
cursed animal. It hadn't been part of the plan to
have a great wet dog with large sharp teeth mo-
nopolizing the afternoon.

He said, "Iris, you can't stay pinned against
the wall for the rest of the day. No telling how—
just a moment."

Returning to the bench Elgin rummaged
through his fishing creel. There was nothing left
of his lunch but a half bottle of beer and two biscuits. Little by little he poured the brew into a
dip in one of the paving stones. Elgin fanned the
fumes in the dog's direction. First the beast's
nose twitched. Then he struggled to his feet and
lumbered over to the puddle of beer, where he
stayed for the last drop. After licking the stone,
he licked the bottle. Then he headed toward Iris
again. He seemed to like Iris and wanted her to
know it.

Elgin blocked the way. Cocking a menacing
eyebrow, he glared down at the dog. Pointing to
the wood he commanded, "Begone, varlet!"

The varlet went as far as his empty beer bowl

and laid down with his face in it, having put one great foot through Iris's hat on the way.

Taking up the ruined hat, Elgin cried, "The Lord works in mysterious ways, a-men!"

Iris clasped her hands, fluttered her eyelashes, and said, "You were *so* brave."

"Yes, I was, wasn't I? It's a little trick I learned years ago in deepest Africa. The old beer diversion. Works on everything from chickens to elephants, with the occasional exception of cats. Shall we walk along the river? I'd hate like the devil to disturb the dog now that I've managed to subdue him."

This time Iris didn't have to run to keep up. Elgin wanted to know more about the house party. Actually, he wanted to know more about the Marquis of Bumpsted at the house party. Iris, in turn, was more than a little interested in what had been going on when Elgin was at home. What his sister's coming-out ball had been like, and, more to the point, what his sisters were like. She didn't ask what his parents were like. She'd already heard the rumors.

When the gnats drove them back to the Ha-ha, they discovered that the dog was gone. The fishing equipment was untouched, as was the basket with the plants. The crushed hat was still there. So was the fish. The beer bottle was nowhere to be seen. Elgin would rather the beast had taken the hat.

In a few days Elgin was gone, too. At first Iris didn't worry. After all, she had asked him to go. She was sure that by the time he returned her grandfather would see reason and approve of him calling on her. Sometimes she even sang softly, happily, while she poked about among the collections. Then, from remarks Prudence made, Iris learned that her family still intended to pursue the Bumpsted connection. With a wink her grandfather confided that he would be inviting the man back for a private unrolling of the mummy.

That news was like the end of the world to Iris. In her heart she believed that Elgin would eventually charm her grandfather and find a way for them to be together. In her head she began to wonder if he could find the way soon enough to save her from Bumpsted. There were times when her eyes were as red as Prudence's. She no longer sang or made illustrations. Each day she felt as though she was being torn further away from Elgin and pushed terrifying closer to a union that would be unbearable.

In desperation Iris tried to explain her feelings to her grandfather. He just patted her hand and said, "Now, now, don't fret so. Young ladies are often apprehensive about marriage, but it's nothing to worry yourself about. Really nothing. You'll survive."

For the first time Iris considered running away. With her education she thought she might find employment as a governess or a companion in a remote place where she wouldn't be recognized. But even ladies and gentlemen from remote places went to London. If it were known that she was missing, someone would surely suspect something, for she had such a striking resemblance to her sisters and her sisters were in London.

So Iris thought that she might be a kitchen maid in a remote place. Cooks would never see her sisters, so they would never recognize her as the one that ran away. Even so a kitchen maid needed reliable references to secure a respectable position. The Huntingtons had never hired anyone without checking their references. A suffocating panic came over Iris when she thought of the stories she had heard about females who left home, never to be seen again. There were reports of unidentified bodies of young women found floating in the river or lying under bridges. Dumped in fields. Iris decided that she'd have to plan things a little better before she ran away. Her mood didn't improve.

Now letters practically flew between Huntington Manor and the grand residence in London that housed the Hubert Huntingtons. The conclusion was that poor Iris, who had gone from songs to tears, was rapidly falling into a dangerous decline. Something simply had to be done about Iris.

· Seven ·

The man said, "Allow me to introduce myself," and confidently crossed the thick carpet of the Egyptian Room with his hand extended. He was of the portly sort, with the thin dark hair from the left side of his head combed carefully over to the right side to cover the balding top. His beard, however, was thick and trimmed square at the bottom. He wore a well-tailored black suit. Gold-rimmed spectacles pinched his florid nose and magnified his eyes to an alarming size, yet when he spoke it was in a voice calculated to soothe.

Seated on the edge of an open crate, Obediah Huntington looked up from the intricately wrapped, brass-studded mummy of a small bird. He slipped the thing back into the crate. When he shook the stranger's too smooth hand, he wondered if this might be yet another spy for one of his rival collectors. If so, he was brazen, indeed!

The fellow said, "I am Dr. Ambrose P. Ambrose. Your son Hubert came to see me concerning his daughter Iris. I believe she's in your care."

"Yes, she's here and feeling quite well"—was the squire's guarded reply.

Ambrose glanced around the crowded room. "May I sit down?"

"In the library." The squire left his crate to lead the doctor out of the Egyptian Room and away from his newest treasures. When the two men were safely relocated, the squire said, "Just what is it that you wish to say about my granddaughter?"

Coming directly to the point, Ambrose said, "Her father fears that her mind has become dangerously unbalanced. Did I understand him correctly when he said that at a recent social gathering in this house the young lady in question left in the middle of a cultural demonstration and went upstairs, where she removed and set fire to a piece of her underclothing?"

"That's what happened, but—"

"That's an unsound attitude toward one's intimate apparel, an obvious indication of repressed sexual cravings. Were there any questionable gentlemen attending that party? Anyone who might have inspired such a wanton action? Are you certain? Your son also tells me that for no good reason at all the girl has refused to consider marriage, a very respectable marriage, saying that she wasn't inclined to take a husband at the present time." Ambrose looked to the squire for confirmation of what he'd been told.

The squire sighed and said, "Iris once told her mother that she would rather become another Florence Nightingale than marry someone she didn't fancy."

Dr. Ambrose didn't like the way that busybody

Nightingale was complaining about dirt in army hospitals when men were dying. Like many others, he thought she should be at home, minding her own business, with a husband and family like God intended. Ambrose, however, didn't allow himself to become distracted. He said, "Is it also true that after another confrontation regarding the proposed marriage this same young woman took her brother's razor and used it, if you'll pardon my bluntness of speech, to shave her legs?"

Once again the squire sighed and nodded. Ambrose leaned forward and dropped his voice. "Is it also true that she's been having *opinions*?"

The squire threw his hands up in dispair. "She has opinions on everything as of late. But I fail to see how—"

"My God, man, she is a *female*! You can't expect her to have the same reasoning powers as the male of the species. Any rational man of science knows that men think with *superior* brains. Women, with their *lesser* brains, can hardly think at all. They merely react according to the dictates of their female organs. They can't help it. It has been proved that men have larger heads, with correspondingly larger brains. Women's heads are smaller; therefore their brains are smaller, so they can't think as well as men. It is a physical impossibility!"

"That may be so," said the squire, "but now and then you do meet up with a man who is as thick as a diggers boot. Then there are women, a few at least, who have displayed unusual mental abilities."

"So there are. But stupid men and smart

women are all freaks," insisted Ambrose. "They are freaks, along with two-headed goats and four-legged ducks, and I have seen a four-legged duck with my own eyes. None of these conditions is normal. We must address what is normal. Your granddaughter, I'm afraid, has slipped past the bounds of normal. May I ask if she has displayed unhealthy eating habits?"

"Not at all. Iris eats like a horse. So you see—"

Ambrose shook his head. "I'm sorry to hear of her exaggerated interest in food. It isn't a good sign, you know. Now tell me, is she given to unbridled laughter?"

"Well," said the squire uncomfortably, "not very often, but she is inclined toward amusement when—"

"I see. She lacks that restraint as well. Does she argue?"

"Until recently Iris has been the picture of sweetness and obedience, though arguments now arise when she has one of her opinions. I can't imagine what's got into her. She's a young woman of twenty years, or thereabout, but perhaps she's twenty-one, I lose count with so many of them, but she should know better."

"Fear not!" intoned the doctor, lifting a soft beefy hand in benediction. "We are fortunate that medical science has found a way to save these unfortunate souls. It has been shown that the removal of the ovaries will return these pitiful females to a placid and obedient state, just as God intended them to be!"

Horrified, the squire said, "Not *surgery*!"

The doctor sighed compassionately. "I'm afraid so. I have, however, performed over one hundred of these operations and can assure you and your son that the results are always the same. Though every one of these women had to be forced by their husbands or fathers to have the operation, they were invariably better behaved after recovery."

"But there are bound to be complications from infection!" cried the squire. "How many of your patients have died?"

In his perpetually soothing voice Ambrose said, "Some, of course, but let us speak of the ones who have lived. The majority, about three-quarters of them, actually, have survived. To look for a greater recovery rate would be an unrealistic expectation of any medical man. Instead of dwelling on the morbid possibilities of death, we must think of the fate that awaits your granddaughter if nothing is done about her present condition.

"In view of what she has already done, you can be sure that she will soon develop *intemperate desire*," said the doctor in tones that promised a rapid descent into hell. "The burning of her undergarment is an indication that the dreaded condition has already begun to manifest itself. That desire, in turn, will cause tuberculosis and venereal disease. Nasty things, I assure you. The fact that these abominable complaints run rampant among the prostitutes of our larger cities is *proof* that an unhealthy sexual appetite has caused them. Facts, sir, are facts. And facts cannot be other than what they are."

"But if Iris has this surgery, she won't be able to have any children."

"True, but if she doesn't have the surgery, she

will end up in an insane asylum. Surely you wouldn't want her to have any children in a place like *that*! Don't you love your granddaughter?"

Shoulders sagging in defeat, the squire asked, "What, exactly, does Hubert have in mind for Iris?"

The doctor leaned back in his chair, clasped his hands over his ample abdomen, and stared at the squire through goggly eyes. "There is only one course of action possible if your granddaughter is to maintain her sanity, physical health, and a respectable position in society." As the squire made no comment, Ambrose continued. "I've brought everything required to perform the operation, needing only a sturdy table in a well-lighted room and a few able-bodied men to take hold of the young lady and keep her down until the chloroform can take effect. I always regret the use of force, of course, but none of these women are ever capable of understanding what is best for them."

Ambrose then paused to check his watch. With a confident smile he said, "We're in luck, for it's barely noon. I can perform the surgery and still catch the train back to London for my supper." The watch went back into his pocket. "There is one more thing. Can you provide me with an assistant who won't faint at the sight of blood? I say, Huntington, you look as though you could do with a spot of brandy."

When the men finally left the room and their voices had faded away down the passage, Prudence came out from behind the library door. She had nearly been squashed against the wall when her brother swung the door open, not knowing that she was on the other side. It had taken a moment for her to catch her breath. In that moment she heard that the stranger in her brother's company was a doctor and feared the worst for Iris. In the next few minutes those fears were confirmed, and she decided to discover the whole of the plan. Despite feeling terribly guilty because she had been eavesdropping, Prudence went in search of her niece.

After peering into the Grecian Room, her bedchamber, and the closet where the kitten had slept, Prudence found Iris alone in the ladies' parlor, reading a magazine. After closing the door, she hurried to the girl's side, a finger across her lips requesting silence.

In a frantic whisper, she said, "Iris, you must leave the house *at once*! You must hide *quickly*!"

"Have my parents sent down another man for me to marry?"

"A doctor has come from London to commit surgery. It's supposed to make you more biddable, because you've been doing such strange things, and he insists that you're quite mad, but then you won't be able to have babies, even if you live through it. The deed will be done within the hour if they can find you!" Prudence took a packet of sweets from her pocket, put it into Iris's hand, and closed her fingers around it.

"Hurry!" Prudence urged, taking Iris by the wrist. She peeked into the hallway to see who might be about, then led Iris to an unused side door. It groaned open on rusty hinges to reveal a heavy covering of ivy. "Stay among the vines until your way is safe. Then go into the trees, then

along the hedgerow until you're out of sight of
the house, then to the old boathouse, even
though it does smell ever so musty in there. It
will have to do for now. I used to go there years
ago when I wanted to escape from my governess
to read the books I borrowed from the housekeeper, though she didn't really want to lend
them to me, but she did. Stay hidden until I
send someone for you, but heaven only knows
who it will be, for that dear Mr. Farley has yet to
return to us. My goodness. Do be careful." Prudence gave Iris a push out the door.

Dr. Ambrose had arranged an operating theater in the sunlit conservatory. For the surgery he
had selected the same table that had supported
the mummy for the unrolling. Now that he was
ready to begin, he expected Iris to be brought in,
only to learn that she couldn't be found. He was
told that when she wasn't seen in her usual
haunts, a search was undertaken. After an hour
had been spent waiting Dr. Ambrose was clearly
annoyed. He wasn't accustomed to having his
valuable time wasted, his skills unappreciated.
After repacking his instruments, he left for the
train in disgust. He intended to send a bill to the
Huntingtons that would compensate him rather
nicely for the inconvenience to which he had
been subjected.

Having seen the doctor off, the squire was
caught between anger and worry over Iris.
Bursting into the ladies' parlor, he said, "Prudence, I've had the house and grounds turned
upside down to no avail. Do you know where Iris
might be?"

Quite unable to lie about it, Prudence twisted

her handkerchief, and said, "She *might* be in the boathouse."

"Egad! Why would she want to go to the boathouse?"

"I don't suppose she would *want* to go there, actually. It is so musty, and I believe things do creep about in the dampness, for the big doors haven't been opened in so long, not since the boats began to leak, you know, so I don't think anyone would *want* to go there. Not really."

"Has she ever gone there before?"

"Oh, I hardly think so."

"Then why would she want to go there now! Is she in her room?"

"No. I looked in her room."

"Where was she when you last sought her out?"

"When I last sought her out? My goodness. She was right here in this room reading a magazine. Would you like to see it? There's an interesting natural history article on icebergs and the animals that—"

"Not now!" The squire rubbed his throbbing forehead and sank into the nearest chair that had a footstool. After elevating the toe that had begun to nag him, he said, "Do you think the girl could be someplace playing with the kitten?" Prudence said no. The squire tapped his fingers impatiently, then stopped.

"I've got it," he said grimly.

"Oh?" said his sister, twisting her handkerchief more tightly.

"I haven't been blind to what's been going on, you know."

"Oh?"

"Who has Iris been interested in?"

"Well, I—"

"Who has Iris talked about? And who did Iris want to see one afternoon?"

"Let me see now . . ." The handkerchief split.

"The gypsies! *That's* who! Iris has gone off to the gypsies! Are they still about the neighborhood?"

"I don't think so, Obediah. When Sofia called here, she said they were getting ready to leave. They might even be in Wales by now."

"Then that's where poor Iris has gone. To Wales with the gypsies. Ah, me. If I ever doubted her degenerated mental condition, this is proof of it. It's a sad day for the Huntingtons."

"Where are you going, Obediah?"

"I'm going to send someone after Iris, of course, starting with the campsite, in case there are any clues as to which caravan she might be in. If it weren't for this damn toe, I'd go myself!"

The search party found the gypsy camp deserted—horses, caravans, everything gone, the ashes cold. There were no clues about Iris.

Late that afternoon Prudence ventured into the Egyptian Room with a small bottle of tincture of artichoke leaves to relieve her brother's gout. He was sagged in his chair with his foot up. She tapped a teaspoon against the bottle, and he opened his mouth like a bird and swallowed the stuff, washed it down with a swig of scotch, and continued to stare at the mummy that had been partly unrolled. Through his brain ran all the wondrous things about mummies that he never had the opportunity to describe.

Some of the ghastly bits about the preparation process were for the ears of gentlemen only, things he would have divulged over a glass of port after dinner, or in the privacy of the all-male billiard room. Ladies simply didn't go into the billiard room.

Recorking the medicine bottle, Prudence said, "Obediah, Elgin Farley is downstairs asking to see Iris. It seems that he has a little something she requested him to bring her from London. He said he has come directly from the train station and hasn't even been to Westbourne Hall yet. Isn't that nice? He is such a dear man. Shall I tell him that Iris has run off with the gypsies?"

"Hell no! We can't let a thing like that get out. Tell him that Iris has taken to her bed with the toothache." Before Prudence reached the door, he said, "Wait! Don't tell him that or he'll just return tomorrow with some other excuse for admittance. Tell him . . . tell him that she's gone back home. To be married. That should send him away with a flea in his ear. The fact that Iris has run off is actually a blessing in disguise for him if he but knew it. Keeping company with a madwoman can turn a man's brain to mush. Haven't I always said that a female can make a man's brain mushy?"

"Yes, Obediah, you've always said that. I shall explain it to Mr. Farley."

The squire looked to heaven for understanding, closed his eyes, and shook his head. "Just tell him that she's gone home to be married."

Prudence found Elgin exactly where she had left him in the small reception room near the front door. Upon entering she folded her hands, cleared her throat, and recited, "Iris has gone home to be married."

The color drained from Elgin's face. Prudence had been wondering how such news would affect him. His stricken expression said a great deal. Stepping closer, she smiled and whispered, "I was told to tell you that Iris has gone home to be married instead of saying that Iris has run off with the gypsies, though she is really in the boathouse. She is also in great danger. Don't let anyone see you going down there."

Elgin now looked at Prudence with something new to consider. Everyone had always known that she was, well . . . *scattered*. He just hadn't realized that she had been scattered quite so far and decided that the best thing to do was jolly her along until he could find out where Iris really was.

He said, "Well, then, Mrs. Chumbly, just what is this danger that Iris is in, hmm?"

A shadow fell over Prudence. "It's a wicked doctor."

"Ah, yes. The old wicked doctor problem," said Elgin gravely. "There's been a great deal of that going around."

"Indeed there has," said Prudence. "I didn't think you knew about such things. He's done it over one hundred times, you know. Imagine that. *One hundred times!* It's too dreadful to think about."

"Indeed it is, so let's not think about it, shall we? Where did you say Iris is to be found?"

"In the boathouse. I sent her there hours ago, though you mustn't tell anyone of her whereabouts. Her grandfather thinks she ran off with the gypsies."

Elgin was awfully confused and looked it. "You first said that she had gone home to be married."

"That's what I was supposed to tell you instead of saying that she was in her room with the toothache."

"Is she in her room with the toothache?" asked Elgin, glancing toward the door, wondering if someone would come along and take Prudence off to a happy corner where she could talk to the fairies.

"Of *course* not! She's hiding in the boathouse. I sent her there myself."

"Well, that would explain it."

"You must save her quite soon, for there's no one else to take her away. I can't even take anything to her for fear I'll be followed."

"That wouldn't be any great surprise, would it?"

"Not really. You see, my brother has had people looking for Iris. Do take a warm blanket when you go. And food. All she has are a few sweets, but not any real food. Not a crumb."

"Food. Quite so," replied Elgin. "Tell me, whatever happened to the wicked doctor?"

"He's gone back to London."

"Ah, yes. They do that sort of thing. Dash off when you least expect it, though I assume you were glad to see him go."

"Indeed I was! The thing is, if Iris is found, he'll come back."

"Is there any other way that I might see Iris?"

"No, only in the boathouse. She is—"

"Hiding, yes. How could I forget?"

"You must go by way of the river. If you leave here and go directly there, it would surely arouse comment, I should think, and we wouldn't want to do that, would we?"

"Goodness no!" said Elgin. "Will you be all right if I leave you? I mean, is there anyone who might be looking for *you*?"

"Oh, no. I'm not missing. You just run along and do remember the blanket, if you please, though it might be difficult to explain why you're going to the river with a blanket at this time of night, for it's almost this time of night, though perhaps you might say that you want to sit on it while you watch the stars, or something. That would do it."

"Yes, I imagine it would. Now I really must be going." When Prudence extended her hand Elgin took it gallantly and said, "Good evening, Mrs. Chumbly. It was good of you to see me. Do give my regards to your brother."

Prudence whispered, "The boathouse."

"Of course. The old b.h." replied Elgin, and politely said good-bye.

King Henry knew exactly where he was supposed to go. When there wasn't anyone at the station to meet him Elgin usually hired that horse from the livery stable to carry him to Westbourne Hall. While the horse plodded along Elgin dwelt upon the whereabouts of Iris. He supposed it was possible that she hadn't been allowed to see him. Hadn't even been told he was there.

By the time he climbed into bed that night Elgin was still at a loss. After unsuccessfully sorting through the logical reasons why Iris hadn't come downstairs to see him, he was forced to consider the illogical reasons. The least logical of them all was that Iris, having been threatened by a wicked doctor, was hiding in the boathouse in need of food and a blanket.

By stuffing his face into the pillow, Elgin was prepared to dismiss the thought. Boathouses, indeed! He'd had too much sun, too much traveling, and one too many disjointed conversations with Prudence Chumbly. As lying very still with his eyes closed didn't do much to dismiss these unwanted thoughts, he flopped onto his back, stared at the darkened ceiling, and continued to ponder the whereabouts of one rather small, amazingly resourceful female. It became obvious that wherever his search might end, it would have to begin with the boathouse.

A few minutes later Elgin was up, mostly dressed, and eyeing the blanket on his bed. A very good-looking blanket. Wool, woven in Scotland from the look of it. He left it, certain that it would be missed if he borrowed it.

An impatient search of his wardrobe for a warm covering revealed the suit he had just been wearing, one tweedside jacket, one shooting jacket, knickerbockers, peg-top trousers. Mourning clothes, evening clothes, shirts, a Chesterfield coat, and an opera cape. He went back to the shooting jacket, took it out, and put it on. It had big pockets. There was an elegant silk dressing gown with quilted lapels. He'd hardly worn it. Beside it hung an old flannel robe. The footman who served as his valet when he was at the Hall had once suggested that he might want to

donate it to a worthy cause. Elgin thought Iris
was a worthy cause, but the robe just didn't look
warm enough for a night in a boathouse. He considered the Chesterfield, but took the opera cape.

It—that is, the cape—was black woolen stuff
with a velvet collar and a red satin lining. Elgin
supposed the thing must have been hanging
there since last winter. He and Maxwell had
been delayed in town at a private party, having
to board the train in London wearing their evening clothes. They hadn't had time to return to
their lodgings to change clothes because they'd
been compelled to take refuge in an old powder
closet of their host's home until they could climb
out a window to escape an insistently amorous
opera dancer. Recuperation from that revel
needed a full day of sleep and headache powders,
though it had taken another week for the tooth
marks in Elgin's shoulder to disappear.

Remembering all that, Elgin put the cape back
in the wardrobe. He felt uncomfortable taking it
to Iris. Then he reasoned that someone hiding in
a cold boathouse really would need a warm cape.
Before blowing out the lamp and leaving the
room, he took both candles from the glass can-
dleholders on the mantel and dropped them into
his pocket. He was out in the passage before he
remembered to go back for the matches.

He went downstairs as casually as possible. It
wouldn't do to look as if he was up to something.
Before he could get to the kitchen, however, he
was met by a footman in his shirtsleeves. The
fellow looked boldly at the cape Elgin had
thrown over his shoulder. It was the way any
number of young men went off to meet a bird—a

female—in mother nature's own downy nest in the tall grass or a hay pile.

The footman's cheeky smirk said *anyone I know?*

Elgin's supercilious glare said *it's none of your damn business!*

The footman cleared his throat apologetically and stepped aside.

Elgin left the house in a poor mood, his anger cushioning his fear for Iris. Not wanting to give away his destination, he started down the drive as though he were going to the village. The cheeky footman watched his moonlit figure from the window of a darkened room and didn't think Elgin was going as far as the village. He knew it had to be the old mill. His smirk returned. He'd gone there himself, with a rug thrown over his shoulder.

Tom's cottage was dark. Elgin stepped quietly to the door, blessing the rose-covered trellises that concealed him. He knocked softly; two quick raps, then a pause and one rap. It was the distress signal that three boys had devised so many years ago. When there was no response after a minute or two, Elgin repeated the pattern. It was difficult for him not to beat a tattoo on the door.

When the door opened it was just enough for Tom to slip out. "This way," he whispered. Elgin followed. Once they were hunkered down behind the shed, Tom said, "Have you got her?"

"Good heavens, does everyone know she's gone?"

"Couldn't help but know it the way the squire sent out hunting parties. Had someone go up to the Hall in case she be on a visit there. They even went to look in the village and the old gypsy camp. Then all of a sudden we hear that the lady be found asleep in her bed, and that she be going back to London right away. It did sound queer."

Tom shifted around so he could tie his shoes and said, "Tonight my cousin comes by. The one that works in the Huntington dairy. She says that the kitchen maids up to the Manor be saying that nobody's found the lady, asleep or otherwise, and the maids don't know why they're saying they found her when they didn't. So I think that Miss Huntington be gone for sure, but the family don't want anyone to know."

"Your common sense shines through once again."

"Have you got her?" Tom persisted.

"No, but I know where she is. I'll be going there as soon as I can get some food and a blanket."

"Do you need anything else?"

"I don't know, but then I don't really know what's going on. Mrs. Chumbly seems to think I've got to take Iris away immediately."

"Does Max know what you be up to?"

"Max is up to his neck with family problems just now. Besides, you're in a position to help me more than anyone else, if you will. I couldn't even get into the kitchen at the Hall for food without being interrupted. Dash it all, one of the footmen thought I was on my way out to meet some petticoat for a romp in the shrubbery!"

Tom muffled a laugh. "Stay where you be and I'll fetch what you need."

*   *   *

As Prudence had instructed, Iris dashed from the house to a line of trees, then ran along the hedgerow into the wood to the old boathouse with the weathered paint. She was panting when she got there and leaned against the side door to catch her breath. After resting for a moment she pushed herself away from the door, slid back the wooden latch, and tugged ineffectively at the handle. After a few more reviving breaths she tried again, bracing her feet on the stone slab in front of the door and pulling with both hands. The door creaked open. She hurried forward and choked on a scream.

Spiderwebs.

They stretched across the doorway. Instinctively retreating, she grabbed the front of her skirt and frantically rubbed her face to remove the wispy, clinging threads.

She went around to the double doors—the ones facing the water. Locked. Returned to the side door. As her survival was at stake, Iris dispensed with the niceties. Getting down on her hands and knees, she squashed in her hoops as much as possible and crawled under the webs, into the moldering boathouse. Closing the door behind herself was easy enough, for she simply took hold of the bottom edge and drew it in. What gave her gooseflesh was having to reach up behind the spiderweb to close the latch from the inside. The slide and tap of wood against wood told her that she was safe—safe in this place where a gloomy light crept in through the cracks around the doors and fell through a hole in the roof.

As her eyes adjusted to the dimness, Iris could see four overturned boats in a neat row. She didn't know how long it had been since anyone had used them.

Shaking out the wad of skirts and hoops, Iris then addressed the twigs and leaves and chips of paint that were stuck in her hair. She hurriedly picked them out as though getting the last little piece was important. That's when her hands began to shake. Her insides felt the same way. Crossing her arms, she hugged herself tightly to keep from falling apart. She was overheated from running and cold from fear and sank to the dirt floor exhausted.

With her eyes squeezed shut she whispered, "Elgin, please hurry," and forbid herself the tears that stung her throat. The next minute her head snapped up, and her eyes flew open.

Voices.

She was certain that she heard voices. Men talking, laughing far away. Then not so far away. Iris held as still as a hare, breath shallow, eyes wide. The voices were closer now; arguing about how a rake handle came to be broken. One of the men hacked and spit.

Please hurry. . . .

The voices faded, heading downstream toward the Ha-ha. Iris began to feel giddy. Those men had just been passing through. It was doubtful that anyone except her Aunt Prudence knew that she was missing from the house. Not yet. Then they would begin looking for her in the collection rooms, or the garden. But they'd search the house through and through before they considered the boathouse. She crawled over to the nearest boat and leaned against it, cushioning her face against her arms, grateful that the men who came so close had been so intent upon the condition of a rake handle. Otherwise they might have noticed that the grass had been trampled down around the boathouse. Iris was gooseflesh all over again, knowing that she had been only a glance away from detection and the threat of the doctor's knife. Perhaps a glance away from her own death.

Feeling the tentacles of panic creeping over her, Iris thought she'd better think about more pleasant things. Like the day Elgin rescued her from the apple tree. That was the memory she trotted out the most whenever she was sad, or when life appeared disastrous. Sometimes she would concentrate on the wonderfully ordinary things, like the birthdates of her brothers and sisters. And their children. And the names of their dogs and cats. And the mouse.

Her second youngest nephew Russell had a pet mouse named Sir Quinsy Teenyfeet. Iris hadn't thought about Sir Quinsy in a long time. He had especially fine whiskers and lived in a large brass birdcage with a swing in it that he had learned to use. His little bed had been made of a cheese box covered in purple velvet. It hadn't taken Quinsy long to chew the velvet cover into more comfortable bedding, which made Russell's sister cry, for she had cut and sewed it with such exquisite care. Thinking about Sir Quinsy was almost restful.

With twilight came a soft grunting and snorting and the crackle of dried leaves from beneath the boat. Iris awoke, interrupting a dream about pigs. Lots of pigs. It was too dark to see much of anything now, but she knew what was making those noises. Somewhere among the shadows was a little spiny hedgehog that continued to grunt and snuffle as he left his nest beneath a boat. Waddling about the dirt floor on his diminutive legs, he paused to gobble up something crunchy before going outside through the furrow he'd worn beneath one of the double doors. Curious things, hedgehogs. Iris had always found them rather dear. The gypsies found them delicious.

Tonight Iris envied hedgehogs, along with butterflies, and birds and Aunt Prudence's cat. Hedgehogs came and went as they pleased. While she was forced to hide away consoling an empty stomach, there were hedgehogs all over England that were feasting on tasty tidbits from forest floor and hedgerow. Iris dug one of the sweets from her pocket and sucked on it. Peppermint. Aunt Prudence swore by peppermint as an aid to digestion. Iris thought it would be nice to have something to digest. And she wondered how Elgin felt about spiders and hedgehogs.

Any warmth from the day had already faded, and Iris was chilled. As modesty wasn't necessary in her present situation she pulled up the back of her skirt and wrapped it around herself like a shawl. Iris knew that her aunt intended to send someone to help her, but who could possibly risk coming out here? Glori and her husband were planning a trip. They might be gone by now. No assurance of help there. Elgin probably wouldn't return for another week. Iris knew she couldn't remain undiscovered for that long.

Where could she go? She would just have to make her way to Elgin's home in Kent. It wasn't the best answer, but it was the only one she had. It would be a long walk, for she didn't have a penny with which to bless herself or hire transportation.

Taking another of the sweets that Prudence had given her, Iris considered where her next meal would come from. She thought she might get something from the kitchen garden after everyone was asleep. There would be a few apples in the orchard. To carry her provender she tore a large square from her undermost petticoat, which wasn't easy to do. She had to start the tear with her teeth. Iris also decided that she would have to start out as soon as her bindle was full, because the search for her would surely be intensive. The trampled grass around the boathouse would be noticed, and she was determined to be far away from Huntington Manor by then.

· *Eight* ·

By stepping back into the deeper shadows among the trees, Elgin was able to observe his surroundings without being seen. He was certain that no one had followed him to the boathouse, yet he waited. For as impatient as he was to see Iris and find out what the devil was going on, he didn't relish the thought of entering that building to get coshed over the head with a boat paddle. Iris might do that. In the dark she wouldn't be able to see that it was a friend who had come to call, not someone trying to drag her back to Huntington Manor and the wicked doctor.

The solution, however, proved simple. Elgin knocked softly on the door, confident that Iris would understand. Surely she would know that a villain wouldn't announce himself in such a way. He gave another gentle *rap-rap* before he even attempted to slide the latch and pull on the handle. Then he hoped that such an abrasive squeaking of hinges in the quiet night wouldn't attract unwanted attention. Anticipating spiderwebs, he swung a stick around inside the darkened doorway, quickly stepped inside, and closed the door.

He whispered, "Iris?" and listened. "Iris, are you in here?"

Nothing but a dull, damp echo.

He dropped his sack and gave the stick an angry slam; it cracked against a wall and plopped to the floor. The place smelled of mildew and mice and rotten wood . . . and the slightest hint of the honeysuckle scent Iris wore. Iris, who wasn't there anymore. He jammed his hands into his pockets and muttered, "Bloody hell!"

Through the inky darkness came "Elgin?"

The worry he'd felt was instantly replaced by an odd mixture of relief and anger. "Why didn't you answer before?"

"I didn't know who you were. I couldn't identify a whispering voice."

"Oh." The anger faded. "Oh, I see. Yes." He cleared his throat. "Are you all right?"

"I'm frightfully hungry and rather cold, actually."

Elgin took a candle and matchbox from his pocket. Scrape-scratch and a sizzling splatter of bright light became a sulfurous flash, then a flame. Iris was there, sitting on the floor beside an overturned boat. Blinking and dirty-faced, her hair was a mess of dusky curls stuck with twigs. Elgin thought she looked positively enchanting, but it wasn't the time for such confessions. He dug a hole in the dirt with the heel of his boot and packed the butt of the candle into it. Their shadows leapt up, then slunk against the walls like sinister giants that followed their every move.

"Will bread and cheese do?" he asked softly while churning things around in the sack. Every-

thing was coated with flour dust. Locating the
loaf of bread, he broke off a crusty chunk. Iris
took it with greedy hands, tore off a smaller
piece with her teeth, and chewed determinedly.
Her teeth were still complaining from tearing
her petticoat. Elgin pulled out the opera cape
and held it open. Iris shivered into it. A moment
later came the *squeak-pop* of the cork being
twisted from a bottle of water. After a few gulps
Iris wiped the back of a dainty hand across her
mouth and reached for a piece of cheese. The
sack then produced two apples, a cold pasty, and
several raw carrots.

While Iris tucked into the pasty, Elgin's gaze
drifted to a small gray moth that fluttered
around the candle. There was an almost whimsi-
cal tone to his voice when he said, "It would
seem that the search for you has been called off.
Your grandfather thinks you've run away with
the gypsies."

Iris gave him a quizzical look but kept eating.

"Your Aunt Pru said you were in hiding because of a wicked doctor, who, by the by, has returned to London. At least for the time being."

Elgin glanced at Iris. He thought she had gone
a bit pale, though it was difficult to tell in such
dim light. Even so he could see that her face had
become a well-disciplined blank. He had to listen
closely when she said, "That doctor came to perform an operation that is supposed to make a female like me more co-operative."

Elgin felt the hair prickle up the back of his
neck, for he finally understood how monstrous
was the threat to Iris. He'd heard about such
operations—about the parts that had been re-

moved from unfortunate women, then passed around on plates to be viewed at meetings of the Medical Society. A paradoxical aspect of a seemingly gentile, virtuous society.

He pulled Iris roughly into his arms and held her tightly, shutting his eyes against the awful thoughts. A second moth joined the first, flirting dangerously with the flame, singeing its wings. Elgin's voice had an edge to it when he said, "This dreadful business, this surgery—it won't happen to you. I'm going to get you away from here."

"When?"

"I don't know yet."

A sniffing at the door sent Elgin diving to slap his hand on the candle. The move sent Iris sprawling on the floor. In the darkness neither spoke, neither moved. Whatever was sniffing now scratched at the door. Elgin knew that Ozzie, Huntington's gamekeeper, had a dog. He also knew that Huntington had the fellow out looking for poachers, but Ozzie had a reputation for staying close to his hearth at night. Still, there was someone's dog out there. It went sniffing around the building until a sharp whistle called it away.

After what seemed like forever Elgin whispered, "I'll get you away tonight. Have you had enough to eat?"

"Yes."

Patting the ground, Elgin found the candle. The thing was broken. It didn't matter. He felt his way back to the boat where he'd left Iris. Straightening the wick and relighting the candle, he stuck it under the boat. Iris began to put things back into the sack. They could hardly see anything, but such an arrangement made it less likely for anyone outside the boathouse to see the light.

"Iris?"

She turned; he smiled.

"What can you possibly find so amusing?"

Leaning back against the boat, Elgin said, "You, me, us. This place. The sticks in your hair." She reached for the sticks. He reached for the cheese. "Would you mind going through the woods at night?"

"Will it take me far away from here?"

"Yes, eventually, but first you'll have to go to a place that's even more humble than this is. I'm not even sure what's left of it. Max and Tom and I built the thing when we were boys. It's a hut, a positive hovel, actually, in the wood on Westbourne land. We were going to use it for a hideout if we ever decided to become *gentlemen of the road*."

When she heard the word *yes*, Iris took the cheese from Elgin and put it in the sack along with everything else.

Elgin could see that the haunted look had left Iris, and he was glad of it, but the expression she assumed was discomforting in another way. When she looked at him now, he could see eyes filled with infinite trust. It was enough to send a profound uneasiness creeping into his bones. She seemed so sure that he would be able to make everything right. So sure that he could save her from anything and everything. He knew the truth to be something very different. He hadn't even been able to save his sisters when they needed saving so many years ago. They had looked at him in much the same way Iris did, but only rarely had he been able to distract their father during one of his bellowing rages. Sometimes Elgin felt that he had only made things worse when he interfered.

Yet he couldn't let anything happen to Iris.

Making an effort not to let his own misgivings show, Elgin brushed some dirt from Iris's face the way he would brush his sister's face. Iris gazed up at him, her lips parted ever so slightly. His voice was gruff when he said, "We'd better go now." He impatiently collected the sack and candle, went to the door, then looked back at Iris. A dog barked in the distance. A gust of wind stirred the trees, and branches scrubbed the boathouse wall. The candle flickered. Elgin still looked at Iris. He finally said, "Are you ready to face the world?"

She spread the cape wide and wrapped herself in its satiny wings. It brushed along the ground when she joined him at the door. He blew out the flame and lead the way out.

Sticks and stones didn't break her bones, but they bruised Iris's feet through the soles of her slippers. Her face and hands were scratched. Every tree in the wood had grown claws that grabbed at her clothes and pulled her hair. In addition to the obvious problems that slowed their progress, a great deal of time had been spent trying to locate the wretched hideout.

It was no help that it was the middle of the night and Elgin hadn't seen the place in years. Not since the roof began to sag. It made him think of the warm kitchen in Tom's cottage.

There would be a place for Iris to hide with no servants to carry tales. But Tom had an observant lad of three, who spoke quite well. So much for Tom's cottage.

Elgin now thought that a barn loft, any barn loft, sounded like a villa by the sea. He knew where the barns were. The trouble was that any number of people might see Iris on the way in or out. That would be a disaster. Barns were beyond consideration. There must be no one else to let anything slip out. Besides, the consequences suffered by anyone caught abducting, or aiding in the abduction of, a lady of unsound mind would be as drastic as the law would allow. After all, there was a doctor who would swear that Iris was of unsound mind, though he hadn't even seen her, but he was a doctor so that was all that mattered. So as miserable as it was, Iris would simply have to grace the lowly hut with her refined presence.

When they came upon another pile of brush that might be the sought-after hideout, it was so dark that Elgin could only guess where the entrance might be. He began to pull away dried branches from what he thought to be the right place. That's what he was doing right before he disappeared. Iris found this rather alarming. Then she heard him moving around and realized that he must have gone underground. Soon a soft light became visible.

Iris watched in grim fascination as Elgin emerged from a gap in the sticks and branches, a specter rising from the grave. Surely she wouldn't be expected to spend the night *there*. Rabbits slept under brush piles. Young ladies did not. Iris distinctly remembered that she'd recently enjoyed tea with a duchess. She'd had her pearls restrung. In her wardrobe were at least three Worth dresses. She could speak French remarkably well and play the flute. Last winter, with cleats on her boots, she had climbed over a glacier in Switzerland. She had promenaded in the South of France. Was she now to live in boathouses and brush piles with creepy things? It simply wasn't done. Such things didn't happen. Not to *real* people. Not to a Huntington. She gave the cape an indignant tug.

After an equally indignant sniff she thought about what else was available. She didn't really care to return to her soft warm bed at Huntington Manor and the dangers that awaited her there. That's when she decided that this might be an unusually *nice* brush pile, as brush piles go, and she wasn't afraid of rabbits.

Dusting off his clothes and pushing back his hair, Elgin said, "I've tidied the place a bit—cleared off the furniture. We haven't had guests in ever so long. Never had guests at all, actually. You might have noticed that it isn't Buckingham Palace; however, it's all ours. That is, all yours." He picked up the sack and gestured toward the gap in the brush pile. "Shall we?"

"Aren't you afraid that whoever it was with the dog will see the candle?"

"Huntington's gamekeeper has no business this far onto Westbourne land, so let's get on with it."

Iris tried. "I can't go in there."

"Oh?"

"My skirts. I'm all tangled up in branches and

skirts." She stepped back from the brush pile and raised the hem of her dress. Elgin discreetly looked away. He didn't have to ask what she was doing. After unbuttoning the correct waistband, she hopped up and down and her hoops fell to the ground, a flattened collection of graduated steel rings run through twill casings in a cotton petticoat. Lifting her drooping skirts, Iris stepped over the stuff at her feet the way a fairy princess might tiptoe over a puddle. Then she took up the hoops, squeezed them in, and held them all to her. They looked like an elongated figure eight. A figure eight taller than she was.

Arranging herself with tremendous dignity, she said, "*Now* I'm ready." Elgin turned around and laughed. She said, "Shhh!" He did his best.

Taking hold of her free hand, Elgin led Iris down the four stone steps to the square room beneath the sagging pile of branches. In a niche in the earthen wall burned a candle. The one that wasn't broken. Back when the room was dug out, platforms had been left along three of the walls to serve as benches. Elgin sat on one of these as there wasn't enough room for him to stand up straight. Iris had plenty of space overhead.

Surveying this sanctuary, Elgin said, "We had hoped to have the entire hideout underground but ran into limestone before we got deep enough. That's why we had to bend branches to make a domed roof."

Iris looked up at the domed roof.

"After that the supporting branches were covered with canvas scraps that we sewed together. Little by little we got axle grease and rubbed it in to make the covering waterproof, and it was, if it didn't rain too hard."

Iris looked up at the domed roof and nodded in understanding of the rain and axle grease.

"The brush pile went over the canvas to keep it from blowing away, and to keep bigger animals from walking over the roof and crushing it, and for camouflage. You can still see tatters of canvas if you look."

Iris looked again. There were indeed tatters of canvas. She took in as much of the place as she could with such limited light, then she, too, sat on one of the benches. "It would appear that you were a fairly accomplished architect."

"Yes, it would seem so, but I wasn't. Neither was Max. Most of the ideas were Tom's. Most of the work was done by Max and myself while Tom worked in the stable. Sometimes Tom's dog came with us. Samson had a bed over there so he wouldn't get stepped on." Elgin pointed at a bay carved close to the floor into the wall that didn't have a bench. Samson couldn't have been a very big dog.

Iris counted more compartments in the walls, places for all sorts of treasures that shouldn't be sat on or stepped on. In one of these nooks Elgin put the broken candle, the box of matches, and the remainder of the food.

The sack appeared to have the magical ability to produce whatever was needed, because a thick blanket came out next, making one of the benches into a narrow bed. While arranging it, Elgin reminded Iris that she would end up on the floor if she turned over too quickly. Then he sat down again and swung the sack up next to

Iris. "There are some traveling clothes in there; however, Tom's wife is more bountifully constructed than yourself, so expect a generous fit. Do you know what time it is?"

Iris reached beneath the cape she wore and touched the gold watch pinned to the bodice of her dress. She turned toward the light, pulled in her chin, and looked sideways at the timepiece. "It's five minutes after two."

"Close enough. When you change clothes, put your own things in the basket—there's a basket in the sack. Leave whatever you don't want to carry. Just make sure that you don't leave anything that can be traced back to you. Am I going too fast?"

"Leave what I don't want," repeated Iris. "Don't leave anything of my own."

"Precisely. Right now we're across the river and beyond the outbuildings of Westbourne Hall. When you go outside—assuming that you can think of this as inside—go down the hill until you reach the river, then turn left. Follow the river to the road, turn right, go over the bridge. Have you got it?"

Iris repeated that, too.

"Follow the road into Little Woolton. Buy a second-class ticket on the four o'clock train to London. I'll be traveling in first class until the next stop, when I'll join you and we'll both go second class so that we don't become separated."

During this spate of directions, Elgin had taken out his wallet, removed some notes, and put them in the nook. Then he thought of happy mice running off with the money to make expensive nests. Reclaiming the notes, he reached for the front edge of the opera cape that Iris had on and shoved the money to the bottom of an inside pocket. That's when he wondered what he may have neglected to remove from those pockets the last time he wore the cape. He excused himself to Iris to find out.

While this pocket searching progressed, Iris said, "I don't mean to sound ungrateful, but I do hope we're not heading for another boathouse or brush pile on your property in Kent."

"Hmm? Oh, no. We're going to see Mims. Known him for years. He's a minister now, though he doesn't live in London. Even so I'll have to get a ticket to London, because I'll be recognized at the Little Woolton station, and they'll expect me to buy a ticket to London. I always buy a ticket to London. This isn't the time to be doing unexpected things that people will remember."

"Where does this Mims live?"

"In a blot on the map in Berkshire. You'll need a ticket all the way to London, too, because so many people go there, and you'll just be one of the crowd. When I join you at the stop after Little Woolton, I'll explain where we'll leave the train." Elgin found nothing in the pockets of the opera cape but ticket stubs.

Now his bravado was failing fast. It was time for him to go, and they both knew it. Iris would be left alone in the wood, under a brush pile. He'd rather stay and watch over her through the night, the way he would watch over one of his sisters, of course, but the fact was that he had to get back to Westbourne Hall before it got light. It wouldn't do to have Iris disappear, then him-

self disappear as well. So far only three or four
or five other people knew of a connection between them, and he didn't want that number to
grow.

To make sure he got himself out of there, Elgin
hardly looked at Iris again. Especially not at her
face, with those big trusting eyes. And not her
hands, either—her hands were so soft—and not
even at the twigs in her hair. He simply had to
leave.

"Well, good night," he said gruffly. "Don't leave
the candle burning any longer than you must."
Yet he stayed a heartbeat longer before he left
her, though it gave him physical pain.

Iris watched Elgin go, then snuggled into the
warm cape, rubbed her cheek against the velvet
collar. It had the smell of him, of his cologne,
something. She heard him covering the entrance
to her hiding place with branches. Then came a
whispered "Do take care . . . and wash your
face."

When she could no longer hear Elgin's foot-
falls, Iris moved to the wall farthest from the
candle, extended her arm, and let go of her
hooped petticoat. It wooshed open, performed a
few throbbing adjustments, then settled into
something like a sagging wheel of cheese. The
fight having gone out of the thing, it slumped
against the wall and throbbed no more. Safely
rid of it, Iris climbed between the layers of blanket and blew out the candle.

It was impossible for her to sleep. There were
things out and about. One of them scampered
over the brush pile, and bits of something fell on
her face. She pulled the blanket over her head,

which kept her free of whatever, but soon decided it wouldn't matter much after she suffocated. Out she came. In a little while more whatever fell on her.

Iris found the matches and relit the candle. Then she recovered her hooped petticoat and stood on her bed so that she could jam the waistband of it between some of the branches that made up the roof. Then she returned to bed. The great skirt hung over her like a tent over a bed in one of those tropical places. Satisfied with the result, she wiggled out, extinguished the candle, and felt her way back in. More whatever fell, but not on Iris.

Genius, she decided smugly, was its own reward.

Beneath her tent Iris hugged her covers and reveled in the plans for her new life. There would be no more exercises to give her nicely plumped arms. She would never again stand with her hands over her head, fingertips touching, bending from side to side. Aunt Prudence would no longer need to stand by and remind her to sway like a flower in a breeze. Iris had done those exercises for ten minutes, twice a day, and thought they were positively stupid. Nothing at all happened to her arms, except sometimes they cramped.

There would be no more dimpling machines to make the desired dents in her cheeks, all because the Marquis of Bumpsted had made favorable comment about a lady with charming dimples. In fact, there would be no more Marquis. Or anyone like him.

Neither would there be another minute spent

in the stretching device to make her taller. It was fashionable to be tall, because the Princess of Wales was tall, but the Princess of Wales didn't have to spend any time at all with her head in a sling that was hooked to a rope that went over the top of a door. When Iris's father packed her off to the Cotswolds in disgrace, he had neglected to pack the sling. Iris had never mentioned the omission.

And there would be no more Genuine Patented Inflatable Undulating Bosoms!

Iris sighed contentedly. No matter that her bed was hard and her corset pinched. Life was going to be wonderful. Elgin said that they would be going to see a friend of his. Mims. A *minister*. All they had to do now was get on the train. So simple. Iris finally slept.

After leaving Iris under the brush-pile, Elgin made his way back to Westbourne Hall in record time. He approached the back door as quietly as he had when he and Maxwell were in their rutting years. No dog barked, no owl hooted. When he applied his latchkey to the oiled lock, the door opened on silent hinges. Only the footman was there. The same one that had been so determined to know where he was going and with whom he was going to do it. Ha! Now the cheeky fellow was asleep in a chair, perhaps waiting to let him in. How thoughtful. How kind. How bloody nosy. The whole house knew that he had his own key, and that he'd come and gone like one of the family for years. Elgin crept up the back stairs.

The next morning he slept much later than expected and had to wash in cold water or be later than ever. He had to take care not to let anyone see how anxious he was to get on with his plans, or they might wonder too much about what those plans were.

As it happened, Elgin still arrived in the breakfast room before Glori and Maxwell did. The soft blush of a lazy morning was still upon them when they got there. Elgin concluded that whatever problems the newly wedded might have, Max and Glori had overcome them. Elgin smiled and said good morning. Glori smiled and said good morning. Max presented him with a rather idiotic grin.

While spreading jam on his toast, Elgin said, "It was only an hour ago, during that period of enlightenment that comes between being asleep and awake, that I divined the answer to a difficulty I'm having at my place in Kent."

Maxwell said, "Is that so?" and Elgin implied that the problem had something to do with bad drainage. Maxwell understood the evils of bad drainage and why Elgin would want to hurry home to correct them.

In Elgin's favor it must be said that he experienced a pang of guilt for deliberately deceiving his old friend as to why he was leaving, who would be with him, and where they were going. The pang didn't last long. Elgin applied a little more jam to his toast and consoled himself with the fact that he was protecting the entire Rutherford family from an ugly scandal if anything went amiss with Miss Huntington's rescue—or abduction. It depended on one's point of view. There was a time when he and Max would have rescued Iris together, but since Max had taken a wife, Elgin thought such an adventure might be inadvisable. Of course Glori had been a friend through all this, so he'd be a friend in return by not allowing Max to become involved in anything that might get him clapped in jail as kidnapper if anything went wrong.

When the carriage arrived, Elgin hoped to see Tom driving it, but no. The driver was one of the older boys from the stable, who had just been allowed to take a carriage, not just a cart or wagon, into the village. Elgin asked the fellow to make the first stop Huntington Manor. It was perfectly reasonable that a gentleman would say farewell to the neighbors before he departed. Nothing suspect in that.

At the Manor Prudence Chumbly left her pressed-flower arranging to join Elgin in the reception room where she had seen him only yesterday when she told him that he needed to get Iris out of the boathouse. While there were any extra ears about Elgin remarked upon the weather and asked Prudence if she would be so kind as to find him a remedy for rough skin, for he would very much like to give it to one of his sisters. When they were quite alone, the servants gone, he whispered, "I'll be taking Iris away today." Chumbly ambled into the room just when Elgin was saying that he would be on the four o'clock train to London.

"Ho now," said Chumbly. "London, is it? I have some business there myself. I'd be glad of your company. Have you a carriage to convey us to the station? Give me five minutes." He hurried away.

Prudence looked horrified. Elgin didn't look much better. She said, "Whatever shall we do?" and he said, "I don't know, but I'll come up with something."

Giving her hand a reassuring pat, Elgin left Prudence fidgeting beside a table furnished with her favorite yellow flowers.

When Elgin returned to the carriage, Chumbly was waiting in it, clutching a worn carpetbag. Elgin hardly acknowledged his unwelcome companion, sat as far away from him as he could, and signaled the driver to roll on. He suspected Chumbly was protecting a supply of spirits in that bag. The rudiments of civility didn't allow him to toss the fool out on his arse, so Chumbly stayed.

Too bad.

Every so often Chumbly tried to stir up conversation but gave it up as Elgin added nothing to the pot. When the carriage stopped in front of the station, the driver would have got down to carry both pieces of baggage, but Elgin carried his own valise. Chumbly wouldn't have parted with his carpetbag in any case. Elgin purchased a first-class seat on the four o'clock to London, then turned to Chumbly saying, "You needn't hang about waiting for me. I've got something to do before I leave, so you may as well take an earlier train." Elgin consulted his watch. "It will be along soon."

Chumbly sensed a free drink if he stuck with Elgin, so he said, "Isn't that a coincidence. I, too, have a few things to do." Then he bought a ticket identical to Elgin's and just stood there, waiting to go wherever Elgin went.

Elgin just stood there waiting for Chumbly to go away, but he didn't. Elgin headed for the nearby pub. The hope was that this shadow of his would get so drunk that he wouldn't be able to follow him onto the four o'clock train.

It was no accident that Elgin chose a table with a view of the station. Unfortunately he had to sit right next to Chumbly to get that view. After a while it paid off. When he was ordering Chumbly's fourth stiff drink, he noticed a small woman taking a seat on the bench on the railway platform. Her clothes were bunchy. She wore a shawl and a sunbonnet—the kind of bonnet farm women wore in the garden. The way the brim stuck out in front and curved down the sides it completely hid her face. She never looked up. On her arm was a basket. Whatever was in the basket had been covered with a white cloth. Leaning against the bench beside her was a flour sack. A flatish, roundish something was twisted up in it. This female was eating a carrot. Iris. Elgin smiled and bought Chumbly another strong drink in a larger glass.

It wasn't enough. Elgin had underestimated Chumbly's considerable tolerance to alcohol. What Chumbly needed just to steady his hand every day would put the ordinary man under the table. Instead of quieting down, Chumbly got louder. By three-thirty he was swatting the barmaids on the rear end and promising them the delight of their lives if they treated him well. He thought he was terribly amusing and laughed until he coughed and wheezed and his belly bounced. When he got his breath, he took out a monogrammed handkerchief, wiped his sweaty face, then winked and jabbed his elbow into Elgin's ribs. Elgin wasn't laughing, and his belly never bounced. Leaning closer, Chumbly murmured:

"There are places in London that you've never seen. Palaces of Pleasure, if you get my meaning. Just mention my name and see what happens." Elgin gave him a laborious smile and leaned away from Chumbly's alcoholic fumes.

After another long swallow Chumbly smacked his lips and said, "I'll tell you what. Because you've been such a jolly good host, I'll treat you to a visit to Mother Purity's Private School. The thing is, you'll have to wait until after I conduct my business." He patted his carpetbag. "I'll have plenty of money then, don't you doubt it!" After getting elbowed in the ribs again, Elgin said that he didn't doubt it in the least.

Chumbly was right in supposing that Elgin had never been to Mother Purity's. He was wrong in thinking that Elgin wanted to go there. The promise of a romp in a dungeon with women wearing black hoods and swinging whips had never lifted him on passion's wings. The catalog listing had been quite clear as to what went on in that particular establishment. Elgin and Max had laughed when they'd read about the place years ago. But that was long ago, and Elgin wasn't laughing now.

At three fifty-one the London train steamed in, and a crush of people got off and got on. Some waved, some cried, some pushed and cursed the ones who waved and cried. Babies were held up to train windows to be kissed. Ladies and gentlemen of leisure mingled with persons who worked, though they didn't mingle deliberately. Trunks were moved from here to there to here, and all the while the great engine steamed and hissed.

When Elgin dropped a generous supply of coins on the table to pay the bill, his interest was focused on a particular female with the flour sack at the train station. She made her way toward the front of the train. Unfortunately Elgin lost sight of her near the middle compartment of the car nearest the baggage trolley. He left the pub at something short of a run and gained the platform, but still couldn't see Iris. He simply had to assume that she had got on the train, so he did, too.

Chumbly stuck to Elgin like gravy on his tie. Took the center seat next to him, then wanted a window seat. Wouldn't shut up. The whistle blasted and the train began a jerking roll before it picked up speed. Elgin leaned back, pulled down the brim of his hat, folded his arms over his chest. He propped one ankle on the other knee, shut his eyes, and held very still. The image of a man asleep. He was trying to figure out how the devil he was going to join Iris at the next stop without Chumbly tagging along.

While Elgin frowned in thought, Chumbly smiled and patted the pocket where he'd squirreled away some of the coins Elgin had left on the table in the pub.

Though the train rolled on with a hypnotic *clickety-clack*, Chumbly showed no signs of falling under its restful spell. He jabbered on as though someone were actually listening. When Elgin sensed that they were slowing down for the next stop, he became more tense than ever. He simply had to get rid of Chumbly, but thought someone would notice the fuss the bugger made when he got pushed out the window. With a mind of its own, Elgin's foot began an impatient jiggle.

Chumbly gave Elgin another elbow in the ribs. "Has your foot gone to sleep or do you need to pee?"

Elgin's eyes flew open, and he said, "Yes! Yes, I do! That's the very thing. I'll give it a go at the next station."

When the train stopped, Chumbly got up to follow Elgin. Elgin said, "You'd better stay here or we're sure to lose our seats." Chumbly didn't seem to care. Elgin said, "We might even lose our bags in this crush." Chumbly sat down.

Elgin got off the train. Espying a porter he indicated the carriage he had just vacated and asked the man to go in and discreetly remove the maroon valise from beneath the empty seat beside a man embracing a carpetbag. When he got it, he should take the valise into the station. The porter smiled. Rubbing the coin that had found its way into his pocket, he assured Elgin that the job was as good as done.

Now all Elgin had to do was find Iris. She would have to be in one of the carriages up ahead, but perhaps she hadn't been able to get a seat next to the window, because he couldn't find her. With all the people milling about, Elgin could hardly get close enough to see where Iris might be.

He picked a window and stood tall to look inside. The first time he tried it, he met up with a child's wet nose and sloppy mouth puffing against the glass. At least he supposed it was a child. The next time all he could see was a very big, very ugly hat on a woman with a mustache. She gave him a come-hither smile, and he moved on. When he finally got inside a carriage for a look-see, he couldn't get out again because of the people pushing in.

A little old woman saw his plight, brandished her umbrella, and cried, " 'Ere now! Mike room fur the toff comin' ou'!" It didn't help much.

The whistle blew, the train rolled, and Elgin looked out the window to see Iris waving at him from the platform.

· *Nine* ·

A glorious breeze bellied the draperies in the Egyptian Room, but Obediah Huntington hardly noticed. He was shouting, "What the devil did Farley want *this* time? I don't believe it was a simple act of neighborliness. And don't tell me he came back to deliver something else to Iris, because I won't believe that, either. He was after something!"

Prudence was fidgeting again, which caused profound distress to another handkerchief. "Mr. Farley first spoke of the weather," she said meekly.

"A poor attempt at deception if I ever heard one. I promise you that he positively did not have atmospheric conditions on his mind. What else did he say?"

"He asked me to provide him with a remedy for his sister's troublesome skin. It has bothered—"

"And you believed that?"

"Well, I—"

"He probably doesn't even have a sister. What else?"

"He said he was about to leave for London and—"

"The man just got back here!" Huntington shook a knowing finger at his sister. "It's obvious that Farley was making one last attempt to see the Egyptian collection. Now he's going back to London to tell whoever sent him out here that he hasn't been able to gain access to my treasures. I *knew* it! Did you let him get upstairs?" Huntington waved aside any reply. "No matter, the room is locked. I told you Farley couldn't be trusted. Didn't I say he couldn't be trusted?"

"Yes, Obediah, you said that, but I didn't take Mr. Farley upstairs. He didn't even mention your collections. However, when Chumbly came in—"

"Egad! What did Chumbly want?"

"He wanted to go to London with Mr. Farley on the four o'clock train. Mr. Farley didn't care for the idea, not a bit, I could tell he didn't, but they left for the station together nonetheless. Now—"

"Now I won't be plagued by either one of them. Wonderful! But Chumbly will run out of money and come back. He always does, damn his hide. Still, we must count our blessings. The important thing is that Farley is gone, and he's taken another problem with him. For that we must be thankful."

"Yes, Obediah, for that we must be *very* thankful." The problem Prudence had in mind was Iris, not Chumbly, though she wondered how that dear Mr. Farley would keep Chumbly from seeing the girl. Chumbly was too annoying. Then she wondered if Iris might simply leave Little Woolton on a later train instead, then Mr. Farley could meet her at the other end. Prudence thought that would answer quite nicely. Leaving her brother to contemplate his collection of blessings, she slipped quietly from the room.

Just as quietly Prudence went to her own bedchamber, placed a chair to face the clock, sat down, and waited. When the hour chimed four, she stood tall, chins up, and went bravely into Chumbly's room. First she looked behind the wardrobe. The carpetbag was gone. Then she opened the blanket chest. At the bottom, way in the back, wrapped in tissue paper, was a fine example of old Roman glass. An unguent bottle. The *missing* unguent bottle. Prudence had put it there herself.

It had been only a few days before that a maid with a feather duster had found the worn carpetbag wedged behind Chumbly's wardrobe. Having been trained to put everything in its place, the girl took the bag to Prudence and asked what she was supposed to do with it. Prudence said she would attend to it herself and she did. When the maid left, Prudence opened the bag and discovered the unguent bottle inside, wrapped in a towel. What she substituted for the unguent bottle was a master ink bottle. Though of pottery and the slightest bit heavier, the ink bottle was close enough to the desired shape. When the carpetbag went back behind the wardrobe, no one could tell by looking at it that anything had changed. Not without actually opening the bag and undoing the towel. That, however, would have taken time. Today Chumbly hadn't had time. He had been in a hurry to get to the train station with Elgin Farley.

Selecting the required key from the great ring of keys she kept hidden, Prudence let herself into the Grecian Room. After choosing a likely crate she carefully laid the unguent bottle inside. Humming softly, quite pleased with the day's work, she took herself outside to sit on her garden bench for a while. When she returned to the house, she went to the stillroom to prepare a little something for Elgin's sister's troublesome complexion. She gave considerable attention to her remedy books, plus a box of receipts written on odd pieces of paper. Eventually she decided upon a face cream that had to be mixed in a warm marble mortar. A friend who suffered from eczema had recommended it most highly.

At the same time that Prudence was measuring out four ounces of almond oil in the stillroom at Huntington Manor, Elgin was wedged inside a second-class carriage of the Great Western Railway watching Iris wave at him from the platform as the train pulled away. As soon as he could, he opened the door of the railway carriage for an unscheduled departure. This caused a round of bawdy cheering and whistling, for Elgin's fellow travelers had seen Iris and heard his impassioned expression of frustration. He tipped his hat to his enthusiastic companions before jumping from the moving train.

As he skidded and tumbled down the roadbed, the old woman with the umbrella leaned out of the train and shouted, "Give 'er me love!"

Elgin's leap onto the stones had taken seconds, but he had to sit still for several minutes before he could get up. His acrobatic performance would undoubtedly produce exquisite bruises, yet he didn't mind all that much because he'd left Chumbly behind, or ahead, as that's where the train had gone with Chumbly in it. A satisfied smile crept over Elgin as he watched the train becoming smaller and smaller in the distance and imagined his antagonist inside that train shrinking to the size of a bean.

Even after the brushing off Elgin gave himself, he still appeared decidedly shabby when he limped back to the station. He had landed rather heavily on one knee. Of course Iris thought Elgin had been positively heroic again and wanted to tell him so, but discretion triumphed. She said nothing. For Elgin's part he found this rescuing business more taxing than ever. Once again he considered the merits of a quiet life with a quiet woman. Being a hero had become a dangerous occupation.

The manner in which Elgin returned to the train station didn't lend itself to the inconspicuous visage one would prefer for secret abductions or clandestine rescues. In fact the methods he had employed thus far lacked a certain finesse of which he was now painfully aware. There weren't many gentlemen who compensated a porter so well for retrieving a valise on the sly. Not many gentlemen then got back on the train without that valise, only to jump off beside the tracks to make a mess of their clothes and dignity.

At this point Elgin realized that he had done exactly as he should if his intention had been to make himself conspicuous. That is, to make an ass of himself. Having done a frightfully good job of it, he would certainly be remembered. So would Iris if he paid her any attention. That's why he pointedly ignored her now, though he knew she was watching him, but that didn't make her any different than anyone else. Everyone was watching him.

Because of this Elgin concluded that one good thing had come of this railway misadventure—two good things if he counted getting rid of Chumbly. The disgraceful spectacle he'd made of himself had turned out to be a monstrously fine diversionary device. If Squire Huntington ever suspected that Iris hadn't really run off with the gypsies, he would certainly make inquiries about a young woman traveling alone. Elgin didn't think anyone would ever recall seeing the small female in drab, badly fitting clothes. Not now. Even so he felt it necessary to maintain his position in the limelight lest anyone's attention wander.

Elgin swaggered up to the ticket window and knocked on the counter. In a voice loud enough for everyone to hear, he said, "A ticket for the next train to Reading, if you please!" Reading was a stop on the way to London.

"One first class to Reading," said the agent as he laid out the ticket, then took in the money and muttered something under his breath about the upper classes being routinely dropped on their heads as infants.

Elgin left the window believing Iris had understood that she was to get off the train at Reading. Since he'd made himself memorable, Elgin didn't dare ride in the same carriage with her to explain where they would be going, or what would happen after they got there. He picked a bit of something from the sleeve of his coat, turned toward the light to inspect a hole in the elbow, sent a slight nod in Iris's direction, and went to retrieve his valise.

Iris didn't purchase her second-class ticket until shortly before the train rolled in. Though she'd clearly heard what Elgin said, she supposed he had been trying to mislead everyone else into thinking that he was going to Reading, when he actually meant to go on to London. So Iris purchased a ticket to London, getting on the train and out of sight as soon as it rolled in.

When the trail pulled into Reading station Elgin hurried out of his carriage and onto the platform to wait for Iris. And wait for Iris. The whistle blew, the train began to roll away, and he still couldn't see Iris. By the time she pushed her way through the crowd with her basket and bulging flour sack, Elgin was nearly frantic. The knot in his chest came loose as soon as he saw her. Their eyes met, he turned and strolled toward town. She followed. When Elgin figured they were far enough away from the station, he waited for Iris to catch up to him, then took her sack and carried it with his valise. Iris kept the basket. They made a wonderfully odd-looking pair, rather like a stud horse and a stewing chicken.

Without looking her way, Elgin said, "What took you so long to get off the train?"

"I thought we were going to London."

"We aren't."

"I was half asleep when someone said, 'Blimy, there's the toff from the other station. I wonder if he fell off the train again.' I opened my eyes,

and there you were on the platform. So I got off
the train. How did you come to be so dusty and
raggedy?"

"I shall endeavor to explain D and R when we
have sufficient time and privacy. More important
is the fellow in your carriage who alerted you to
my exalted presence on the station platform.
Otherwise I would have had to get back on that
train without a ticket. As it is, I'm overjoyed that
you got off instead. I'll remember your keen-eyed
traveling companion in my prayers."

Iris said, "Do you have any idea where we're
going?"

"We're going to find respectable lodgings for tonight, leave our things there, then we'll eat. Tomorrow you can sleep as late as you like in a
real bed with a real pillow while I go to the
bank. After that we'll shop, if you like."

Iris looked down at her baggy dress and said,
"I suppose we could shop, if you insist."

"After you've purchased what you need, we'll
be off again in search of my old friend Mims."
Iris was glad to hear it.

There weren't any problems for at least half
an hour. Not until they tried to secure those respectable lodgings. Suspicious keepers of public
houses didn't think the pair of them looked all
that respectable. In fact those publicans made it
quite clear that they didn't think a well-tailored
gentleman would take a young woman in country clothes to a private room for respectable reasons.

Elgin kept Iris in the background while he and
the next hosteler negotiated a price for overlooking their unusual circumstances. For double

the price they could have one small back room and use the back stairs. As one room simply wouldn't do, Elgin pressed on. For triple the price they could have two rooms, but they still had to use the back stairs. It was, after all, a respectable establishment. Elgin was also told that if he didn't like what it cost, he could go to a cheaper place where no one cared who was sleeping where, though it would be none too safe. Elgin paid up.

In a gravelly whisper the innkeeper said, "We'll have no indecent noises up there."

Dropping the keys into his pocket, Elgin hurried Iris up the back stairs. After inspecting both rooms, he put her sack and basket into the room with the better lock on the door. Before they went back into the passage, he said, "By the by, we're registered as Mary and John Smith, sister and brother."

The new Mary Smith smiled and said, "I'd like to tidy up before dinner. Shall I knock you up when I'm ready?"

Her new brother John said, "Please do," then went to his own little cell across the hall.

They were in good spirits when they descended the back stairs to search out a suitable evening meal. The innkeeper knew exactly when they left, then used his own keys to get in and inspect both rooms. He took away the blanket from the room in which the woman's belongings had been placed.

Iris and Elgin were in high spirits when they returned by those creaking back stairs, having been well fed and well entertained at an establishment with a newly painted sign over the door

that identified the place as the Muddy Hog.
There had been a young man about the
place—an especially fine-looking fellow—who
had recently arrived with a talented parrot. A
blue and gold parrot. Since the bird's first appearance its antics had improved the floundering
custom of the pub to such an extent that the
owner took the young fellow on as a minor part-
ner. It was the best way to get him to stay there
with his bird. Shakespeare—that was the parrot's name—talked and sang, mostly hymns and
rhymes, except for a sailing song that had
naughty bits.

It was while the customers waited about for
the naughty bits that the most beer and roast
beef were sold. After the naughty bits the most
handsome tips were laid down. With the rolling
gait of a sailor the bird went round the table it
used for a stage to collect the coins. One by one
he dropped them into a tobacco tin that had a
large slot in the top. After the coins were collected, he got a slice of apple and considerable
applause.

When Iris held out a shilling, the bird hopped
from side to side and said, "Kissy kissy kiss."
Then he took the coin and added it to the others
in the tobacco tin.

After Iris and Elgin finally left the pub, she
declared that she had never had such a great
good time. She had never been inside a pub before, either, and Elgin might well be denounced
for taking a lady to such a low place. Even so,
they were still in a jolly mood when they made
their way up the back stairs by the light of the
moon that spilled through the windows over the

stairwell. But the smiles slipped away by the time they reached Iris's door. Whatever had been so amusing fled their minds and left a crackling silence in its place. Elgin could feel his heart beat in his ears. He lifted a hand to touch Iris, then paused and combed his fingers through his hair instead. She tilted her face up to his, her shadowy eyes dark and inviting, her mouth . . . He shut his eyes so he wouldn't see her mouth. A soft, yielding mouth. The knot was back in his chest.

She giggled and whispered, "Kissy kissy kiss," and he said, "I owe you a shilling." As quickly as he could, he unlocked her door and pushed her into the room. He stayed where he was until he heard her turn the key in the lock from the inside. The knot in his chest was still there, and he felt irritable, but didn't really know why.

It was hours later that Elgin was awakened by a light tapping sound and a gravelly voice that whispered, "I got a warm blanket for ya, missy."

Wearing nothing but his drawers, Elgin was out of bed and into the passage in a flash. He looked murderous but said nothing. He extended his hand, and the innkeeper thrust the blanket at him, then stomped off with his candle. If Elgin had been in a bad mood when he got into bed, it was even worse when he got out. Returning to his cubicle didn't improve his disposition. After considerable groping he lit the stub of a candle the management had provided, found his trousers, pulled them on, and grabbed up his shirt before he hurried across the hall.

After what was supposed to be a calming breath, he tapped on Iris's door and whispered,

"It's Elgin, do open up." As he was doing up a couple of the buttons on his shirt he could hear the bed creak and bare feet pat across the floor before Iris opened the door a crack. She only peeked out around it, wide-eyed and startled. As a lady wasn't supposed to notice improper things, like a man who was only partly dressed, she didn't know quite what to say. If it had been anyone else, she would have shut the door. But it wasn't anyone else. It was Elgin, all rumpled and tired and he had dashed to her rescue again. *Dear* Elgin. She looked at him like he was a plum pudding, and he almost choked on a laugh.

Making a rapid recovery, he said, "Your previous caller was the host of this respectable establishment. It would appear that he has a lusty inclination for your charming company. Perhaps it would be best if I spent the rest of the night with you in your room. He does have a key, you know."

Iris looked down the gloomy passage where anyone might be hiding and said she thought it would be a good idea if Elgin stayed.

It wasn't until Elgin stepped inside the room and closed the door that he reconsidered the wisdom of what he was about to do. Iris had jumped back into bed, now all but lost in a high-necked nightdress of some striped stuff that had come from Tom's wife. In addition to that she wore the opera cape for warmth because she'd been without a blanket. She had pulled her knees up and the cape down to make certain that her bare feet were decently covered.

Elgin tossed Iris the blanket he'd got from the innkeeper, held the candle high, and looked at the bed. So did Iris. Then he looked around the room. So did Iris. They could plainly see that the bed wasn't very big, yet there wasn't enough space in the room to bring in another bed. He watched Iris move to the edge of the mattress and draw the cape even closer around a body that was so small that she was lost in her wrappings. Only a dark curly head and an apprehensive face looked out from the pile of fabric.

Elgin strongly suspected that such a sleeping arrangement would interfere with sleep to an alarming degree. He handed Iris the candle and said, "Hold the door open."

A quick trip across the hall secured his valise and the rest of his clothes, which he dropped on Iris's bed—except for his boots, which went on the floor. Then he went back and took hold of his mattress and dragged it into Iris's room, the bedding trailing behind. His bruised knee protested. He ignored it.

There were soon enough candles lighting the passage for Elgin to see reasonably well, as several people had left their rooms to find out what the noise was about. The shocking sight of a half-naked man flinging his bedding about sent some of them scurrying back to the safety of their closed doors. The shocking sight of the same half-naked man kept others right where they were so they wouldn't miss whatever it was that he might do next.

There was a caustic remark from one disgruntled guest who thought Elgin should do it in one bed at a time like normal men and minced no words telling him so. Elgin thanked him for his concern and said he would certainly try it sometime. The innkeeper didn't appear again, which probably kept him from getting his nose broken.

After he got the mattress through the doorway Elgin moved the washstand out of the way. Then he shoved Iris's bed over as far as it would go, laid his mattress on the floor, and pushed one edge of it under the side of her bed. That's the only way there was enough room for the mattress to lie flat. And there was no way anyone could get into the room unless he pulled up the other edge of his mattress so that the door could swing in.

While Elgin was arranging his bed and Iris was locking the door, what was left of the candle sputtered and died. Elgin said something, but when Iris asked what it meant, he said she wouldn't understand and he meant to keep it that way, that he'd forgotten to bring his pillow, and he couldn't find his damn coat, and would she please light another candle!

"I don't have another candle."

"Did you bring any from the hideout?"

"I didn't know I would need them."

"Then we'll do without," he grumbled, smoothed out his covers, and climbed beneath them. His voice had a note of irritable finality about it when he said, "Good night."

Iris said good night, spread out the blanket, and wondered what it would be like to snuggle up with Elgin. She reminded herself that it wouldn't be much longer before she'd know, for they were, after all, on their way to his friend. His friend was a minister. Why would anyone want to go to so much trouble to reach a minister unless he was supposed to marry them? She wiggled round to get the pillow just right and thought of sleepy things.

Elgin was all too aware of Iris wiggling around in the bed and couldn't manage to think of sleepy things. His eyes had adjusted from candlelight to moonlight. From where he lay he had a view of the underside of her bed. He could just make out the sag she made in the canvas nailed across the bedframe that supported her thin mattress. A mattress with one small woman with a soft laugh and soft hands and other soft parts that he shouldn't be thinking about, but he thought about them anyway. It was like telling someone that they would win a fortune if they wouldn't think of the word *walrus* during the next hour.

Elgin listened to Iris breathing. Soft and steady. He supposed that meant she was asleep and recognized the wonderfully awful possibility that they might be spending another night like this before they ever reached Mims. If that happened he'd likely end up in her bed if she didn't end up in his. Then he tried to remember that this was Iris, Iris who was like one of his sisters. The word here was *restraint*, not *walrus*.

But restraint lasted only so long in such a situation when he found himself far from indifferent to the woman in the bed above him who looked nothing at all like a walrus. He reminded himself that the reason they were in such an awkward situation was so that he could keep Iris safe from other men. Then he thought he'd better keep her safe from himself as well.

Elgin rolled over onto his belly. He tried to ignore Iris and go to sleep, but his wayward mind would insist upon fleshing out what he didn't know about her. It was a dangerous situation that he had to face if he had any sense at all. Tomorrow, while Iris was shopping, he'd attend to it. The ounce of prevention that was more valuable than the pound of cure. A means of limitation that the polite world referred to as protection from disease, if they referred to it at all. The Society For The Suppression Of Vice took exception to any form of population interruption, insisting that all such things were evil. Even so, Elgin thought he'd best step round to a tobacconist or apothecary to make a discreet purchase. A packet of English Overcoats or French Letters. Devices of the Devil.

Whatever anyone called them, the treated appendix of the humble sheep had served man amazingly well for a long, long time. The things were given a jaunty red ribbon with which to tie them on. So festive. An army officer could special order them with ribbons in his regimental colors if—

"Elgin, are you asleep?" came whispering through the night.

"No, not quite" was the strained reply.

"Why aren't you asleep?"

"Oh, I was just thinking."

"About what?"

There was a pause before Elgin said, "Sheep."

Iris stretched and sighed and said, "Tell me about sheep."

There was a longer pause before Elgin said, "Handy things, sheep. Did you know that British sheep and the dogs that watch over them are much different than Continental sheep and their

attendant dogs? One mustn't go switching them
about without courting disaster. Oh, no. You see,
sheep in Britain haven't had wolves or bears
threatening them for centuries. They wander
about to graze, which is less destructive to the
land. The dogs don't need to guard them from
wild predators; they need to find and herd them
in when the farmer wants his sheep." Elgin
rolled over to stare at the dark ceiling, folding an
arm beneath his head. "In many parts of the
Continent sheep wouldn't last long if they wandered about. They move about in a cluster, and
the dog stays with them like one of the fold, a
dog that will run off a wolf and guard his flock."

"What an awful lot to think about," mumbled
Iris through a yawn. "I was thinking about that
parrot. How long do you suppose it would take to
train a bird to do that?"

Elgin said, "We'll talk about anything you like
in the morning."

There was a sleepy smile in Iris's voice when
she said, "Kissy kissy kiss."

Elgin thumped his hand against the side of
her bed, then rolled toward the door and tried to
think of parrots and walruses instead of sheep
and their numerous benefits to mankind.

It wasn't until the following evening that Iris
and Elgin reboarded the train at Reading station
and stepped off the train at Hungerford station.
There they needed to hire a carriage to take
them to the parsonage of the New Church near
Chilton Gate. With some difficulty Elgin tried to
make the coachman understand where they
wanted to go. The fellow was quite deaf. It

helped considerably when he brought out his ear trumpet and Elgin shouted into it.

While this obstreperous transaction was being conducted, Iris wondered if the coachman knew that ant eggs and onion juice placed in the affected ear was recommended to treat deafness. The directions were given in one of Aunt Prudence's books, though Iris had wondered how anyone was supposed to hear better with their ears packed with ants' eggs. And then what was one to do about the ants if the eggs hatched? She concluded that the coachman, deaf as he was, might be better off with his ear trumpet.

By the time their trunk was loaded onto the roof of the carriage, Iris and Elgin had been loaded inside. Iris was grateful for it. She had become more concerned with immediate comfort than their destination or the coachman's ears, maintaining that the cause of goodness and mercy would be better served if she wasn't breaking in a new pair of factory-made footwear.

With the exception of her shoes, the lady had moved through the day quite comfortably in a sensible dress of brown serge that almost fit. It didn't drag along the ground, and there were modest hoops beneath it. Her brown felt hat was also sensible, though it sported a frivolous yellow taffeta ribbon. To complete her costume Iris had added a cloak, rather plain, also brown. She had removed the hat as soon as they got into the carriage and placed it on the seat beside her so that the ribbons wouldn't get crushed. Elgin sat across from her.

Because ready-made clothing wasn't that easy to come by—unless one went to the warehouses

that supplied mourning clothes without delay—
Iris had to change the way she shopped. With no
time for dressmakers many of her purchases had
come from an establishment that advertised
Clean, Previously Owned Clothing of Good Quality. It would have given her family palpitations if
they had known Iris had ever gone inside such a
place. "A Huntington," she told Elgin in arch
tones, "simply wouldn't."

The only problem Iris found with any of the
clothes she purchased was the unflattering color,
yet that's the very reason she had chosen them.
With her coloring she was all but invisible in
brown. This drab redecoration of a young lady
who had been presented to the queen in snowy
white with roses in her hair was no accident.
She and Elgin had agreed that it was safer to be
drab and invisible than attractive and found out.
At least for now.

As though she'd done it all her life, Iris had si-
dled up to the counters in the shops where the
baker's wife and the butcher's daughter got their
corset stays, fancy hatpins, and rubber garters.
She asked other women about preferred makers
of this and that and where to find better stock-
ings.

Of all the things Iris had acquired it was the
shopping bag she particularly liked. She had explained to an amused Elgin that she'd never before had such a thing. In fact she had never
before used money to shop, or carried things af-
terward, and thought it was all a great lark. Before this whatever she had purchased was added
to her father's accounts at the *better* stores, and
her maid carried everything that wasn't being

delivered. Yet her good humor wasn't entirely due to the shopping bag. It wasn't her stiff new shoes, either. It was because Elgin had told her about Chumbly as a traveling companion, and jumping off the train and all that.

Of course Iris thought Elgin had done a brilliant job of outwitting Chumbly—not that Chumbly had much wit at his disposal. But Elgin, ever alert, had avoided Chumbly's company through a series of comings and goings from trains that Iris saw as nothing less than brilliant. Even though Elgin's recital of the events had been conducted with an ample dose of chagrin, Iris knew how gallant he truly was. After all, he had rescued her from that apple tree years ago.

Soon enough the rocking carriage put the finishing touch to the last few days that had provided Iris with high excitement but insufficient sleep. Her mainspring had run down. Her brain had nearly ceased ticking if one was to judge from her drooping eyelids and the way she struggled to follow the conversation.

Recognizing the signs of extreme fatigue, Elgin moved Iris's hat out of harm's way and lay his protesting companion down on the seat, using his valise as a pillow. Then he propped his foot against that seat so the jolting of the carriage wouldn't throw her onto the floor.

When Elgin saw the lights from cottages, he suspected that they would soon be coming upon the New Church. He shook Iris ever so gently to waken her, then sat her up and took the seat beside her. She smiled and leaned against him.

Elgin thought about, then thought better of,

putting his arm around her. Such thoughts led to other thoughts. Cozier thoughts. The idea was to wake Iris up, not make her cozy. What she needed was an awakening thought. He said, "Iris, have you given any consideration to the fact that you are now ruined? Cavorting about the country without a proper escort will do that for a young lady."

The young lady yawned and mumbled something that sounded like "bowsly."

"Please?"

"I said how silly. It was perfectly silly for that innkeeper in Reading to think that I was your . . . what did he call me? Never mind. It must have been *quite* rude." Another yawn. "It's the innkeepers who should worry about their own respectability."

Elgin said he thought so, too, gathered his thoughts from where he'd left them, and said, "There is the possibility of assistance from Mrs. Mims with this respectability business. I should think that Mims must certainly have a missus by now. Ministers are encouraged to have them, you know. Helpmates and all that. Someone to deliver potions and elixirs to sick people who don't want them."

Iris gave a sleepy sigh and said, "The shopping was perfectly delightful. I should like to do it again some time, but not too soon, except that the house slippers really don't fit too well. They're blue."

"A minister's wife, even without the potions, would surely give you some amount of credibility, just in case it's ever possible to reestablish your virtue. For some reason women need so much more of it than men do. If the opportunity ever arises, we might even say that you traveled in the company of a minister's wife. Perhaps Mrs. Mims herself, if she'll go for it."

"Even if they don't fit too well, they should be warm. Did you notice the fleece inside?"

"Yes, I think Mrs. Mims can surely provide the solution to this conundrum. You'll be living a perfectly respectable life the moment you step inside the portals of the parsonage with its resident wife. Of course we needn't broadcast the fact that one night has been spent on the road—or on the track, as the case may be."

Iris yawned again, leaned a little more. "Next time I'll get red slippers. Mother doesn't think red slippers are quite respectable. Would you object if I had red slippers?"

"I suppose it might be advisable for me to put in a solitary appearance somewhere, just for effect, just in case anyone wonders if we might be together, but perhaps that won't be necessary. Thanks to your grandfather and the story that you've left the manor to be married, it should all go much easier. The country folk will think you're in the city, while the city folk will think you're still in the country. A capital arrangement, when one thinks about it."

The carriage jolted along the rough road through the fading light. White cows could still be seen in dark fields. Elgin said, "Did I tell you about Mims? I suppose I didn't. His name is actually Mimford. The Reverend Mimford L. Jones. *L* for Leonard. It has a rather grand ring to it, don't you think? Too bad he was never suited to the church, though as the third son from a noble family, it was his destiny. You know how it is: The oldest son gets the title, the second son gets a commission in the army, the third goes into the church, like it or not. There's a fourth brother who got out of reading law by borrowing enough money for a one-way ticket to New Zealand. Now he raises sheep, or some other fuzzy things with lots of legs."

Iris thought it sounded like he could be raising caterpillars.

When the carriage came to a standstill, the driver pounded on the roof with the butt of his whip to announce their arrival at the New Church. Elgin and Iris were soon left in front of the parsonage with a valise and one trunk filled with almost new clothes.

A lamp burned in a downstairs room of the modest house. Wooden venetian blinds made stripes of the golden light that fell across the front garden over a mass of unkept rosebushes. A cat sat in the shadows watching the night, watching for mice, watching. Holding Iris by the hand, Elgin opened the picket gate with a rattle, closed it with a clatter, and followed the stone walk to the doorstep. The house was built of dark brick, the door of dark oak. When Elgin pulled a knotted cord beside the door, they heard a bell tinkle inside. A minute or two later a tall slender man answered the call while putting on his coat.

Elgin said, "Mims, is that you?"

"Right-O. Do come . . . Farley?"

The man called Mims drew Elgin into the lighted hall. "By Jove, it *is* you! What brings you here, not that it matters. It's jolly good to see you!" When he went to shut the door, Mims was startled to see Iris standing there. "Is this your wife? Do forgive me."

"Ah . . . not my wife, no. Allow me to introduce Miss Iris Huntington." Elgin took her hand. Iris stepped forward.

Mims looked at his old friend suspiciously.

"Oh, nothing like *that*," said Elgin impatiently. "Iris and I are somewhat betrothed."

"How do you do," said Mims, somewhat relieved.

He led the way to the best parlor and lit another lamp. His guests arranged themselves on the uncomfortable mahogany furniture, all of which was covered in stiff black horsehair upholstery.

While lighting a fire in the stove, Mims said, "Did you have a good trip?" Elgin said yes. Iris said nothing.

What Mims wanted to ask was why Elgin had brought this female here, but he wouldn't say such an ungenerous thing in front of the female herself. Still, he was glad that his old friend hadn't brought a different sort of woman to the parsonage. He couldn't forget that this was the same Elgin Farley who had been known to put a pig—or the occasional ferret—where one would least expect to find one. They messed up the bedding something awful. But with or without the livestock, it was rather late to be entertaining unattended, unmarried young ladies in the parsonage. Even so, what else could he do?

When he got the fire burning, Mims turned toward the tired lady on the sofa and said, "Could you do with a spot of tea?"

Iris said, "Yes, please," and Elgin said, "She would do better with a bed or a warm chimney corner in which to sleep. Perhaps your wife might do something with her."

"Wife? I don't have a wife," said Mims as he headed toward the kitchen for refreshments. From there he called, "I have a housekeeper who'll be back in the morning."

"It's thoughtless of you not to have a wife just now. We need a respectable lady in residence. In fact, we're in a frightful bind without one. I don't suppose you have an aunt or cousin in the neighborhood?"

When Mims returned with a loaded tray, he put it on the tea table in the center of the room. The apple pie looked especially good. He said, "No aunts or cousins here. My family won't come near this place. Far too rustic. The fact is no one beyond the village comes here. I say, your betrothed has nodded off."

Elgin looked down at the head resting on his shoulder. Smiling indulgently, he held Iris upright and removed her hat. She blinked once, twice, and would have slumped into the corner of the sofa if Elgin hadn't put an arm around her. "Perhaps there's a lady in your congregation who—"

"There isn't a congregation."

"You are a minister?"

"Duly ordained."

Mims poured a cup of tea for himself. Knowing Elgin of old, he skipped the tea and passed him some pie. As Elgin couldn't eat any of it and hold Iris at the same time, Mims retrieved the pie.

Elgin said, "You do have the living of this place, with this house and a church?"

"But no congregation."

"Why not?"

"No services, that's why not. The local people prefer the rather splendid old church in Chilton Gate, not that I can blame them. The place has an organ and a choir. It has bells and bell-ringers to ring the changes. My small, quaint, but rather dismal church"—Mims pointed next door—"was built by a pious lady during the last century to accommodate those of an invalid condition who might not attend services if they had to travel too far away from home, especially in bad weather. For all the trouble she'd taken to build it, the place satisfied everyone's curiosity after the first few months. There is, however, the occasional funeral here when the roads are too bad to go to Chilton Gate."

Mims paused to rearrange his lanky self in his chair, then said, "Now and then someone stops by just to talk about cows and things. I rather enjoy that. I even give advice if anyone wants it, but there aren't regular service, no. My predecessor hadn't managed to attract a congregation in the ten years he was here, and he gave it a jolly good go. There's just something about organs and choirs and bells. I understand he did a great deal of reading after his ecclesiastical efforts failed. He translated obscure classics and contemplated the universe. Invented some sort of long-handled watering can, though I never saw the thing myself."

"So you snapped up the living here to provide

occasional conversations about cows and have enough time to read."

"Not exactly. You see, no one else wanted it. The stipend provided by the will of the lady who built this place is far from adequate. Couldn't afford to stay on if I didn't have a bit of my own drawing interest."

"Then why do you stay?"

"I like it here. It's so marvelously uneventful. Hardly anything ever happens."

Elgin's expression was eloquently blank. Mims said, "I know it sounds rather dull, but there are the gardens, and I've been doing a great deal with them. We—that is, the staff and I—now grow enough vegetables for myself and a few others all year round. I'll have to show you the late strawberries after we get your wedding out of the way, if it doesn't take too long. At least I suppose that's why you've come here." Mims was about to dig in to the last of the pie when he said, "You know, you're the last person I expected to see with a wife."

"The thing is, old chum, I didn't actually think of coming here to get married, but to find a refuge for Iris."

· Ten ·

"No, marriage wasn't what I had intended when this latest adventure began," said Elgin. "Since then, however, my life has become so entwined with Iris's that an immediate matrimonial is the only answer to our predicament. I've got to watch out for her as best I can, though it's a daunting prospect."

"Must you marry her to watch out for her?"

"I don't know of any way around it, not without a safe place, a proper place to leave her. Installing her here with you certainly wouldn't do, even if your housekeeper lived in. Besides that, I've been significantly instrumental in her flight from home sweet home, and we've been together ever since then. You can see how it is."

Mims didn't look as though he could see it.

Elgin didn't think Iris looked all that comfortable, so he shifted her around, and then she looked even more uncomfortable. He gave up and drew her to his side and held her there. She sighed and slept on. He said, "Conditions within the young lady's family had become so threatening that we became engaged as a safety precaution. An excuse to prevent her from being married off to someone disagreeable. It wasn't intended to be a *real* engagement, not with a wedding and all that. Then a new danger arose that made the previous threat seem like a day at the seaside. That's when it became apparent that I must remove her from an otherwise insurmountable danger, so here we are."

"You're not in love with her or anything like that?"

"Oh, no, nothing like that."

Mims puckered up and thrummed his lower lip with his finger, frowning in perplexed thought. He said, "Do I understand you to mean that you're not in love with this young woman, the one arranged so nicely in your arms, but you're willing to marry her for the sake of propriety, because you personally spirited her away from her wretched family?"

"Something of that sort. The frightful thing is that we might go through all this only to have her father find her and take her away."

"Good heavens! Is she really so young?"

"I don't recall, but we can ask her in the morning."

Mims resorted to further lip thrumming, then gave it up and said, "No matter. For the past forty-some years parental consent has been nice to have but not actually necessary for the marriage of minors. Still, I'd like to find out how well you know this female. I do feel a responsibility here." He watched as Elgin ever so tenderly arranged Iris's cloak around her. She smiled and cuddled closer without waking. Mims cocked a speculative eyebrow at Elgin.

As for Elgin, he was neither as relaxed as Iris

nor as curious as Mims. Though he found it a relief to know that parental approval wasn't necessary for the marriage, he feared that Iris's father
might decide that she was too unbalanced mentally to embark upon marriage no matter what
the law said. If the man could discover the
whereabouts of his daughter, it wouldn't be at all
difficult to snatch her up and lock her away
someplace. If that happened Elgin feared it
would be difficult, even impossible, to get her
back. To add to his concerns, the evil doctor still
lurked in the background, waiting to exercise the
surgical technique that was supposed to return
Iris to something called normal.

There was, however, a limit to how many skel-
etons Elgin would drag out of the closet, even for
Mims. He said, "It's a long story. The end of it is
that Iris is an old friend and I've become accustomed to watching out for her."

"Ah, yes. Old friends," said Mims. "Remarkable things, old friends."

"Exactly. We just haven't been *intimate*
friends. However, the concern isn't how well
we're acquainted, but that we haven't made any
preparations for marriage. For instance, we
haven't got a license."

Mims had stretched out one long leg and used
his foot to adjust the draft on the front of the
parlor stove. "If you're sure you want to do this,
to get married, you needn't worry about a license. After I get you tied up there isn't anything anyone can do as long as the lady hasn't
been coerced."

"What about posting banns?"

"Oh, don't worry about that. Who's to say the

notice hasn't been nailed to the church door for an age? I think it must have been. There's something hanging out there that no one has ever bothered to read. I say Farley, are you feeling as poorly as you look?"

"I'm just tired. We've had a few busy days and sleepless nights." Elgin idly slipped his finger through a curl of Iris's hair and rubbed it with his thumb. He supposed it would feel even silkier in the middle of the night when she was bathed in honeysuckle, her breath whisper soft against his throat when she wrapped her arms around him, and then he noticed Mims watching them. He dropped the curl and cleared his throat and said something inane about Iris having something caught in her hair.

Mims grinned and said, "Quite so."

Elgin missed the implication. Being so aware of Iris leaning against him, he was wondering how his parents had ever come to hate each other so. And he wondered if he would get to be like them without even trying. Like the dog that learns to kill birds by being around another dog that kills birds. Jumbled thoughts were wrapped in old hurts and past fears, stained by the tears of the child he had been.

It was the first time Elgin had wished he didn't look so much like his father.

Never having been an accomplished mind reader, Mims sprawled out in his chair to organize his impressions. In some ways it seemed that his old friend Farley was as opposed to marriage as he ever was. Even so, there was this young woman in his arms that he said he didn't love, but felt honor bound to wed. Yet the attentions he showed her had little to do with honor. If one didn't know better one might think such gestures had been inspired by affection. Curious indeed. Mims concluded that Elgin didn't know what he wanted. That, however, didn't alter the fact that the young lady in question had been compromised by being in his company. No matter how chivalrous Farley's intentions had been, he was stuck with her.

Mims then considered the other half of the proposed nuptial. Though she hadn't had anything to say for herself, he was of the opinion that the female in Farley's arms was quite willing to become Mrs. Farley. Yet he wondered how she dealt with Farley's not wanting to be married to her, now or at any other time. He could only suppose that because they were such old friends, they had already puzzled it out between them.

Mims pushed out of his chair and said, "Sit tight, old chum. There's no one else about, so I'll go upstairs and get a bed ready for Miss Huntington. Then you can just toss her in, and we can finish the pie and catch up on the news. Did I get her name right?"

"Yes, quite right, but that isn't a problem. My lamentable wardrobe is if I'm going to stay on and marry Iris. I'll need to get a wire off to my man at home so he can send some clothes. The trunk waiting beside your gate is filled with feminine things."

Iris awoke the next morning all turned around in her cloak, the heel of her shoe caught in the patchwork quilt with the date 1824 stitched into the corner. Her hooped petticoat had put ruts in her legs while she slept. She'd been dreaming that she was stuck under a boat while having tea with her Aunt Prudence and a hedgehog. Someone knocked on the bottom of the boat and woke her. Whoever it was knocked again.

"Come in."

A pretty young woman with a long blond braid opened the door to Iris's room, then smiled hesitantly. She said, "Good morning," and crossed the floor to place a large can of hot water on the washstand. "My name is Grace." Grace pushed aside the curtains and swung the window out, felt the chill draft, and shut the window. "Your Mr. Farley sent me up to see if you'll be ready soon. Mimford—that is, the Reverend Jones—is eager to get on with the wedding."

Still groggy, Iris was having some difficulty orienting herself and looked around for the hedgehog. The little animal was nowhere to be seen, but her trunk was there on the floor. She sat up slowly and waited for her head to clear.

Though Iris believed that Elgin had brought her here to be married, she hadn't expected it to happen quite so soon. Even so, she wasn't about to complain. She yawned and rubbed her eyes and said, "What time is it, please?"

"Almost noon. Follow me and I'll show you the path to the privy."

By the time Iris returned, Grace had opened the trunk and taken out the best dress she could find. It was the same one Iris had been wearing the afternoon she fled Huntington Manor for the safety of the boathouse. The fabric showed distinct signs of life on a dirt floor. It was remarkable that the homely blue dress of a few days before would now be her wedding finery.

Grace stayed long enough to help Iris undress and get out of her corset, saying, "Pull that bell cord over there when you've done bathing, and I'll bring up your breakfast." She left with the dress, as it was badly in need of brushing. As soon as Grace was gone, Iris scratched blissfully. It felt sooo good to be out of tight lacing.

When she rang for breakfast, Grace had the dress over her shoulder and a feast on a tray with a vase of pink snapdragons. Crisp bacon was piled beside an omelet made with chopped peppers. There were hot muffins and marmalade. Fresh fruit in a bowl. Hot chocolate and tea. Porridge.

Grace said, "We didn't know what you might like, and Mr. Farley said you were probably near starving, so Mrs. Hill gave you some of everything."

Exhibiting regrettably poor manners, Iris merely nodded her thanks with her mouth full. While she gobbled her omelet, Grace attempted to put some order to her disorderly hair. Before and after looked much the same. Curls all over. Even when Iris's hair had been long it was a problem. No matter how carefully it was pulled back into a bun, or how tightly it had been braided, determined curls worked their way out and an unruly halo would soon appear. Her father had complained that she looked like a waif no matter what.

While polishing off the muffin with the marmalade dribbling out, Iris considered the familiar blue dress that was now draped across the back of a chair. She almost choked when she laughed at how different this wedding would be from the elaborate affair her mother had planned for her marriage to the Marquis of Bumpsted. The guest list had been drawn up over a year ago. An elaborate gown had been designed to be fashioned of crimson brocade for a winter wedding or pink watered silk for summer. The bridesmaids had been chosen from among the children of the better families. The ceremony was to be held in Westminster Abbey, of course.

Today's bride wouldn't have been allowed inside Westminster in her smudged dress. But today's bride was radiantly happy the way she was.

A *tap-tapping* on the door announced the brief appearance of Mrs. Hill, the housekeeper-cook. Something about her reminded Iris of Aunt Prudence, though she was neither as short nor as round. The lady fairly twinkled when she said, "These are from Mr. Farley," and handed Iris a bouquet of yellow chrysanthemums, an armload of sunshine to be carried against her tired dress.

Until the flowers arrived, Iris had been reasonably well composed. Now she wiped her eyes and said, "He is such a dear man, and I love him shamefully," then blushed a deep pink.

When the two young women descended the stairs, Elgin nodded politely to Grace and greeted Iris with a gentle smile. Taking her hand, he said, "They're waiting for us in the parlor. Have you sufficiently recovered from our travels?"

Iris was teasing when she said, "Would you call it off if I hadn't?"

He said, "No," and they entered the parlor to stand before Mims. Only Grace and Mrs. Hill were there as witnesses. Mims clasped his hands, cleared his throat, and looked at Iris.

"Your name, please, your full name?"

"Iris Anna Ester Louise Huntington."

"Well, then, Iris Anna Ester Louise, do you want him?"

"Yes, I do."

"Elgin, will you have her?"

"Of course."

"The ring, please."

"The ring?"

"It *is* customary."

Elgin twisted the gold signet ring from his little finger, right hand, and slipped it onto Iris's ring finger, left hand.

Mims cried, "Good show! You're man and wife, a-men." Then he added, "I dislike dashing off like this, especially from the first wedding I've ever performed, but the day is getting on and I've got to be someplace else this afternoon. Mrs. Drake's melons will be at their prime between noon and three. They were nearly ripe when I smelled them yesterday. Do make yourselves comfortable and fit in wherever you like."

"One moment!" called Elgin to the back of the departing Reverend Jones. "Was that legal? Aren't we supposed to sign something?"

"Yes, but we can do it later."

"We can do it *now*!"

Exasperated by the additional delay, Mims said, "Very well," and led the way to his study. After going through a monstrous stack of botanical journals and the contents of several drawers, he produced two copies of the sought-after certificate. Iris laid aside the flowers and signed with the others. Only Mrs. Hill dabbed at sentimental tears with the corner of her apron.

Mims handed the first copy of the document to Iris, "With my very best wishes." When he presented the second copy to Elgin, he said, "At first I wondered if this was all a joke. I would have lost money betting on it."

"Betting on what?" asked Iris suspiciously.

"On the wedding," replied the grinning Mims on his way out the door. Grace smiled shyly and followed him.

Mrs. Hill said she would leave some dinner in the cupboard, then she, too, left the house.

Iris had gone to the window, more to put a little distance between herself and Elgin than to admire the weeds around the church.

She was ominously quiet.

Elgin jammed his hands into his pockets, and a seam gave way. Then he plowed finger-rows through his immaculately groomed hair. As calmly as he could, he said, "About the wedding . . . it isn't quite how Mims made it sound."

She said, "Perhaps not, but you do look as though you've been hit with a brick."

"You don't understand."

She turned then and said, "I do understand. You're brave and kind and would do anything to save me from disgrace or the Marquis of Bumpsted. You're my dearest friend, but you shouldn't have gone this far."

"You're doing it up a bit too sweet, though I would certainly try to keep you from anything

unpleasant. Besides, most marriages are arranged for practical reasons."

Iris shook her head and said, "I thought you
. . . oh, never mind what I thought," and hurried
from the room.

Rather shaken himself, Elgin stared at the
draped and tasseled doorway through which Iris
had passed. He honestly didn't know if it would
be best to leave her alone or go after her and
point out that in some marriages the couples
didn't even like each other. Yet the last thing he
wanted to do was to charge after her, railing like
a bully. Like his father. He told himself that everything would be fine if he just didn't become
overly emotional, except that Iris was ready to
bolt, and he was ready to punch something.

After a few trips around the room Elgin decided that he'd just have to hang on and ride out
the storm. But just in case it took longer than
anticipated, he thought it might be prudent to
put his copy of the marriage lines in a safe place.
Except that he couldn't find his copy on the desk
where he'd left it. It wasn't on the floor, either. It
was gone. Once again Elgin looked at the doorway through which Iris had passed.

It was hours later that Elgin observed Mims
coming across the lawn and hailed him. Mims
adjusted his course, making directly for the man
in the canvas hammock. He glanced about for
Mrs. Farley.

"She isn't here," Elgin informed him dryly.
"She shut herself up in her room after everyone
else left the house after the wedding."

"I shouldn't wonder," replied Mims as he collapsed into the fat cushions of a wooden lawn chair. "Pitched a fit, did she?"

"Nothing of the kind. She said something to the effect that I'd been nice about the wedding, but I shouldn't have done it, then went upstairs. And she didn't pitch anything, she was perfectly calm."

"Good heavens, you are in trouble."

"Dammit, Mims, she took exception to what you had to say about not believing I'd ever wanted to get married."

"And it's true, though there's more to it than that. She took exception because she was hurt and insulted by the way you felt about the whole thing, not that I can blame her."

Elgin sat up and swung his feet to the ground and hung on. He wasn't too happy with Mims to begin with and more angry because he'd almost gone backward out of the hammock, and said, "I'd like to remind you that she didn't know what I thought until you told her! You could have kept your silly mouth shut, and she would never have known a thing!"

"Oh, really?" said Mims in a placid, unsympathetic voice. "If you would have just said you loved her—"

"I said I'd marry her. I didn't say anything about loving her."

"You're noble as hell. Of course, anyone else might say you've got your brains where your bum goes."

"You're a wonderful friend, Mims. Always there to buck a fellow up."

"And you're a wonderful ass, Farley. Just tell the girl you still love her and be done with it."

"That's not how it is."

Mims wagged a scolding finger. "Lightning will strike you for telling lies like that." Then he frowned and asked. "Have you *ever* told her you loved her?"

"Well, no."

"I take it all back. You're not a wonderful ass. You're a *spectacular* ass! You'd better decide what you want before the lady decides that you're not what she wants."

"But Iris wouldn't—"

"When they've jumped ship once, they can do it again. How long do you expect her to wait? Tell the truth, old chum. Have you ever carried off any other young woman from whatever danger was threatening her? Have you cuddled up with any other young woman who fell asleep in your arms when you were out visiting? Stared at her while she slept? Played with her curly locks?"

"I told you that she had something in her hair!"

"She certainly did, you dunce, it was your fingers! The truth now—how long have you been in love with her?"

Elgin only glowered at Mims, left the hammock, and strode off across the lawn. Mims grinned as he watched him go, then whistled his way into the house and kitchen to see what Mrs. Hill would be serving for dinner, the turnips having been especially fine of late.

Elgin picked up a stick and went along whacking the tops off weeds, sending the dry seeds flying. He was so angry that he hadn't been able to trust himself to say anything to Mims. It wasn't anyone else's business what he said or didn't say to Iris. As for Iris, he supposed he *might* love her, in a way. He loved his sisters, too. But after thinking about his sisters, he conceded that he didn't love Iris *quite* that way and whacked the top off another weed. Besides, his sisters had found their own husbands. He didn't have much to do with it. Iris was another matter. He never had been able to find the right man for her. Under the circumstances he just had to fill that position himself. He thought anyone could surely understand why. Anyone except Mims. Mims would ask why he felt that way. Why indeed! He would simply tell him . . .

What would he tell him?

Would he say that the very thought of another man touching Iris couldn't be endured? Would he say that Iris had affected his animal urge for propagation of the species in a way that he had no intention of revealing to anyone? Would he actually tell Mims that the happiest moments of his life had been spent with Iris? . . . though the most maddening moments of his life had also been spent with Iris. Elgin knew he wouldn't say any of it. That, however, was beside the point. Loving Iris was the point, yet it was considerably different than being *in love* with Iris. But what did it matter? What difference did it make? None. *Whack whack whack.* Then again, it might perhaps make some slight difference now and then under certain conditions.

For instance, Elgin had already decided that being in love was like prancing across hot coals, emotionally dangerous stuff with which to mess about. A fire-breathing dragon better left undis-

turbed. He thought it was fine for poets to ram-
ble on about love and all that, producing piles
and pages of sentimental nonsense, but in life
one must be less emotional. Not like poets and
certainly not like his parents. Being extremely
emotional, his parents had antagonized the
dragon, and everyone else had been burned.

The subject now, however, wasn't his parents
and the dragon. It was himself and Iris and the
same scaly beast. Himself and Iris. Elgin gave a
resigned sigh, and the next weed got a half-
hearted poke. He found that it was no longer
possible to imagine himself without Iris. He
cared a great deal about her. That should be
honest enough for Mims. Some things, however,
needed to remain private. Privately Elgin didn't
think he could have left Iris at the parsonage
and gone away even if Mims had kept four
chaste wives, three kneeling bishops, two pious
aunts, and a partridge in a pear tree in residence. In a burst of self-imposed honesty Elgin
admitted that he loved Iris so fiercely that it
could wake the dragon and all its fire-breathing
kin. He was over the moon, canoodling-in-the-
hay in love with Iris. He adored her eyes and her
hair and lusted after her body. There, he'd said
it! But not aloud. Still, he thought it should have
made him happy.

Instead it scared him, but he wouldn't say that
to anyone, either. He walked a little faster. Took
him a long time to get back to the parsonage.

Mims was already at the dinner table when
Elgin returned to the house. As Iris wasn't
seated there, Elgin supposed she had taken a
tray in her room. Damned if he'd ask. Mims

passed a platter of boiled knuckle with rice. Elgin took it and said, "I don't know."

Mims said, "You don't know what?"

"I don't know how long I've been in love with Iris."

"That long?"

"It would appear so."

"What are you going to do about it?"

"I don't know that, either."

"Well, then," said Mims as he passed what was left of the French beans. "I'll tell you what the smithy did when he'd got himself in hot water over a really stupid remark he'd made about the bloomers on the carter's comely sister the day she slipped on something awful in the cow shed."

"Must you tell me now?"

"I'm afraid so. After attempting an apology that wasn't accepted—the smithy's wife didn't say no, thank you, exactly, she hit him on the noggin with a sauce pot. Anyway, he spent the next three days keeping out of her way. In your case I should think only one more day should do it as there was neither another woman's drawers nor a sauce pot involved."

"Mims, please tell me that there's a purpose to all this."

"Indeed there is. When the smithy noticed that his wife and the pot had cooled down sufficiently, he walked into the kitchen and took up the day's events as though nothing had been amiss. He apologized for being a consummate ass and they lived happily after, until he made an unfortunate remark about her cousin's notable bosoms dipping into the mint sauce when she reached for a pickled egg at the grandmother's sixty-fifth birthday celebration, but that's another story."

"Thank God."

"I'll be working in the gardens again tomorrow if you'd care to spend the day there. We could use another man."

"That will hardly be necessary. I'll be able to solve this little problem quite nicely before that."

Dust.

Flour dust, actually.

Iris was wearing a fine layer of it. She'd spent two days successfuly avoiding Elgin, and now she was making bread. Rubbing the tip of her nose with the back of her wrist, she held her breath so she wouldn't sneeze. After a moment she returned to the long maple table and the flour-coated lump of dough. It seemed to her that she had punched and rearranged it quite enough, but conceded that she really didn't know much about making bread, this being her first attempt.

At the opposite end of the kitchen table stood Mrs. Hill expertly kneading a larger lump of dough. After she divided the roly-poly thing in half, she said, "This way dear," and folded sides to center, pushing it in with her fists, shaping the two pieces into fat rounded loaves that she dusted with more flour.

Iris watched closely and kneaded her dough almost the same way and made her loaf practically round, with some flour on it, too, then stood back to admire it.

"Well done," said the male voice behind her.

Iris glanced around at Elgin and squeezed out

a pleasant "Thank you," and decided that her dough needed more pat-patting into shape. Busywork.

It was the first time Iris and Elgin had actually exchanged words since she'd left him standing in the study after the wedding. He had tapped on her chamber door last night, but she hadn't answered. Even so, she knew that he knew that she hadn't been asleep. It made things a bit awkward now, but nothing insurmountable.

Iris reshaped the dough and sprinkled on more flour. She didn't know if she could be this close to Elgin without losing her composure. She'd spent a night and a day wondering what she would say to this man who had almost been her husband. He hadn't wanted to marry her, not really. As it turned out he was free after all, and she had decided to tell him so today. But here in the kitchen with the cook wasn't the place to discuss such things.

Mrs. Hill put her loaves of bread onto a floured board and scored a cross in the top to let the devil out. Iris watched and did the same. Mrs. Hill covered her loaves with a light cloth. Iris did that, too. The bread board was then put in a warm place near the oven so the dough would rise. But when Mrs. Hill put her hand inside the hot oven and began to count, Iris didn't do it. In fact she looked at the woman very strangely.

Elgin's smile came easy. Having spent so much time in the kitchens as a child, he knew what was happening. "If you can leave your hand in the oven until the count of seven—that is, until the quick of your fingernails can stand the heat to seven but no more—then you know the temperature is right for something like bread or that pan of buns. Just don't touch anything in the oven when you stick your hand in, or you'll get burned."

Mrs. Hill slid the buns into the brick oven and closed the iron door with a folded towel. After glancing at the clock, she took to the rocking chair by the window to peel apples. A sleek gray cat lay asleep in a block of sunlight that came through the window and warmed the floor.

Iris's smile looked rather pinched when she said, "Yes. I mean yes, I understand, but no, I wouldn't touch anything in the oven." Her composure had begun to slip. She moved away from Elgin and got a cloth to wipe the table.

Elgin thought he recognized a spasm of maidenly modesty and filled the conversational gap with trite but pleasant things about the big kitchen he knew as a child. That's where he had learned his numbers, by counting jam jars and spoons. Then he added, "If a staffing emergency should arise, I'm certain that I could still trim the pie crust away from the edge of the pan as neatly as I ever could. And pinch together little animals—mostly turtles and fish—from the scraps of pie dough that fell away. Our cook had a very small gallery of very small works of art—mostly by yours truly—with a cat or two of marzipan sculpted by the knifeboy, who was considerably more talented."

As Iris was still listening, Elgin assumed that two days had healed her injured feelings, and he was anxious to get back to the way things were when he and Iris first arrived at the parsonage. They had been good friends then. They had still been friends when he carried her upstairs to bed that night. He'd wanted to ease down beside her and stay there. Instead he nuzzled her ear and whispered good night, and she smiled in her sleep when he tucked the covers under her chin. The covers were thick, the pillows soft. The mattress hard. That made him wonder if Iris might take a little nap this afternoon. Iris. His wife. In that bed. Both of them might have a little nap. Then again they might not.

Elgin yawned and smiled. He smiled again without the yawn.

Mrs. Hill noticed the way his gaze followed Iris and how Iris tried to avoid looking at him. Knowing that theirs had been a runaway marriage, she suspected that the young lady had never had the benefit of a mother's advice and counsel to prepare her for this momentous time in her life. Mrs. Hill also knew that Elgin had spent the night on the sofa in the parlor, because there was still a pillow and blanket there when she arrived this morning. Yes, there were a few things that wanted explaining when she and the young lady were alone.

In her chair by the window Mrs. Hill cut away jagged red ribbons of apple peel that curled and collected in the wooden bowl on her lap. She looked up at Iris and said, "Thank you for your help, but I can manage now. The table is clean enough, go along with your husband. You and I can have a nice little chat later on."

Being resigned to another sort of chat that she must have with Elgin, Iris hung up the damp cloth and untied her apron. Not suspecting what was to come, Elgin cheerfully tossed the apron over a chair, steered Iris toward the coatrack in the hall for her wrap, then out the back door. He had often heard that fresh air could leave one longing for a nap.

He said, "Would you care for a guided tour of the great achievements of our host? I mean his gardens. Today I helped Mims dig a hole as deep as my arm and set a stone slab in the bottom. Then we planted a fruit tree. Peach, I think it was. When the tap root can't go down any farther than the stone slab, the tree won't grow any bigger." In addition to the dirt smudges on the knees of his borrowed trousers with the cuffs rolled up, Elgin wore a dirt-stained shirt beneath a jacket that showed how far he'd been into that hole.

Iris looked around the lawn and yard without seeing anything that looked particularly productive. There were a few trees, the usual outbuildings that included a carriage house, but no garden walls.

Elgin extended his arm. "Allow me."

Iris allowed, hoping there would be a place where they could talk, for she had to get through what she had to say before another day was out. They walked down the drive and along the empty road while Elgin went on about the immediate neighborhood, saying, "According to Mims, this bend in the road once had a pub. Right over there." He pointed to a place where a cow grazed among the stone foundations of a long-gone building. Iris also noticed the weed-choked hole in the ground that used to be a cellar. Farther on were a few cottages. Elgin explained that the families that lived in them earned their livings on the local farms. Mrs. Hill, he said, lived in one of those cottages with a niece and her husband.

Farther down the road on the opposite side from the parsonage was a house of more spacious proportions, though still not what one would call a grand residence. This was where Elgin and Iris turned in, following the drive to the back, where they stopped.

"My goodness!"

"Yes, I said something like that myself the first time I saw it. I'm told that Grace actually assisted Mims with repairs to the brickwork on one of the walls. They're devoted to each other." Elgin paused, expecting Iris to comment on a woman doing brickwork. She didn't. He wasn't even sure how closely she was listening.

"The house is that of Grace and her parents. Her brothers are in the army. The old man served in India and did very well for himself, considering that he wasn't an officer. When he retired he built this place on the site of his humble boyhood home, because he wanted to be with the people he'd missed while he was away all those years. The fellow went at it with remarkable vigor where the garden was concerned. Had an inclination for digging about and growing things, but never quite got it right until Mims arrived and took the place in hand. The garden and the structures built into the garden walls take up a little over an acre." Some moments were spent in quiet contemplation of the place before Elgin said, "Come inside and look around."

Strolling beneath the Gothic arch in the garden wall, Iris found neat beds of vegetables. An early crop of peas now climbed poles near the cooler north-facing wall. Yellow chrysanthemums and pink snapdragons grew among the cutting flowers along each side of a central walk.

Carrots and beetroot, salsify and scorzonera bordered the narrower gardens of the south-facing wall. That's where cherry and apple trees were espaliered against sun-warmed bricks. Iris couldn't see what was in the cold frames and wondered if it might be sea kale. Elgin looked and said it wasn't. Behind a hedge of lavender grew gooseberries and white currants.

Spade in hand, Mims called out, "Have a look about and be sure you see the strawberries. We'll have some at dinner."

While admiring those fine berry plants, Iris quietly said, "Elgin, I simply must talk to you. Privately."

Elgin smiled. He liked the idea of private anything with Iris. In fact he had been thinking along those lines himself. He walked her over to the potting shed, scooted her inside, and pushed the door shut with his foot.

In an instant Iris was swept into a playful embrace by the only man she had ever loved. He growled kissy kissy kiss and delivered a line of smacking kisses along her neck before he chewed on her ear. Iris tried not to giggle too loudly. But then the teasing stopped and the kisses didn't smack. Iris didn't giggle. Her composure was in tatters, and his self-control was going straight to the hot place.

He said, "Sometime, when I wasn't paying attention, you grew up. So did I." He lowered his mouth to hers and got the jolt of his life. The electric fluid of lightning couldn't have done a more devastating job of it on his nerve endings. Her yielding sigh teased a response of his own, and he forced himself to hold her away so he could catch his breath. His heart pounded in his ears, but the throbbing wasn't that confined. His eyes were little more than misty blue rims around dilated pupils.

Iris, feeling somewhat dazed, wondered if Elgin's lips felt as tingly as her own and lifted a hand to his mouth to find out. At her touch he wanted to climb out of his skin. For the first time he missed his hat. If he had it he would have held it.

"We really shouldn't be doing this," came Iris's breathy whisper. "Not now."

"And not here."

She took a deep breath. "We really must discuss this."

He said, "Later," and put his arms around her. She wiggled her hands up against his chest and pushed; he stepped back. Noting her flushed face, his grin became nothing short of wicked. He touched her cheek and said, "Perhaps we don't have to talk."

Iris's knees weren't as strong as she'd thought. She took another deep breath. Elgin's eyelids drooped seductively.

She shook her head and said, "Lust."

"Would you please repeat that?"

"We might call it *friendly* lust."

"We might indeed!"

Fingers tightly knotted, she said, "Elgin, we aren't really married. Under the circumstances there are some things that we can't do, delightful as they are. All that breathing and hugging and kissing and breathing. I've noticed a dangerous amount of breathing. It's inadvisable for us to indulge in activities so stimulating to the passions. Such behavior can lead to *other* behavior. So under the circumstances . . ."

Elgin leaned against the door and stuffed his hands into his pockets. "What is this about not being married?"

"We aren't."

"Did you take my copy of our marriage lines?"

"Yes, however, that hasn't changed a thing. The certificates are altogether intact. We simply aren't married."

"You seemed to think we were until Mims delivered his asinine remark."

"The legality of it all has nothing to do with Mims's remark. It has to do with requirements."

"What's the matter with you? Mims married us. We have witnesses and papers to prove—oooh, I know what it is. It's those requirements. You think we skipped something. That business of the banns. Besides that I expect you're hesitant about sharing a bed—don't gape. Makes you look like a fish. Just remember that I'm not insensitive to the situation."

"Elgin, we truly aren't married!"

"Oh, no? I've got something to show you. I think you'll find it reassuring, under the circumstances."

She hesitated. "I must know if we're still friends."

With one slender finger he rubbed the worry lines on her forehead. "Never doubt it."

Elgin led Iris out of the potting shed, through the garden, down the drive, along the road to the church. As they walked the overgrown path to the front door, the weeds and thistles stuck all over her skirt and picked at her legs when they snapped up inside her hooped petticoat. Reaching the step, Elgin read aloud the words written in a scrawl on the weathered paper tacked to the oaken door. It was the paper Mims had spoken of. The one nobody bothered to read.

"The banns," said Elgin. "You will notice that according to this document one Elgin Farley and a Miss Iris Huntington announce their intention to marry. According to the date, it's been here over a month."

Iris looked and didn't doubt that the paper had been put up that long ago, but with some other message on it. She said, "Did you do this?" and he said, "Of course not. It's the work of the Reverend Mims. Please note that we have now completed the requirements. Ceremony, certificate, and posted banns. In fact I think I'll keep this. Save it for our children along with our marriage lines." Elgin removed the tacks, stuck them back in the door, then folded and pocketed the paper. Rather full of himself, he turned to Iris and cranked up a triumphant leer. "Do you feel at all tired? Might you like a nap?"

"That wouldn't be appropriate, as we aren't married," repeated Iris.

"The joke is *over*."

"Elgin, it isn't a joke. To be married a couple must have done three things: purchased a license or posted banns, have two witnesses to the event, and have it recorded in the church registry. Three things." She wiggled three fingers on her left hand. None of those fingers wore his ring.

"Are you certain—I mean about the registry?"

"Quite."

"How do you know?"

"I read it in Mims's book of Ecclesiastic law."

"Then the remedy is simple enough. All we have to do is put it in the registry."

Iris shook her head. "I won't sign it."

"Why not? I thought you wanted to get married."

"I did. But you didn't. You only agreed to an engagement after I badgered you into it, and then you couldn't very well get out of it. I simply cannot allow you to make such a sacrifice."

"Iris—"

She stubbornly shook her head again. "It wasn't until Mims spoke up that I finally realized how terribly unfair I've been. Isn't it surprising? Now I'm saving you."

"Iris, I don't *want* to be saved."

"Oh, Elgin. You've always been so decent about everything. Now there's one last thing with which you can be of assistance. You see, I haven't planned what to do next. The work at which I'm skilled is the illustration of antiquities. Unfortunately, women aren't employed for such things. Still, I might be able to give French or flute lessons to children. Can you tell me how to go about obtaining such a position?"

"Iris, I don't *intend* to be saved."

"I'm *so* sorry to have done all this to you, truly I am. If—"

Elgin put his hands to Iris's face like bookends and laid both thumbs across her mouth. Having gained her complete attention, he said, "Do listen carefully, as I'll say it only once. I've spent my last night alone. When I want to be saved, I'll apprise you of the need." He removed his thumbs.

Iris stared into his eyes, searching for doubts, any sign of reluctance, the smallest hint of duty. In a very soft voice she said, "Are you absolutely certain?"

Just as quietly he said, "Yes, I am," and released her.

"You aren't simply doing the proper thing?"

Hand on his heart he said, "Propriety is the farthest thing from my mind."

Iris gave his answer considerable thought, then said, "Oh," which was followed by another silence that seemed to go on forever.

Elgin looked at the sky and at his shoes and at the weeds, then looked at Iris and said, "I do like you tremendously."

She stared back and said, "How do you know?"

He was about to return a brilliant sally, but the expression on her face held him back. She was expecting him to say something else, something about loving, not liking, but he couldn't. She just didn't understand how dangerous such emotional confessions could be, but he didn't know how to explain it without sounding like an idiot. The longer he stared back at her, waiting for inspiration to manifest itself, the more he became aware of the shape of her mouth, of lips that parted to form a word he didn't hear, watched the tip of a pink tongue slide across a rosy bottom lip close enough to kiss if he just leaned . . .

But they were on the front steps of the church. Quite public. Too public. Iris waited for him to say something more. Elgin still thought about kissing her and said, "Not here and not now." It was the rumbly soft voice of a man who wouldn't be spending another night on the sofa.

· *Eleven* ·

After leaving Iris at the church, Elgin went to help Mims in the garden. It was the most sensible thing he was able to do at the time. When Iris returned to the parsonage, she stopped at the back door to pick weeds from her skirt. It was all she was able to do with any amount of coherent thought. Going around in her head was a strange mixture of delight and disappointment, because of what Elgin said and didn't say. But she reasoned that life was like that, and she wasn't about to turn away from what she and Elgin had because it wasn't precisely everything she wanted. If he couldn't quite *say* he loved her, then she would make do with knowing that he *meant* he loved her. At least she *supposed* he meant he loved her. But if he loved her enough, he'd say it, wouldn't he? When she finally entered the house she was assaulted by conflicting clues and the smell of fresh-baked bread.

Seeing Iris pass the kitchen door, Mrs. Hill cheerfully offered her a cup of tea. Iris stepped into the room, and the good woman asked her to close the door, if you please. Once again Mrs. Hill was sitting in the rocking chair near the window where the light was brightest. This time she wasn't peeling apples. She had a frock coat lying across her lap that belonged to Mims. Stitch by stitch she was taking out the lining and pockets, as the gray wool and red sateen parts of the garment had to be cleaned separately.

"Now, my dear," began Mrs. Hill as Iris sat down at the table with her tea. "I don't mean to intrude, but I've got the idea that you have had very little preparation for married life."

Iris said, "Thank you for the tea, but I really must be going."

"Oh, *do* sit down, dear. This won't be so awfully bad." Discreetly keeping her eyes on her work, the housekeeper said, "I quite understand the difficulties of an elopement, though you mustn't think this will be a lecture on what happens when bees buzz in and out of flowers. I should think your governess and teachers must have given you at least a few lessons concerning the fertilization of plants and how seeds grow. Did they have you dissecting flowers and making drawings?" She looked up for only a moment to see Iris nod, then returned to picking out stitches, satisfied that the girl before her wasn't completely ignorant of the facts of life. "You must remember that your husband cares for you. I can see it in the way he looks at you. You're very fortunate. And I can see that you are anything but indifferent to his attentions. Even so, the pleasures of anticipation are generally greater than those of realization."

Iris didn't know quite what to make of that remark and looked it.

"When two people are strongly attracted to each other, knowing what to do after marriage in the bedchamber is rarely a problem, though if you are ever tempted by the evils of venereal excesses, you should find relief in reciting The Lord's Prayer. And do remember," Mrs. Hill said in her most reassuring tones, "whatever your husband expects, even if it seems peculiar, you must cooperate but still remain a lady. To do otherwise might find you wanting in moral character. Either obstinacy or wanton aggression will surely put him in disgust of you. A lady is quietly submissive." Mrs. Hill was almost whispering when she added, "A lady simply doesn't feel these things the way men do. She wouldn't be respectable if she did."

Iris was still wondering about those *peculiar expectations*, like what they were, and poured herself more tea and shoveled in too much sugar.

"Then there's the matter of making babies," said Mrs. Hill.

Iris choked on the tea and blamed it on the sugar. Mrs. Hill overlooked it. She'd had this talk, or a variation of it, with several nieces and one other young lady in a great house where she had been employed.

"Babies," continued Mrs. Hill, "are most easily conceived just before or just after your monthly. The least likely time is right in between, though there are those who think conception can happen at any time." She collected little bits of thread and put them on the stool she had placed beside her rocker. "If you prefer one sex of child over the other, there are ways to go about it," she explained knowingly. "To have a boy-child the woman must be passive and the man the aggressor. To have a girl the roles must be reversed. And then there are those who think it's the moon, with girls being more likely at the full of the moon and the boys at the new moon. Your husband will explain more about the *other* things."

Now Iris wondered about the peculiarities *and* the other things. They weren't comforting thoughts.

"Then there's the food," continued Mrs. Hill. "To produce a boy the prospective father must eat highly seasoned food and be physically active for at least two weeks before the attempted conception. The mother must become as passive as possible, eating very plain foods. To produce a girl-child the man lives quietly and eats plainly, while the woman has the spicy diet and greater activity."

Iris was thinking about Mr. and Mrs. Sacks. Sacks was a merchant in Little Woolton, a slight mouse of a man who wore his shirts too big and a too small bowler hat perched squarely on top of his head like the lid on a tea caddy. His wife was an overbearing Wagnerian sort of woman, who wore too much perfume. Yet they had produced nothing but sons. Six of them. Whoever would have thought that after dark Sacks would become so remarkably different than he appeared to be during the day.

Mrs. Hill was talking but not to Iris. The girl that came in to clean was being given instructions for beating the rugs. Iris put her cup aside and slipped out of the kitchen, glad that Elgin hadn't popped in to hear this lecture the way he had popped in to watch her make bread.

When Iris reached her chamber and flopped across her bed, she had plenty to think about besides the fact that her bouncing hoops exposed an absolutely indecent amount of petticoats and drawers. Fortunately there wasn't anyone about to notice. She was still occupied with what Mrs. Hill had to say. And she remembered that a long time ago one of the girls at boarding school had said she thought a woman could have a baby from kissing a man, and someone else said babies were caused by something that happened when a man and woman were asleep together, which caused the dormitory maid to giggle. She said babies didn't happen either way. It was the same maid who sold a love potion made of juniper berries to some of the girls. Recalling the trouble one of them got into, Iris thought the philter must have worked too well.

Iris found that it had been unbelievably easy to get into trouble at school, though it wasn't from any laxity of supervision. It was because there were so many rules she didn't like. For instance, she had been scolded for wearing thin-soled shoes. The headmistress insisted that wearing such shoes led to mental disturbances, displacement of the female organs, and consumption, which would be perfectly dreadful, because consumptives mustn't marry, because they would produce consumptive children.

Another problem was that Iris hated to wear woolen underthings all year round. Actually, she didn't like wearing woollies anytime at all. And she was forever in trouble for laughing too much and too loud. "A sweet smile," she had been told, "is quite enough for a lady." And then there was the day the headmistress called her into the office for a scold. Iris was firmly reminded that young ladies only learned mathematics to supervise household accounts. "Young ladies," the woman had said, "are not to concern themselves with compounding interest on stocks and bonds. Young ladies have no business asking about such things." So that Iris wouldn't repeat the offense, she wasn't allowed any dessert that night. As it turned out, she didn't care all that much for stewed plums and didn't consider the loss a deprivation.

The headmistress, however, wasn't the most memorable of the instructresses. It had been the one they all called The Prune. She was the music teacher, and the girls snickered about her in private. No matter what piece of music the woman began to discuss, everyone knew that she would end up reminding them of the evils of *secret bad habits*, which she said would do more to ruin one's constitution than thin-soled shoes. Everyone agreed that The Prune was the most pious and strict of their teachers. With a shrill voice and pinched lips she said things like: "Erotic propensities threaten one's chastity and are exacerbated by pernicious examples of flummery, fashion, and ruinous vanity!"

Unfortunately no one knew what most of those words meant, except Suzzan Hepplewhite, and that was because she was frightfully intelligent and liked to read the dictionary she had purloined from her father's library. She had the small volume hidden in a bottom drawer among her woolen underwear. Suzzan had boasted about knowing words like *sperm* and *orgasm*, but wouldn't tell what they meant. Then she said that she'd tell them what The Prune meant in her most recent lecture if the rest of the girls would compensate her in liquid assets. The girls talked about it and thought they might be able to get hold of some extra hot chocolate, until Suzzan said she wanted money, and the girls said she should have told them that in the first place. After considerable effort they handed over nearly eight shillings. It's all the group of eleven- and twelve-year-olds could collect between them, as spending money was a restricted commodity. What they learned for their money was that their pedantic music mistress had meant dancing when she spoke of erotic propensities.

This same woman had also said that children should begin music and dancing lessons early in life, by the age of five years, and certainly no later than six years, so that such things were tasks rather than pleasures. "This arrangement," she insisted, "will conduce to rigid morality instead of the dissipation and excitement that will lead to a revolting and indecent character." None of them quite understood what that meant, either, but they couldn't afford any more explanations from Suzzan Hepplewhite.

Now Iris propped her chin on her hands and grinned, remembering how they had managed to use The Prune's depressing sentiments to their own advantage. To get what they wanted they simply had to say they didn't want it. The more they objected to dancing—with Suzzan's honest objections adding strength to their own dishonest lamentations—the more music and dancing they were given. The lot of them never got their pound of flesh off Suzzan that term, but they got eight shillings' worth just watching her puff and sweat and whine about the dancing.

Catching hold of a pillow, Iris pulled it over and hugged it. Her grin softened to a smile as she began to weave a glorious fantasy in which she danced pleasurably with Elgin, her chastity threatened at every step by erotic flummery. She fell asleep in the midst of a dissipating waltz, for which she wore a shimmering blue gown with a ruinously low neckline that revealed her indecently magnificent bosom.

It was, after all, a fantasy.

There were indeed strawberries at table that evening, along with a boiled round of beef, suet dumplings, peas, turnips, and baked apple pudding. Mims himself had taken great care to arrange the berries in bowls with leaves and vines tucked among them for decoration. So attractive. Elgin was relieved when his friend expounded upon the subject of his garden, not their disreputable school days together.

"Have you seen the root store?" Mims asked Iris. "More parsnips were put in today. Packed in layers in dry sand on the floor like the other root crops. Did you know that there are two assistant gardeners? Perhaps you didn't see them. Both are terribly good at arranging things for market. The root store is done up every bit as nicely."

Mims hoisted a forkful of peas and explained that one kind of vegetable was separated from another by boards between the neatly arranged stacks. He didn't want Iris to think his magnificent produce was all jumbled together, and wanted her to know that potatoes didn't need sand. They were simply piled up.

Having been a curious child, Iris had been in and out of the root store at Huntington Manor many times and knew the arrangement well, but it wasn't necessary to say so. It would have been unkind to dampen Mims's pride and enthusiasm in his own achievements. Thus her mind wandered, but it didn't wander far. Only back to Mrs. Hill's teatime lecture.

More to the point, Iris wondered what Mrs. Hill had left out. Wondered about those *other things* that husbands were supposed to know about. And what, precisely, need the aggressive party *do* to produce the desired progeny? That is, what form did this aggression take? It sounded dangerous, even frightening. And Iris wondered if her Aunt Prudence would be able to tell her, but she truly couldn't imagine Prudence knowing much about such things. Not *those* things. Not about what men and women do when they're together at night, because Chumbly was rather revolting. Elgin, however, wasn't revolting in the least. Elgin made her toes curl when he kissed her. Elgin had eyes that . . .

Elgin looked across the table at Iris over an arrangement of fall flowers, cocked an eyebrow, smiled. If only he hadn't smiled. Iris thought he looked as though he knew what she'd been thinking. She turned pink, and Elgin turned away, grinning. Mims turned over something in his salad and said, "Have I told you about hand-pollinating the exotics? I've had some interesting results with botanical consummation. All you have to do is tickle the little parts with a camel's hair brush."

Elgin credited earnest prayer for the fact that Mims had nothing more to say about pollinating anything. Even so Iris was understandably apprehensive when the three of them gathered in the parlor after dinner for further conversation. Before Mims could say God only knew what, Elgin inquired after the progress with the vinery.

Mims was delighted to comply. "We'll have four cows to heat the place during the cold months," he waxed enthusiastically. "At least four to start with. Need more. Cows are devilishly warm beasts. We're in the process of building stalls to accommodate them. Then the vines will be trained up the wall and hung from the beams, getting plenty of sunlight through the glass roof, though we have yet to install the glass roof, and the fruit will hang down for convenient observation and picking, but too high for the cows to reach. Cows are considerably more economical than steam boilers to heat the place, you know, even with underground heating pipes. Besides, the existing boiler has never worked properly, and cows are dependably warm."

Elgin agreed that cows were both dependable and warm, and Iris said yes, they were.

"Two of the beasts have already been moved into the vinery," said Mims. "I do hope they're liking it. They still hadn't settled in when last I saw them. Kept looking like they wanted to go home." Addressing Elgin, he said, "I think I should have a look-in at them. One wants contented cows and all that. Would you care to come along, old chum?"

The old chum said, "Thank you, not this time."

Mims then asked if he was certain, and Elgin said that he was, so Mims said not to wait up.

It had been difficult for Iris to control an unladylike burst of levity, though she did. This urge to laugh was due in part to Mims and his restless cows. The rest of it was nervousness because she knew that with Mims gone, she and Elgin would be alone and it was getting late and she was sure he would want to go to bed soon and she didn't know how to go about it. And then there were those *peculiar expectations* and the *other things* of which Mrs. Hill had spoken. Iris glanced at Elgin. He didn't *look* peculiar. He never had, but how could she really tell if he was?

Iris took a calming breath, folded her hands neatly on her lap, and smiled brightly before she said, "Well, how are things at home in Kent? It's time for the hops to be harvested, I believe."

Elgin said, "Yes, it is. Let's go to bed. I'm not at all accustomed to hard labor, and I ache like the devil."

Iris turned a shade of apprehensive gray, and Elgin said, "Oh, hell. Have you been given the same ridiculous instructions my sisters got about marriage and husbands and all that?"

Iris thought for a moment and said, "How would I know if it was the same or not?"

Elgin shook his head. "I got hold of some books on the subject, you see. Books written especially for young ladies, God help them every one. Those printed and bound wonders were brought into

the house for my sisters. A medical doctor wrote
one, a doctor of divinity wrote another, even a
matron of good family had her advice preserved
for posterity. From what they had to say I'm
amazed that the night sky hasn't exploded with
plaintive invocations. The Lord's Prayer, and glorious thoughts of England, issued by terrified
young wives while shrinking beneath the panting attentions of their slobbering husbands!

"Gads!" he went on, rubbing the tight muscles
at the back of his neck. "The lower classes have
been spared a great deal of suffering by simply
being unable to read those damn books! Who
knows how many of those publications are lurk-
ing about, waiting to frighten the hapless females who are instructed by them? We'd all be
better off if a few of the more refined madames
would provide a little advice."

"What, exactly, is a refined madame?"

"A refined madame," he said slowly, "is a dignified woman who ... whose business it is to
know about what men and women do."

"Does that have anything to do with why
you're angry?"

"I am *not* angry." A breath later he said, "Yes,
I am."

"Why?"

He shook his head, stood up, and held out his
hand. She took it.

"Elgin?"

"I'm not angry at you. It's simply that we're
being cheated by a lot of people who have some
silly ideas about what's respectable and what
isn't." At the bottom of the stairs he lit a candle.
Iris could see that he was smiling when he said,

"I'd be ever so pleased if you found my attentions in the bedchamber as pleasurable as my attentions in a potting shed."

"But a respectable lady—"

"Is a wonderful thing to have at one's side in a ballroom, for a ride in the park, in another man's box at the opera, but not in one's bed."

At the top of the stairs they turned toward Iris's room. She was saying, "I've been told that a good wife—"

"Is an absolute must in the parlor, the nursery, and when a man is out of town."

"Of course, but—"

He laid a finger across her lips. In a soft rumbly voice he said, "I've felt you shiver when I held you, and I know it wasn't from the cold. But young ladies aren't supposed to know what passion is, poor things. A decent woman is supposed to be, or pretend to be, as cold as a witch's tit."

"What is a witch's tit?"

Elgin shut his eyes and sighed. "It's a mole or wart or something of the sort, supposedly used by witches to suckle their familiars, and those are usually in the form of black cats or black birds, and you can stop looking at me that way because I didn't mean you. I meant a female designed by the writers of books like *Correct Conduct For Young Ladies Of Good Family*, with chapters on public meetings, private homes, courting, and the nuptial chamber.

"Oh."

He said, "I'd like a lady in the ballroom and a wife in the parlor and a mistress in my bed. I want you the way you are when we're cuddling in a potting shed. What do you want?"

"Elgin, is that peculiar? The part about the mistress?"

It was a moment before he said, "I suppose the people who write those dreadful bedtime etiquette books would think it's peculiar."

Iris was quiet for much too long, comparing what she'd heard and what she'd read, to what her older sisters had said, with what Mrs. Hill had told her this afternoon, then measured it against the remarks society makes all the time. Years of lessons all confused and contradicted in a few minutes by what Elgin had just told her.

Looking every bit as perplexed as she felt, Iris said, "I'm not saying that I understand it, but it seems that if it's peculiar it's to be expected, and one's husband must be relied upon, peculiar or not, because he knows about *things*. Unfortunately, I don't understand exactly what peculiar *is*, or exactly what a mistress *does*, though that isn't to say that I've never heard of them, because I have, of course, and that they're something like a concubine, but that could mean anything, though I don't think they do housework."

Elgin rubbed the place between his eyes to hide a smile. He said, "You're right about the housework, but the rest of it isn't anything I can explain here in the passage. Perhaps it would be best to forget the books and whatever you've been told, and we'll start over on our own. We can make it up as we go."

They had long since reached the chamber that had been hers alone, and Iris had slowed to an awkward stop. Elgin tilted her face up and whispered, "A lady in the ballroom, a wife in the par-

lor, and a mistress in here." He tapped on the
door. "I would appreciate it if you wouldn't get
them mixed up." He turned the knob and pushed
the door open.

When Iris still looked uncertain, he said,
"Kissy kissy kiss." She laughed softly but didn't
move. He bowed her into the room, lit the lamp,
and turned it low. "See here, Mrs. Farley, you're
dawdling. You owe me a shilling for those sweet
bird-words, and I know exactly how to get it."

Iris looked up at Elgin with a shadowy smile
as sweet as his bird-words. He nearly melted on
the spot. She said, "You'll have to sing fine
hymns and sailing songs to get a shilling from
me, Mr. Farley," and pushed the door shut with
her foot.

Far from the little parsonage Chumbly was on
his way back to Little Woolton and Huntington
Manor. He was in a particularly bad mood. Being obliged to ride in a second-class railway carriage was only part of the cause. In addition to
having had to submit to accommodations beneath his station, it disgusted him to be wearing
unbecoming, threadbare clothing. He suspected
that none of it had ever been new, but started
out stained and shabby, stinking of cheap tobacco and fried fish. There was no way to know
where his own clothes were by now. He thought
they could even be hanging on the body of some
inferior person, perhaps some publican, who
didn't know the least thing about what it meant
to be a gentleman.

Shifting his feet in badly worn shoes only reminded Chumbly that he'd had to sell his hand-

made boots, too. Even his gold watch with the diamond at twelve o'clock was gone. And his silver matchbox. It was the only way he could come up with enough money to pay the sizable bill he'd run up at Mother Purity's Private School and buy a train ticket home. He could have easily paid for everything if some scabby thief hadn't taken the old bottle out of his carpetbag. It would have brought him a pretty penny or two. But the bottle hadn't been there to sell when he got to London, and Mother Purity had threatened him with the law if he didn't pay for the instructions he'd received. Chumbly swore that when he discovered the identity of the bottle thief, he'd have a score to settle.

While Chumbly considered the possible identity of the thief, the Linguistic Society of Paris debated whether humans invented language or were born to it like birds were born to fly.

Far away in Wyoming on the western side of the United States of America the wife of Lieutenant Colonel George Armstrong Custer wished he'd get his hair cut.

At Huntington Manor the fire bell rang. The fellow on the rope pulled a slow, steady dirge. The men of the estate made their way to the carriage house, and the women finished whatever they were doing before going to the trough to fill water buckets. Dogs got up and wandered away to a quieter place. Children followed the dogs. An upstairs window of the great house was opened and someone threw out a towel. The terrace doors were swung wide for a maid who carried out a spindle-backed chair. A second maid followed with a magazine and laid it on the chair. When several men had gathered at the carriage house, they rolled the fire engine to the back door of the manor. Half of them took up the greasy leather hose, hauled it inside over the polished floor and up the carpeted stairs to the door of the Egyptian Room. There they waited for the squire. While they waited the wash house burned to the ground.

· Twelve ·

He lay there with one knee bent among her
skirts, blowing at a wisp of hair that curled
against her ear. "We can't stay here forever," he
said in a husky whisper. "Someone is bound to
wonder what's become of us. Then they'll send
out a search party with a pack of hounds."

The delightful attention her ear received persuaded Iris to abandon sky watching and turn
toward her husband. After wiggling her hip
deeper into the cushions, she wiggled her fingers
inside the front of his shirt and whispered, "If
they bring hounds to find us, we'll hear them before they see us," then traced erotic swirls over
his chest—a touching that would have been better left for another time. And another place.

Nearing the moment when he would be unable
to resist the urge to squirm, Elgin sat up and
said, "Would you care for more cider? Roasted
duck? Fruit? A back rub? Alas," he sighed
mournfully, "not a back rub. Too blasted many
layers of stuff and steel reinforcements for such
simple pleasures. Lovemaking in a tree house
has its complications." He felt a chill where Iris's

warm hand had been and put his own hand over that lonesome place.

When he regained something of his composure from the sitting-up exercise, stretching his arms and flexing his legs as though that's what it had all been about, he laid down again. Adjusting the cushions beneath his head, he said, "Just look at that railing. Fine work. Sturdy." He was still thinking about making love in a tree house, where the stairs wound up and around the trunk of the huge beech tree to the cushion-strewn platform. The peeling yellow paint appeared so oddly correct with the smooth gray bark of the tree.

"I think there must have been a table and chairs up here at one time," Elgin continued as casually as he could, acutely aware of the fact that Iris's hand had slipped inside his shirt again. His hard-won control began to wilt. Flashing Elgin an absurdly innocent smile, Iris continued the inspiring designs upon his person. The man himself was determined not to let her know that she was driving him mad. He even sounded deceptively lucid when he said, "You can see the marks from furniture legs, or you could if there weren't cushions on the floor."

Yes, Elgin was having a difficult time of it, trying to think about chair legs and scuff marks while Iris's fingers tiptoed about inside his clothes. But it wasn't only Iris's hand that he'd found so delectably soft. He was quite aware that she was soft all over. And he found himself wishing that night would come sooner, though he knew he'd be better off abandoning such thoughts—at least for the time being.

But he didn't.

He couldn't.

The honeysuckle scent of her teased his imagination, and he was loath to forgo the vision of Iris *au naturel* among the cushions, the warm September sun dancing though coppered leaves to dapple her fair skin with diamonds of light. . . .

To maintain his fragile calm, Elgin counted to ten. Then he counted to twenty.

Iris said, "Is something wrong?" and he said, "I've just got a rather lumpy cushion."

She started to get up, saying, "I'll fix it for you."

He said, "No," and pulled her down, tucking her in snugly beside him.

Iris was as contented as one of Mims's cows. Her eyes drifted shut. It was the same pampered feeling she'd had that warm sunny day when Elgin had saved her from the apple tree. Now cicadas buzzed a grand finale to another summer. The smell of fresh-cut hay floated on the wind. Birds chirruped. Finches, she thought, and inched her fingers inside Elgin's shirt.

Pulling uncomfortably at his collar, he said, "I've been thinking that we shouldn't stay on with Mims much longer. He's been neglecting his gardens. Besides that, I'm eager to get us home." When Iris trailed her fingernails over a ticklish spot, Elgin stiffened ever so slightly and loosened his tie. "I'm really in a devilish fix," he said in a slightly strained voice. "I must get on with telling your family what's become of you. But before they learn that you're married to me, not dancing around a campfire with some gypsies, I have to be certain that they won't do anything to upset you." What he really meant was that he didn't want them to do anything to hurt her.

Iris gave a sort of ho-hum sigh and splayed her hand against his skin, the very tip of her little finger sliding beneath Elgin's belt. He caught his breath. She said, "You needn't tell them for another week or two."

"Wait that long?" Then he shrugged and said, "I suppose you must have a superior understanding of what your family might do if I let the cat out of the bag too soon. If you think it would be safer to wait a bit longer, we'll wait, but not two weeks and not here with Mims." As Iris suggested nothing, Elgin said, "We could go to Bath. Delightful place and it's not far away. Our set hardly goes there these days, you know. The place is awash with merchants taking the waters, so the likelihood of seeing a familiar face is miniscule." After a pause he added, "If you'd rather, we could simply go home to Kent, but then the tabby really would be out and about, and everyone would know where you are. Still, it's time to do something other than roost here like fat pigeons."

Iris shifted her head to a more comfortable place against Elgin's shoulder and murmured, "You're right, of course. I shall think about it directly."

"Hmm. Yes. Good."

Elgin found it amazing that Iris had become so cooperative. So docile. So willing to do as he suggested. He concluded that she had domesticated rather nicely. Who would have believed it? He found it immensely comforting to think that life with this female would be peaceful from now on. They would lead a blissfully uneventful existence in the country.

There would be no more confrontations on city streets with foul-mouthed lorry drivers who mistreated their horses. He'd been rather frightened for her when he arrived upon the scene and found that Iris had nearly run the villainous fellow through with her furled parasol. Yet he had to admit that the horse was better off for the intervention. He supposed the beast was still eating its head off with the others of its species in his own stables. It had been a bloody nuisance to transport the decrepit animal to Kent for rest and recuperation, but Iris was much relieved when he agreed to do it. Elgin rubbed his cheek against her hair and smiled, thinking that it was rather endearing the way she cared for helpless, dumb animals. Iris, sweet Iris.

On the other hand there was that incident with the dead cat. The one she had kept in her pocket. He was pleased that she hadn't displayed any further inclinations to carry such things about, relieved that it wasn't a habit, though he did wonder what had become of the poor thing. Then he wondered how long one could leave one's cloak hanging about before one noticed that there was some unfinished business in the pocket. How terribly inconvenient it would be to inspect Iris's pockets every time they left home. But that sort of thing was surely behind them now.

Yes, Elgin could see that life would be serene, with an adoring amenable wife. All he had to do was puzzle out the best way to tell her family that she was now Mrs. Elgin Farley. For the moment, however, he was content with a sleepy afternoon, cuddled up with her in a tree house.

Iris jiggled him. "Why are you smiling like that?"

"Hmm? Oh," he mumbled through a yawn. "I was just thinking that it's been gloriously peaceful and quiet."

There it was again, she thought. Peaceful and quiet. After shifting around with little success at getting as comfortable as she had been, Iris noticed that the branches overhead had become as restless as she was, and said, "The wind is coming up. I do believe it's going to rain."

He gave her a squeeze and said, "Hmm."

"If we don't go now, we'll get wet."

"Might not."

"The cushions will get wet."

"In that case I suppose we'd best pack up, but not quite yet." Elgin's sleepy smile became wickedly seductive. When he rolled over, it was Iris who caught her breath.

She had changed into dry clothes, but her hair was still damp when she stepped into the kitchen to see Mrs. Hill. The woman looked up from the meat-tenderizing mallet she held in her hand and gave Iris a cheery "Good afternoon, dear. Would you care for tea?"

"No, thank you," replied Iris, distracted by the sound of Elgin coming down the hall stairs. There was no carpet to cushion his clattering descent. He was whistling. She concluded that he had rather enjoyed playing lady's maid, helping to drag off her cumbersome wet clothes, then eventually hooking her into more manageable dry ones. Iris looked up when Elgin reached the kitchen door. He looked in and smiled. She blushed. He glanced back toward the stairway to their bedchamber before continuing on his way. The back door squeaked open and banged shut, the whistling faded away through the rain in the direction of Mims's garden.

Iris paid an inordinate amount of attention to the adjustment of a chair at the table before she sat in it. Folding her hands just so, she cleared her throat, hoped her face wasn't still red, and watched Mrs. Hill sort through a collection of kitchen tools.

"Potato masher," announced the good woman, holding the item like a scepter. It was an egg-sized, egg-shaped piece of wood run through from end to end with a thick wire. The egg sat in the middle like a bead, with the ends of the wire bent around one side of it and twisted together into a handle.

Iris might have asked how such a strange-looking instrument could mash anything if her thoughts weren't scattered in so many other directions. One of those directions was the kitchen itself. Until now she hadn't considered the possibility of missing a kitchen. Such places simply hadn't been a part of her day-to-day life. Yet she had become acutely aware of this kitchen. She had come to know the difference between the sound of a new straw broom or an old one sweeping the brick floor, and to recognize the change in pitch, the hollow sound when a certain part of the hearth was swept. She had become used to the smell of something in the oven—

today it was roasting mutton. Yesterday it was pie. Iris laid her palm on the tabletop were she had rolled out a pie crust. For the first attempt she hadn't sprinkled enough flour on the table before putting the dough down and the roller to the dough. Everything got stuck together. She had used the butter paddle to scrape up the glutinous mess. Now the place felt clean and smooth.

Against the far wall of this particular white-washed kitchen stood a large, solidly constructed cupboard that Iris had come to admire. She supposed that some appreciation of the rather plain piece had come about because of the green color, for it was almost the same shade as the caterpillar of the Wall butterfly after its first molt. On the open cupboard shelves were dishes, jugs, and crocks that never saw the dining room. Many of the pieces were chipped, marks that she now looked upon as proofs of valued service rather than flaws. Beside an ironstone platter stood a jar of wooden spoons that had been used and washed so many times that they had acquired a soft nap. Mrs. Hill had explained that repeated soakings and scrubbings had worn the pulp from the grain of the wood and left them a wee bit furry.

Below the open shelves were cupboard doors. Behind the doors were stored larger pieces of crockery. And a copper jam kettle. Wooden bowls. The butter paddle. A sieve. A larger sieve. One mechanical apple peeler in a box with one mechanical cherry pitter. The meat grinder had a box to itself. And Iris knew that at the very bottom of the cupboard, way in the back corner right side, behind the sugar cutter, was a mouse hole. She'd seen it when she was looking for the butter paddle to get the pie dough off the table.

There were no gilt-framed mirrors here, only a modest looking-glass located near the door. The silvering was peeling off the back in one corner. Everyone and everything reflected there took on a faint blue tinge from the color of the glass. Next to the cupboard hung the picture of a child with a Saint Bernard dog. It had been taken from a magazine and put into a frame that was too big for it, very likely the only frame available.

Over the back door was an embroidered sampler that read *Gone But Not Forgotten*. The verse was surrounded by forget-me-nots and blue ribbons held aloft by hovering cherubim. Iris had seen the sampler many times, but this was the first time she noticed that the cherubim had wings too small to allow them to fly, let alone keep them up there, even without the added weight of the flowers and ribbons with which they had to contend. She concluded that the problem was either poorly designed wings or an insufficient amount of white floss with which to stitch more feathers.

"The handle on this wants mending," said Mrs. Hill. Jarred from her revelry, Iris said something about handles in general and picked up the wire egg whisk Mrs. Hill had just put aside. The wooden handle had split. The next tool had a long metal handle attached to the center of a metal disk with holes in it. Iris thought it looked altogether too much like a medieval instrument of discomfort. "Spinach presser," explained Mrs.

Hill. Iris nodded in recognition of this information and resolved to think more compassionately toward spinach.

Iris said, "My husband and I will be leaving soon." She flattened a few crumbs on the table with the rolling pin. The crumbs were from the toast Mrs. Hill gave her with tea. "The day after tomorrow, I should think."

"Sycamore." The housekeeper offered informatively. She was pointing at the rolling pin. "Sycamore wood doesn't leave a taste or color of its own on the food. I'll be sorry to see you go, dear, though you must be eager to get settled in your own home."

"Yes" was all Iris cared to say. She didn't explain that she and Elgin would be going on to Bath, not his place in Kent. The fewer people who knew of her exact whereabouts the better. "We would be leaving tomorrow, but there's the cow-heated vinery that my husband would like to see finished. He said he might like to have such a place if it looks productive."

Mrs. Hill began the return of the utensils to the basket from which she had taken them, except for the egg whisk with the split handle. Iris put in a single-bladed vegetable chopper and then a double-bladed one. There was a wooden chocolate blender with a long handle that one spun between the palms of one's hands. Two tin graters and a plunger lemon squeezer. A cucumber slicer.

While putting the basket away, the older woman said, "Have you learned flower arranging? Good heavens, of course you must have. All young ladies learn such things. Would you mind doing the arrangement for the dinner table? The Reverend does enjoy seeing his flowers displayed at their best, and I think you must be ever so much better at it than I am. You will? Lovely. I believe you'll find snapdragons and baby's breath and whatever else standing in a pail of water in the stillroom."

The next day Elgin went with Mims to the vinery, and Iris returned to the kitchen. One might suppose that she was soaking up as much of the place as she could. A decidedly odd inclination for someone who had been carefully molded for life as a lady of grace and leisure. Her education had prepared her to converse with the most knowledgeable on the fine points of art and music. Iris had been taught to pour tea from a silver pot into unstained cups for the elite to stir with monogrammed spoons and sip through cultured lips.

In spite of it all Iris now sat in a common dress and a plain apron before an ordinary cup of ordinary tea. There was a half-eaten biscuit on the edge of the chipped saucer. With her elbows on the common maple worktable she was intently watching a common cook, not a chef, cracking eggs for a cake. Iris studied everything in Mrs. Hill's kitchen in much the same way that she studied her grandfather's ancient treasures.

It was Iris who said, "I've heard that an Egyptian shepherd can cook an egg without a fire. When he finds a duck egg in a nest he puts it into his sling and spins it around until the friction of the air heats and cooks the egg."

"I cannot credit that," replied Mrs. Hill. "It sounds like the kind of nonsense tourists love to tell when they get back home. If it would be possible to cook an egg by spinning it, then the grooms at Fairhaven—I used to work at a great house called Fairhaven, perhaps you know of it, it's near Manchester, a lovely place with several picturesque water lily ponds. As I was saying, if such spinning could cook an egg, then the grooms at Fairhaven would have cooked the head of the smallest stable boy the way they used to spin him around by his feet."

"What sort of sling do you think the shepherds might have used if they did it?" asked Iris.

"I suppose it must be the same kind David used to fling the stone that killed Goliath. However, if you should decide to attempt such an experiment, I do hope you'll try it outside, away from any windows or clean laundry." When the cake went into the oven, Iris went for a walk.

That night Iris told Elgin about her progress as a country housewife, and Elgin told Iris how vines grow up posts and across rafters, and they teased about sleepy afternoons in a tree house until there was a whimper of pleasure, a groan of satisfaction, and mingled sighs of contentment.

On the chosen day Mims brought the wagonette around. After the few pieces of luggage were loaded, Elgin gave Iris a hand up from the mounting block in front of the house. Mrs. Hill and the hired girl provided a teary sentimental farewell.

They had hardly gone any distance down the road when Mims said, "Good God! Do you hear honking? Honking and puffing? Yes, definitely honking and puffing! Farley, we'll have to hold the horse. Mrs. Farley, do get down in case the horse bolts anyway." While Mims was telling Iris to move, he was boldly talking hold and swinging her to the ground. Pointing to a place well off the road, he said, "Just stand there." After a minute or two of statuesque boredom Iris discovered the reason for the noise and horse-holding. Up over the hill came a slow-moving, huffing-puffing, steam-powered carriage. Ahead of it was a man on foot, waving a red flag. A second man honked a brass horn, just like the one mounted on the side of the carriage. The horse shifted fearfully, sidestepping, eyes rolling, trying to rear. Mims held the bridle more tightly and talked softly to the creature. It caused Iris to wonder what a horse might like to hear at a time like this.

When the parade drew closer, the finely dressed gentleman operating the machine nodded ever so politely and waved stiffly, the way the royal family waves when on exhibit. Mims and Elgin responded with as much civility as they could for as busy as they were with the horse. The men with the flag and the horn carried on with tremendous dignity, seemingly oblivious to the commotion their passing incited.

When they were back in the wagonette with the horse moving along at a nervous trot, Mims said, "The infernal display you have just witnessed has been disturbing us all this past year. Whoever conceived the law that made it necessary for a flagman to precede a machine like that through town and village should be flogged. Even at a reduced speed the noisy thing still upsets the citizenry and livestock, the flag waving makes it worse, and the addition of the honking attendant makes it worse than ever!" He looked at the clouds rolling in from the west, decided it was going to rain before the afternoon was out, and gave the reins a quickening snap.

Halfway to the train station in Hungerford the conversation was still dominated by the infamous machine. It would seem that the gentleman who owned it had made excursions across hill and dale, pasture and stream. "In one of his own pastures was a bull that took exception to the invasion," said Mims. "The bull didn't exactly attack, at least not until it got honked at. Then it gored the monster rather badly before the gamekeeper responded to the frantic honking and shot the animal. Should have shot the blasted fool with the horn!"

"How terribly unfair," said Iris.

Mims agreed that it was unfair, then apologized for his bad language, and Iris told him that she quite understood, given the circumstances, and then said that she thought it was rather stupid to shoot an animal that was brave enough to defend its own pasture.

"The machine had to be pulled out by plow horses," said Mims. "Don't know how they moved the bull." After a derisive snort he said, "Steam-driven carriages are undoubtedly interesting as curiosities go, but they aren't particularly dependable or even safe. Steam boilers have exploded and burned people. Horses never explode. I sincerely doubt that horseless carriages will ever catch on. If there was any likelihood of that happening, more would have been done about them since 800 B.C. I think it was 800 B.C. when the Chinese made a steam-powered cart. Have no idea what it looked like, but I'll bet it didn't have flag wavers and horn honkers. This horseless-carriage business will fade like the sailing ship."

Elgin decided that this wasn't the time to say that he'd been considering a steam-powered carriage of his own.

Bath: the gem of Somersetshire. Healing waters and elegant assembly rooms. Cobbled streets, beautiful shops, flowers everywhere. Chaucer country. Walpole had said that people arrived well and left cured. Bath, with its Bath chairs, Bath stone, Bath buns, and Bath baths.

The curative properties of the place had been sought after since the ancient Romans settled in, called the place Aquæ Sulis, and built a spa with lots of stone columns. They built a lot of things all over the place, actually, before they were called back home. Hundreds of years later, in 863, Prince Bladud and his herd of swine came down from the hills and found relief for their skin afflictions in the warm, mineral-laden mud. Then it was called Bath. That was long before Beau Nash established himself there as the authority on fashion and decorum to the privileged class. Geologists called it hard Jurassic limestone at the southern end of the great western oolitic range. Iris called it heaven.

This time it was Mr. and Mrs. John Smith— husband and wife, not sister and brother—who were having a gay time of it. And they were having a good time despite the fact that they weren't frequenting the Pump Room or staying at one of

the finer hotels now patronized by wealthy merchants instead of the ton. It was a more modest
establishment that they had chosen. The sort of
place where anyone they might possibly know
wouldn't expect to find them. The truth was that
Iris and Elgin were sharing the air with *trades-
men*. On their first day in Bath they spent delightful hours strolling along cobbled streets
decked with flowers. They looked in the windows
of fashionable shops and stopped for tea. After
tea they stepped into a jeweler's and stepped out
with a proper gold band that fit Iris's third finger, left hand.

It was also on that first day in Bath that Iris
noticed a particularly fine hat in the window of
a shop on Milsom Street. The sign across the
front read MADAME LA RUE. Elgin thought the
place sounded like a bordello, but he didn't say
so, exercising great wisdom. Iris moved from one
side of the window to the other to better view the
work of art displayed on an ornate brass stand.
The blown-glass windowpanes gave a wavy impression of the goods inside. The hat that caught
Iris's attention was of a style called the *wide
awake*. It was of a delicate straw, with lace and
ribbons and two grand plumes, the whole of it
being done in shades of pale blue and violet,
with a stuffed bird clinging to the hat band. The
bird was dyed a darker blue. A violet ribbon tied
in a great bow hung down the back of the hat.
Iris didn't much care for the bird, but found the
rest of the hat especially fine.

"As you like the hat, you shall have it," said
Elgin.

"I don't think so," sighed Iris. "I dare not wear

it. With my clothes it would surely attract more attention than I care to have." Smoothing her gloved hand over the second best of her plain brown dresses, she pulled at Elgin's arm, leading him away.

They gave coins to the hurdy-gurdy man's monkey and stopped to watch a Punch-and-Judy show—the same Punch after whom *Punch* magazine had been named. On another afternoon they rented a horse and carriage and drove out of town, into the hills. There they spread a blanket on a grassy place overlooking the town, read Tennyson, and lunched on buns and cheese and grapes. The bottle of wine had been tipped over in the grass during a moment of distraction, which annoyed some ants that had been caught in the flood. The next day they went rowing on the River Avon—not to be confused with the Avon Canal. Elgin wondered if he'd ever again be able to lift his aching arms to feed himself. After that a walk along the towpath of the barge canal proved far less hazardous, as long as they took care where they stepped.

When Iris said, "I've been told that we can walk from one end of town to the other in twenty minutes," they tried it, of course. It took them twenty-six minutes. That was due to the reappearance of the hurdy-gurdy man and his monkey. Iris would stop to watch the smaller of the two remove his hat for the coins he received.

They spent surprisingly little time in the shops on Pulteny Bridge, their only purchases being handkerchiefs for Iris and a book Elgin found on relics of the ancient world, with endpapers showing a view of Rome. When they left there, Iris's steps leaned ever so gently in the direction of Milsom Street and Madame La Rue's. The hat was still in the window, and she was satisfied with looking at it.

The next day it rained, so they stayed inside reading more poetry and eventually becoming otherwise occupied. It was no surprise that the next morning they got a very late start. The clock struck eleven before they had breakfast and thought about seeing the Abbey Church, with its climbing angles and old tombstones, but they gave it up. They did, however, rouse themselves to go to the theater that evening. Elgin especially wanted to see what the interior of the new place looked like, the old one having burned down some four years before in '62.

The next morning Elgin felt inclined to linger over his new book. Iris felt restless. It was agreed that he would read and she would take one of the hotel maids out and about with her. Elgin had insisted on the attendance of the maid. Once among the other visitors on the streets of Bath, Iris found that the performing monkey was still in good form and the Bath buns as delicious as ever. And she went down Milsom Street, past the hat shop. This time, however, the hat wasn't there. Disappointed, she turned away from the elegant little establishment, then stopped and went back.

"Yes?" The young woman turned around when the bell over the door jingled, looked at Iris, and went back to dusting shelves.

Iris thought the girl was someplace between rude and rather silly. In her more fashionable days she would have had clerks falling all over themselves to be of assistance to her. Now, dressed like someone's lady's maid, she was of no particular interest.

"What do you want?" the clerk said. No attempt had been made to exert herself for the sake of good manners.

"There was a hat in the window. It had blue—"

"It's over there"—she nodded—"on the round table."

Iris thanked her and went to that table.

"Don't touch it!" warned the clerk.

Iris gave her a wooden smile and picked up the hat, then sat down on a brocade upholstered bench in front of a mirror. The hotel maid looked uncomfortably from the woman whose interests she was supposed to guard to the clerk who terrified her. As though the clerk didn't exist, Iris had removed her own hat and set the new one on her head.

"I hope you don't have lice," snapped the clerk.

Iris put the hat on the table and said, "I would like you to remove the bird." When Iris saw the wistful look the maid gave the blue pigeon, she added, "Please wrap it separately."

The clerk looked happy enough when Iris paid with a large bank note, then began to fuss and fawn and speak with a French accent. When Iris and the maid left the shop, there was a young man following them with the hatbox. The clerk had called him André. André wore a black beret that matched his black mustache and possessed the dignity that the clerk had lacked.

It was just after Iris left the hat shop that Billy Shepherd saw her, and surprised he was, though there was a moment of confusion. That was because the clothes were all wrong for a lady like Miss Huntington. Making a quick recovery, he turned his attention to the shop windows, then crossed the street and trailed along as though other window displays now claimed his attention. Ignoring a shopkeeper who threatened his shabby person with a broom, Billy hung back to let some people get between himself and his quarry, but not so many people that he didn't know exactly where she was. Not even cabs and carriages got in the way for long. Because the lady he followed was so small, there were times when all Billy could see was the man who looked like a gypsy that carried her package.

The only reason Billy had been in the way of seeing Iris at all was because he'd spent the night in the hills and had come down through town on his way to the docks. He hoped to be taken up on one of the barges and work his way to someplace he'd never been before.

Patting his dirty coat, he was comforted by the lump of bills in his inside pocket. When he'd heard talk that the squire was looking for the gypsies that had camped near the manor, Billy told him that he had lived with some of those wandering folk when he was a boy. He assured the squire that he knew their ways. So the old man had hired him to find his granddaughter, who, he said, had really gone to Wales with the gypsies, not back to her parents. Billy was sworn to secrecy.

What the squire didn't know was that Billy had never lived with any gypsies, or even known any gypsies. Neither did he intend to go to Wales

to look for gypsies. He had a mind to see a bit of
the country on the horse the squire had loaned
him. After leaving Huntington Manor, he got all
the way to Tewkesbury before he decided that
he'd far rather ride on a train out of the rain. He
could get on and off whenever the fancy took
him, and when it got too cold to enjoy life on the
road, Billy planned to return to Huntington
Manor and tell the squire that the gypsies had
left the country, and there would be the end of it.
So he left the horse at a stable in Tewkesbury,
telling them that Squire Huntington of Huntington Manor, Little Woolton, would make good the
bill as soon as they delivered the animal.

Everything changed when he saw Iris. Grasp-
ing his worn lapels, Billy sort of puffed up. He
saw himself in the way of a small fortune. All he
had to do was let Miss Huntington know that
she'd been found out. Then he'd tell her that he'd
be happy to forget he ever saw her for a price. A
generous price. He had no doubt that he'd collect, as long as he didn't lose sight of her. In-
creasing his pace through the strolling shoppers,
Billy turned the corner and found Iris again. He
began to think about what he'd do with the
money he would get. There would surely be
enough to impress the pretty ladies at the Pig
and Puddle. He might even get a checkered suit
and spats. A new bowler hat. It was going to cost
plenty.

That's when Billy decided that the information
he had would be worth plenty more to the
squire.

Giving the brim of his hat a smart tug to keep
it tight on his head, Billy went about the selec-

tion of a choice cigar butt from the gutter. With such an occupation no one would suspect that he was watching Miss Huntington and her gypsy enter the hotel. A newly painted sign gave the name of the place. When the door closed behind Iris and her gypsy and some girl who was hanging about, Billy tossed aside the chewed cigar and wiped his hand on his coat. Sauntering off toward the train station, he thought about the ladies he would have to disappoint at the Pig and Puddle tonight.

"Be patient," he said to himself. "Be patient."

· Thirteen ·

Billy Shepherd looked around nervously,
clutching his hat, rubbing the brim between his
dirty fingers. Now and then he looked at the
mummy on the far side of the room. Not a stare,
merely a glance. Only the dried head and one
shriveled arm had been unrolled. He had traveled around the country since he was a boy but
had never seen anything like it.

"I assume you have news of my granddaughter," said the squire, impatient for the man to
get on with what he had come to say.

"That I do," Billy assured him, looking at the
squire, then at the morbid sight on the table.
"She's in Bath."

"How can that be? I've been assured that the
entire gypsy band has gone to Wales."

"It were her, I tell ya, in Bath, with a gypsy. I
saw 'em with these own eyes!" Billy pointed a
dirty finger at his right eye so the squire would
better understand the means he had used to de-
tect the elusive Miss Huntington. "It were day-
time, so I looked at her good. Then real careful I
followed the pair of 'em all around town, back

an' forth, inside an' out again, ta this partic'lar hotel."

"Gypsies in a hotel?"

"Not all of 'em. Just one. A bloke as looks some like yerself, but younger, with dark hair an' a great mustache." Billy smoothed his hand both ways over his own whisker-studded upper lip to show the extent of the other man's luxurious growth. "One gypsy. An' yer granddaughter, a course."

"What is the name of this hotel?"

"That I can't say, bein' as I can't read."

"Then what good is this story you're telling me?"

"Bless my soul, I can show ya the very place!" Billy assured him, taking a foul handkerchief from his pocket to blow his nose. "I can find ya the buildin' sure as I know my own mother. Didn't I set off ta Wales like ya said, only ta find the two of 'em gone otherwise? Didn't I track 'em down in a different part of the country? Didn't I go without victuals an' sleep, no matter how much suffering it caused me? It were a masterful job of findin', if I do say so myself, an' I do, an' I know how important an' valuable this information is, an' how glad ya are ta have it from a loyal an' trusted servant such as myself, knowin' that ya can be generous in showin' yer gratitude . . . if ya take my meanin'."

The squire got the meaning very clearly. He was about to get his pocket picked by this loyal and trusted servant that had already been paid to do the job, though he did get his horse back after paying a stiff boarding and delivery fee. Feeling trapped, the squire said, "I have a great deal to consider before I decide what I'm going to do. I'll tell you when I need you." Billy bowed out in the grandiose manner in which he supposed a loyal and trusted servant would perform such an act.

When his informant had gone, the squire slumped into a chair and wondered if he was truly any closer to getting Iris back. Propping up the weary foot with the nagging toe, he began to sort out pieces of the puzzle.

He had already decided that the proposed surgery for Iris had been a dreadful idea, for it would only draw attention to her rebellious disposition. Besides, he had discovered the real reason for her behavior, and it wasn't her mutinous female organs.

The true cause of Iris's turn of mind had come to light after the squire had her bedchamber turned out, looking for clues regarding her disappearance. During the process a book was discovered under her mattress. It wasn't a proper book with morals for young ladies, but a work of *fiction*. Fiction, the most deadly reading. A dangerous piece of work by Bulwer-Lytton.

Furthermore, the squire strongly suspected that this wasn't the first book of its kind that Iris had read. He was filled with dread when he realized that the practice must have been going on for years. No wonder she was so seriously affected. God only knew how many books of fiction had been consumed in that length of time. He only wondered where she got them. The book under her mattress appeared to be well read. But new or old, it was still fiction, the kind of thing that caused the reader to lose all sense of truth and reality. It destroyed manners, morals, and religion. It was known that lunatic asylums were filled with people—especially women—who had read works of fiction. After that they lost their hold on sanity. Went hopelessly out of their minds.

The squire had also read the work by an expert who had proof that fiction reading led to suicide. The indisputable example was that of a young lady who had drowned herself after leaving a note behind. In it she described the feelings of hopelessness that overwhelmed her. When her lifeless body was lifted from the water there was clutched in her cold hand a dreaded book of fiction!

When the squire first read the accounts of the tragedies that impure reading had caused, he didn't actually believe any of it. But now, after what Iris had done, he could no longer doubt it. Iris had been led to the brink of doom by innocent-looking books.

So poor Iris must be dealt with as she was, which was undoubtedly a bit daft. Yet if they still hoped to get her respectably married to the Marquis of Bumpsted, she would have to have at least the appearance of being intact, both physically and mentally. But to get Iris married they had to get hold of her. According to what Billy the shepherd said, they could get hold of her in Bath. But the squire had no assurance that Billy had identified the correct woman as Iris.

"Here you are, Obediah," trilled Prudence as she entered the Egyptian Room with a dainty china demitasse cup centered on a dainty lace doily on a small silver tray. With the cup was a dainty silver spoon with an ornate *H* on the handle. Prudence didn't take any notice of the mummy, having seen it so many times before.

The squire looked; the cup was half full. He sniffed at the contents. "It smells like oil."

"You do have a finely tuned nose, for it is oil. Seep oil from Persia. There are places where it comes right up out of the ground so pure that it is bottled for medicine. It's said to be very good for rheumatism, gout, and distempers that cause painful joints and bones. Do drink it while it's warm." Leaving the tray within her brother's reach, Prudence left the room.

The squire sniffed the stuff again and pushed the cup aside. He was trying to get his thoughts back to the situation revolving—spinning, actually—around Iris. The smell of hot petroleum didn't help him think more clearly. He changed chairs, finding it easier to move himself away than move the tippy cup on the slippery tray. When he started thinking again, he thought to send someone else to Bath to find out if it actually was Iris there with the gypsy. Unfortunately, another search would take more time. Iris might move on while all the detective work was being redone by someone else. Rapping his bony knuckles on the arm of his chair, the squire decided that he would simply have to get a look at the woman in Bath to be certain it was Iris.

The smell of oil had worked its way around the room until it caught up with him. He swore and limped over to collect his cane from where he'd left it leaning against the table supporting the mummy. Slamming the door against the assaulting fumes, he made his way down the hall to the Roman Room. To his great surprise he found the door ajar. He was sure that he'd left it locked. Patting his pocket, he felt the key. Pushing the door open, the squire discovered Chumbly bending over the latest delivery, the crate of things from ancient Crete. Chumbly, however, was too far gone from drink to notice that his brother-in-law was standing there watching him.

In no mood to be taken advantage of again, the squire said, "Are you looking for anything in particular? Perhaps something nice in ancient glass? An old bottle for a profitable transaction?"

Chumbly stopped rooting through the box and slowly turned around. Even more slowly he squinted to focus on the squire. His speech was slurred when he said, "Damn cheeky sneakin' up on a man tha' way! Could gimme a heart attack!"

"You'll never have a heart attack, you old sot. You'll drink yourself to death! Or you might die of a broken pate if you don't keep your hands off my things!"

"You wouldn't dare!" cried Chumbly, waving a statue.

"Ha!" cried the squire, brandishing his cane.

Chumbly dropped the statue back into the crate, sent a rude two-fingered gesture in Huntington's direction, and wove a path to the cabinet where the liquor was kept. Grabbing hold of a bottle, he said, "You can't touch me! Nobody can touch me or I'll take Prudence away!"

"You miserable toad, take the bottle with my blessings! Take another!" To demonstrate how little he cared about what Chumbly was doing, the squire turned his back on him to find another chair and another place to rest his throbbing foot. Another place to rest his mind so he could figure out what he was going to do about Iris and her gypsy. So far all he knew was that he had to get her back, though he couldn't very well creep up and drop a sack over her head and carry her away. Or could he? Or could someone else do it? This time he would provide the man with a photograph of Iris. That way there would be no room for mistakes. He didn't want strange young women stuffed into sacks and dropped off at Huntington Manor because they resembled Iris. Besides being inconvenient, it was probably against the law, and someone might object.

While wondering who he might find to drop the sack over Iris, the squire remembered seeing advertisements by men who offered confidential detection services. Following wayward wives, tracking missing husbands, and all that. Some had addresses on Fleet Street, London. The squire thought he might send a telegraph wire to one of those fellows and have him come to Huntington Manor to learn the particulars. Then he'd send him to Bath to save Iris from a life of corruption and dissipation by returning her to the bosom of her loving family. Then they'd marry her off to the Marquis of Bumpsted as quickly as possible. As long as Iris ended up married to a title, the squire was certain her parents wouldn't care how he brought the event about. All through the day and into the night the squire devised one plan of abduction after another.

By the next morning he congratulated himself

for having everything worked out, at least in his head. He had decided that the detective he would hire could best decide how to deal with Iris when he found her, as long as he wasn't rough or ungentlemanlike. When Iris was safely installed at Huntington Manor, the squire would then invite Bumpsted to return to see the rest of the mummy unrolled. The invitation would hint at the viewing of treasures from Crete as well. What man of culture and breeding could possibly resist all that?

In the morning the squire found breakfast a joy and told Prudence so. The cold potted meat and broiled mackerel had never tasted better. The broiled sheep's kidneys were perfectly done. Never had he praised an omelet so highly. Quite ordinary marmalade and muffins were gifts from the gods. The tea was better and the milk in it sweeter than ever before. In fact Huntington was still sitting at the table long after it was cleared, gazing at the decorative tiles on the fireplace, contemplating the return of Iris and her marriage to Bumpsted. The only thing that tainted his sense of triumph were the bruises he'd seen on Prudence's neck. Her shawl had slipped while she forked up her eggs. Before she pulled it back, he'd seen the finger marks that had begun to turn an ugly greenish purple, and muttered, "Damn Chumbly to hell!"

Into these distressing thoughts stepped a footman, who said, "Mr. Farley is here to see you, sir. I've put him in the library."

"Farley, you say?"

"Yes, sir. Mr. Elgin Farley."

"Haven't I got enough trouble without a spy?"

"Sir?"

"Nothing, nothing at all."

Hobbling out of the oak-beamed breakfast room and down the paneled hall, the squire didn't even look at the grease stains on the oriental carpets. Or at the new dents in an old suit of armor. Or the scuff marks on the newel post and banisters. Pausing outside the library door, he wondered again how Farley had managed to find out about the newest shipment of antiquities. The stuff hadn't been in his possession for three full days, and Farley was back here already to spy it out. No matter, the crate from Crete was once again safe behind a locked door. Of course, the squire knew that it would be simple enough to have Farley thrown out of the house, but then he'd never find out how the man was coming by the information about his shipments of antiquities. For this reason and this reason alone he decided that he would talk to this spy.

Elgin stood when the squire entered the library. The older man motioned the younger one back into his chair and said, "Can I get you anything?" Elgin declined. The squire used his cane to hook a footstool closer to the chair in which he wished to sit. After an exchange of platitudes about the weather and the crops, he said, "I won't ask why you're here, because I know."

Elgin shifted uncomfortably and said, "I'm amazed." He truly was. He didn't know how the squire could know about himself and Iris.

"Well, now," said the squire to the would-be spy. "You had better understand from the beginning that you won't be getting into my collection rooms!"

Startled, Elgin said, "It isn't a liberty I thought to take."

"You hoped to get me to show you the treasures, is that it?"

Elgin could plainly see that the things his host spoke of were of great importance to him. To say that he had little interest in them might well offend the man. It was also clear that it wouldn't be wise to show too much interest in them, either, so he said, "I've heard that your collections are nothing less than remarkable."

"Oh? Which collections?"

"Ahh, the Roman glass, I should think."

The squire studied Elgin suspiciously, then said, "I have everything numbered and cataloged, you know. My granddaughter has made clear illustrations of everything in my collections. Except for the most recent arrivals, of course. She hasn't been here to record the things from Crete. She's with her family in London."

Elgin choked up. The squire was certain that it had something to do with the mention of treasures from Crete. The part where he'd said that no drawings had yet been made of those things. No physical descriptions of what he owned. No proofs of identification. In addition to that there was something else he found suspicious.

Nailing Elgin with an evil eye, the old man said, "You seem to be very well informed about my Roman glass. I hadn't thought such information was common knowledge."

Elgin was on very thin ice, and he knew it. It was obvious that the squire didn't know very much about what had become of Iris. Besides that, Elgin had no idea that the Roman glass of which Iris had spoken so descriptively was kept in such secrecy. That being the case, he couldn't very well say that Iris had told him about it. Questions would be asked about when she'd told him. So he wouldn't say anything about how he knew about the glass. Not yet. Not until he knew to what dangers Iris might be subjected because of what he said.

Trying to look thoughtful, Elgin said, "Word of your expertise as a collector has obviously gone beyond the walls of Huntington Manor. Well beyond the Cotswolds. I can't really say who it was that praised your remarkable collection."

"Humbug! You've been getting your information from someone, and I want to know who!" The squire poked Elgin's foot with his cane. "Tell me about the other spies, and I'll make it worth your while."

Elgin moved his foot. "There aren't any spies."

"Yet you know about my Roman glass! I have a proposition for you. It's one by which we both can profit."

Elgin tried to get up, saying, "For crissakes, there are no spies!"

The squire pointed his cane at him and said, "Be quiet and listen! If you'll do a bit of business for me, I'll reward you with a piece of that Roman glass."

"Sir," said Elgin quietly, "I swear that I have no spies for friends. At least, I don't think so. Neither do I covet your Roman glass."

"Look here. If you'll find someone for me and

keep your mouth shut about it, you'll get the glass."

"Find someone you've lost recently?"

"Ah-ha! I knew the promise of that old glass would change your mind. I want you to find my granddaughter. She's not actually in London with her family. I thought she'd run off to Wales with a band of gypsies. Since then I've been told that she's in Bath with only one of them. A handsome devil, or so I've been told."

"I see" was all Elgin said and prudently so.

"Unfortunately, I don't know the name of the hotel, but I have the feeling you'll find it easy enough, given the way you've managed to find out about my shipments of antiquities. No, don't bother to deny it. Just find my granddaughter."

Elgin cleared his throat and said, "I think I might be able to bring that about, though I need to know what you plan to do with her once you get her back."

"What I do with her is none of your business!"

"It is if you want her to return peacefully. It seems she has a way of slipping off if she's unhappy about something."

"How would you know?"

"She's gone, isn't she? Happy young ladies don't run off, do they? If she thinks she's still going to be unhappy when I bring her back, she might give me the slip."

"Well, then, as you insist upon knowing, she's going to be married. The man is quite respectable. If you don't like the terms, I'll hire one of those fellows from London to kidnap her."

Elgin raised a restraining hand and said, "Let's not be hasty."

"Ah-ha! I didn't think you'd allow a piece of that glass to get away. When can you leave for Bath?"

"When? Now, I suppose."

"Shall I get you a photograph of my granddaughter?"

"No, that won't be necessary. I know what she looks like."

"So you do. Will you need anything for expenses?"

"That won't be necessary, either."

"I'll have a carriage take you to the station. If the connections work out, you could be in Bath sometime tonight, though there is one other thing."

"And that is?"

"Billy. He's a shepherd employed here. He said he knew the ways of the gypsies, so I paid him to find Iris. He said he's seen her in Bath but wants more money before he tells me exactly where. I told him that I had a lot to think about before I decide anything."

"Has he threatened you if you won't pay more?"

"Not yet, though I can't say what he might do with such information. The need for secrecy concerning Iris is vital."

Elgin puckered in thought, then said, "Might I make an effort to resolve the problem with this Billy person?"

"If you like. I'll have him sent 'round, though I suggest you talk to him outside in a good breeze."

When Elgin went down to the stable yard to wait for Billy, he was racking his brain for what to say that would keep him from broadcasting anything about Iris. Not knowing the man, Elgin couldn't say if he might be more persuaded by a blessing from the Almighty or a curse from the devil. He probably wouldn't be the least bit affected by the possibility of losing his position as a watcher of sheep. Britain had a great many sheep that needed watching.

Neither did he suppose that the threat of a beating would do much to bring him around, for he seemed to be of a rough nature that wouldn't be much affected by such a thing. What else was there? Certainly not threatening him with the law, for then the reason for the threat would surely come out. That would never do. Elgin supposed he might appeal to his better nature, but if the man had a better nature, he wouldn't have tried to hold up the squire for more money.

When Billy finally arrived, Elgin just hoped for the best. He introduced himself and explained that it was himself who would be going to Bath. Alone. Then asked Billy if there was anything he could tell him about finding Miss Huntington.

Billy said, "Did ya talk ta him? Ta the squire?"

"Yes, of course," said Elgin.

"Did ya talk to him in the room where he keeps the dead things?"

"Where he keeps *what*?"

"The dead people. Ya know, the ones wrapped up in bandages. Gave me the shivers."

"Oh, those," said Elgin, finally recognizing the description of a mummy. "Squire Huntington collects them." Billy's color went a bit off. With a fiendish stroke of genius, Elgin lowered his voice and said, "Did you recognize anyone?"

"There were only the one bloke partways lookin' out, an' I never saw 'im before."

Elgin said, "That's the last man who tried to cheat the squire." He tapped his head and added, "The old man is a bit strange that way. Spent a small fortune looking for the fellow who nicked him for a few pounds in a card game. After he had him hunted down, he had him stuffed."

Billy looked horrified and said, "It wasn't even a good job!"

Elgin looked at the ground and shook his head. "Poor Sam does look rather used up, so let's not talk about it. I'm getting away from what I came to ask you."

Twisting his hat, Billy said, "If it's about Miss Huntington, ya might find her at the Regent's, or the Rooster's, or some hotel with a *R*. The sign's red an' white, painted new. That's all there is ta know, an' tell the squire I said so, an' I don't need nothin' else, thank ya very much all the same. Now, if ya don't mind I think I'll go see ta the sheep. Good day ta ya, sir."

Elgin was whistling as he walked along the drive to the front of the house and carriage that was waiting to take him to Little Woolton and the train station.

The afternoon sun shown on the statue the squire had taken ever so carefully from the packing crate. It was the figure of a full-breasted woman, taller than a hand span, with great staring eyes. She was wearing a dress with short sleeves and a tight-fitting bodice. The neckline was so low that her most distinctive features were completely exposed. More properly her waistline was as tightly laced as the most fashionable woman of today, though her long flounced skirt had no hoops beneath it. On the very top of her headdress sat a small animal. Perhaps a dog or a cat—the squire couldn't tell. There was no such mistake about the snakes. The woman held one in each hand and two more of them knotted around her waist as a belt. The squire laid the figure in a padded box, the big eyes a blank stare until he covered it with a soft cloth.

Another piece of pottery, a vase, lay partly exposed in the crate. The dark metallic background was evident beneath intricate swirls of yellow and red. After a close inspection it was gently placed on the table. Next was a pot with a light background and black sea creatures painted on it. The largest of the beasts was an octopus with its tentacles wrapped around the pot. Seaweed, conch shells, and squid had been painted around the octopus. This piece went onto the table beside the other, and the squire wished Iris were with him to see them.

The straw used as packing material clung to his trousers and hung from his shirt. It collected on the floor around the table to be blown across the room until the windows were closed. When Prudence came in, the straw stuck to the hem of her dress. She said, "Obediah, have you seen the paper today? My goodness, of course you haven't, because here it is. We have news about the Marquis of Bumpsted."

"Don't say that the old boy stuck his spoon in the wall!"

"Goodness no. It would appear that the gentleman is alive and exceptionally healthy. Healthy enough to have remarried." The squire took the paper from Prudence and began to search through it. She said, "Page six. He has married a widow with twelve children and seventeen grandchildren and six great-grandchildren. My goodness. The bride is none other than the former Iphigena Holingbottom. I happen to know that she is someone the marquis knew and loved in his youth but was forbidden to marry due to her inferior station in life, though she was a beauty and somehow connected to the Taggerts of Devon. It would also—"

"Egad, it's true!" The paper was crushed in the squire's sagging arms. "They were married last week in a private ceremony at the bride's home."

"It must have been quite nice," bubbled Prudence. "The paper says that eight of her children were there, plus ten grandchildren and their husbands and wives, and four great-grandchildren. All those in addition to his own numerous progeny. How interesting to be a bride at that age, whatever it is. She wore maroon. I'm relieved that it wasn't black. So many brides wear black, you know. It is serviceable, especially for the lower orders, but black on a bride is simply too depressing if it can be helped. One doesn't usually think of brides as being anything but young ladies, and they can wear red or blue or yellow, if they can afford to be that impractical, though not everyone can. Obediah, are you feeling poorly?"

"How in the devil can we marry Iris off to a man who already has a wife?"

Prudence gave the question some thought before she said, "I don't think we should. Some people do it, though, for I've read about them, but it's quite improper, so I don't think *we* should. That is, I don't think Iris should. Do sit down and I'll have someone bring you a restorative." Collecting more straw on her skirt, Prudence went to see to her brother's refreshment. Leaving the Roman Room, she deposited straw along the passage, on the stairs, through the hall, and on some of the stained oriental carpets, and down a smaller flight of stairs into the kitchen.

The squire was left among his treasures to wonder what he was going to do with Iris when she was captured and returned to Huntington Manor. The prospective husband was no longer a prospect. If she was going to be brought back only to be locked away, the squire thought she might be better off with the gypsies.

It was a long time before the restorative arrived, then proved to be nothing more dangerous than lemonade. The excited maid who brought it in said, "Did you hear? Mr. Chumbly is in a bad way again. This time it took four footmen to fetch him home from the pub in Little Woolton and get him in bed, all thrashing about and red in the face. The last time it took only two footmen to do it. Mr. Chumbly don't care for being in there, in his bed, I mean. He says there's dragons up the chimney, but Maddy, she looked, and said there wasn't any."

"Is that all?"

"Oh, no, sir. The doctor has been sent for, and

Mr. Chumbly says there's monsters with red eyes under the bed trying to bite him, but Maddy says the monsters came out of his whiskey bottle. Mr. Chumbly has her rooting about under his bed with a broom to chase them out and—"

The squire held up a silencing hand. "I meant are there any biscuits to go with the lemonade."

"Oh, dear! I forgot. So sorry, I'll bring them straight away."

Watching the girl scurry from the room, the squire thought she must be new to the job. Her version of the news, however, was probably more inclusive than it would have been had he received it from one of the better-trained staff. To prove his theory, one of the stiff-necked footmen arrived to say:

"I regret to inform you that Mr. Chumbly has once again taken ill. He is now resting in his chamber, awaiting the arrival of the doctor. Be assured that everything is being done to see to his comfort and ease his fears. Have you any instructions in regard to the matter, sir?"

"How is my sister doing?"

"Mrs. Chumbly is with Mr. Chumbly."

"Are the two of them alone in there?"

"No, sir. The housekeeper is with them."

"Good. Thank you, there's nothing else."

The squire didn't consider Chumbly's monster hunt a crisis. Monsters under the bed of a drunkard weren't particularly unusual. Besides, his presence would probably excite Chumbly even more, so he thought it best to stay out of the man's sight lest he make matters worse for Prudence.

*　　*　　*

Elgin reached Bath late that night. When he finally slid beneath the covers with Iris, she roused enough to smile and ask if his mission had been completed. He said not exactly.

"Whyever not?"

"When I made plans to tell your grandfather that we had been married, I thought your whereabouts would be unknown when I broke the news. It's just luck that I found out that he knew you were somewhere in Bath before I had the chance to say anything. I didn't want him sending anyone else out here—hold on there, take care what you're about, my girl." Iris was brushing her lips across his Adam's apple while he was trying to talk. Most distracting.

"As it happened," he persisted, "your grandfather asked me to find you, snatch you from the clutches of your gypsy lover—he thinks you've run off with the gypsies—and return you to Huntington Manor to be married to a man that they have picked out. He must have meant Bumpsted."

Iris's laugh was more like a purr. "Do you suppose you might warn him off?"

"What should I say? Sir, I don't think it would be quite the thing if you should marry my wife?"

"That might discourage him." Her breath came in warm puffs against his throat.

He put his hand over the spot and said, "Iris, you don't seem to understand that all hell is about to break loose, and I don't want you struck by flying brimstone. Stop it!" He pressed a finger to her marauding mouth. "Now, listen, because this is important. I want to take you home to

Kent, where you'll be safe while I go back to explain the facts of life to your grandfather."

She said, "We'll go together. We are quite thoroughly married, and my family can't do anything about it, unless they wouldn't mind a frightful scandal, and I know they would, so we'll go to see Grandfather together."

"It really isn't necessary."

"Truly it is. I do miss him, you see. Over the years I've spent more time with him than I have with my parents. I couldn't bear it if he thought I didn't love him anymore. Please?"

Elgin's sigh was one of resignation. "All right, we'll leave tomorrow."

"Not tomorrow," Iris whispered. "We can wait another day or two. Surely grandfather doesn't expect you to return quite so soon."

"We've been hiding long enough. Tomorrow it is."

Iris wrapped her arms around Elgin's neck and rubbed her toes along his leg. His voice was soft and husky when he said, "Perhaps another day won't matter, but absolutely no longer."

Iris didn't have another word to say.

· *Fourteen* ·

When Dr. Burdock arrived, he found Chumbly in much the same condition as he had seen him so many times before. The smell of alcohol on his breath only confirmed the obvious. The man was drunk again. This time, however, he was thrashing around and raving worse than ever. He thought there were demons and monsters after him. When he grabbed the doctor by the coat and demanded a drink, the doctor told the attendant to give him water and left the room in disgust.

The squire and Prudence were in the small reception room when Burdock came downstairs. He went directly to Prudence and clasped her hand firmly, lowering his graying head to hers. He said, "My dear lady, you have my most profound sympathy during this time of trial."

Pale of face but otherwise composed, Prudence thanked him for his sympathetic words. The doctor then excused himself and spoke privately with the squire about the less delicate aspects of the case. Prudence had turned her attention to the small table before her where she was choosing the right flowers and weeds for her next pressed-flower arrangement. Separating the layers of blotting paper, she revealed graceful vines with three-lobed leaves, white daisy petals, yellow cowslips, purple violets. Moving them about was accomplished with the tip of a small, soft paintbrush.

After dropping two of the delicate flowers Prudence decided that she didn't have the necessary concentration for the task. Putting the little table aside, she smoothed the doilies on the arms of the chairs until they would smooth no more, then smoothed out her handerkerchief and folded it and smoothed it again, then picked at a bit of green thread that had come undone from a leaf embroidered in one corner of the handkerchief.

Dr. Burdock watched Prudence for a moment, looking as serious as the situation was. He said, "Mrs. Chumbly, I'm terribly sorry that I cannot feel optimistic about your husband's condition. Ordinarily I would recommend three days of purging for our patient, then the shaving of his head to apply leeches to his temples to draw off the poisons from his brain. Unfortunately, his condition, as you may well imagine, is too far gone to wait three precious days. The procedure must be done sooner if it is to be of any help at all. One purging will have to do before the leeches are put to use."

Removing his spectacles, the doctor puffed on the lenses, then rubbed them on the sleeve of his coat. "After a man has been drinking so much for so long, there isn't a great deal anyone can do for him." He put the spectacles on and looked around, apparently satisfied with what he saw.

"I've left the necessary medicine with your housekeeper and given instructions for its use."

When the good doctor was in the midst of relating the significant similarities between Chumbly's case and others of its kind, the new maid hurried into the room. In a rush of words she said, "If you please, Mrs. Chumbly, your husband wants you." She turned to leave the room and was halfway to the door before she remembered to curtsy, then dashed out.

Prudence, only slightly more pale than she had been before, rose from her chair with regal dignity. The squire got up as well, intending to accompany his sister. She shook her head and said, "You needn't disturb yourself, Obediah. I shall manage." Her brother wasn't at all comfortable with that decision, but Prudence insisted. The doctor also appeared ill at ease, knowing how wild Chumbly had become. Yet the men held back at the woman's insistence, and she left the room alone.

The climb upstairs had never been as difficult for Prudence, even though this was the house in which she had grown up. She could remember when going up these same stairs had seemed like mountain climbing to a little child. As a young girl she went up and down as though she had Mercurial wings on her heels. Her mother was forever telling her to go slowly, to conduct herself like a lady. Now there was no need to tell Prudence to slow down. When she realized that she had come to a stop halfway up the stairs, she felt oddly disconnected from her surroundings. It took concentration to make herself finish the climb to the next floor and the room where Chumbly lay.

Chumbly's bedchamber smelled like the sickroom it was. Though the windows were open to admit fresh air, the draperies were drawn to prevent drafts. The lamp on the dresser was turned low because he couldn't stand bright light. A burly groom sat in attendance. When Prudence stepped into the room, she motioned the man to leave. He was unwilling to do so. Prudence insisted. He left then, muttering, "I won't be far away, ma'am, should you need me."

After dampening a cloth in cool water, Prudence took the bedside chair and began to bathe her husband's flushed face. His eyes snapped open. He looked about frantically and grabbed her wrist. "Have you seen 'em?" The slurred words were forced through cracked lips. "They come out from un'er my bed to get me!"

Prudence pushed his hand away and continued to wipe his brow. "Perhaps they won't come out while I'm here," she told him.

Chumbly jerked away to crouch among his disorderly covers, looking wild-eyed into dark corners. Ever watchful, he said, "I'm dying. Don't wanna go to hell. That's where the mons'ers live. Listen . . . they're coming!"

"It's your own heart beating. Don't worry yourself so."

With a sharp cry Chumbly sat upright and began to curse and beat away things only he could see. He picked at his arms, scrubbed his chest, shouting, "Worms! Worms all over me!"

Prudence waved the cloth over Chumbly's arms and chest. "They're gone now. I've chased them away. Just rest." She rinsed the cloth and cooled his face again.

Chumbly grabbed her arm and shook until her cap fell off and her hair came undone. He said, "They're here 'cause I lied!"

Pulling away, Prudence said, "You mustn't carry on so. Your monsters can't take you anywhere you wouldn't go alone. Just rest now and don't frighten yourself."

He dropped his voice so the monsters wouldn't hear him. "No one stole all my money. I was gam'ling."

"I know," said Prudence. "I talked with the bankers who paid the vouchers. It would seem that you are an exceptionally poor cardplayer, but it doesn't matter now. Just rest."

"Your dowry." He had hold of her arms again. "I spent most of it on my frien's."

"I know," sighed Prudence. "I was told that you had been seen with one of those friends in Venice. She was quite beautiful. But that was years ago. It doesn't matter now. Just rest."

"Been sellin' your brother's stuff."

"I know. I think he knows it as well."

"Jewelry," he rasped, his throat dry. "Sol' the stones."

Prudence nodded solemnly. "I knew it as soon as you substituted paste replacements for the rubies in my grandmother's necklace. But that doesn't matter anymore, either."

His eyes were fever bright when he thrust his face up to hers and croaked, "Got rid of your damned cat!"

She patted his hand gently and said, "I know. That's why I poisoned you."

Chumbly's roar thundered along the passage, up into the attics, down the stairs. The groom dashed in to pry Chumbly's hands from Prudence's throat. The doctor came in right behind the groom to support the staggering woman, leading her to a chair away from Chumbly. While she struggled to catch her breath, the groom subdued Chumbly by pushing him facedown and sitting on him. Pointing a shaky finger at Prudence, Chumbly shouted, "She's killing me!"

Wiping her tear-dampened cheeks, Prudence looked at the doctor and said, "I'm afraid it's true."

"My God!" said the doctor. "I hope you don't expect anyone to believe that you drove this man to drink! You there," he called to the groom. "I'll send in someone to help you tie him down so we can shave his head. We can't delay applying the leeches."

Ever so tenderly Dr. Burdock led Prudence from the room. While she insisted, "It truly is my fault," he crooned, "There, there, dear lady. I quite understand how guilty he has made you feel for his own weakness of character. Let us hear no more about it."

A small, private funeral was held two days later.

Iris and Elgin knew nothing about Chumbly's passing or the funeral. At the time of the service they were still in Bath. Iris was trying to decide exactly how much new underwear she needed to buy. As she didn't have her own maid upon whom she could depend, she had to rely on the hotel staff for assistance. A reliable girl of her own would have known where every piece of her clothing had gone and made sure it came back. As it was her lace-trimmed drawers weren't coming back from being laundered and no one seemed to have the vaguest notion of what had become of them. Terribly inconvenient.

She said, "It's too silly, really, having one's unmentionables pinched. I should think the management of the hotel would care. Elgin, did you hear what I said?"

Elgin was standing at the window, hands stuffed into the pockets of his dressing gown, staring down at the street. He said, "Iris, it's time to go home. I've had enough."

"I can't go very far without more underthings, for heaven's sake."

He said, "The place will be in brilliant color by now. A hundred barrels of cider have already been pressed, though not of the Barnack Beauty apples. Those won't be ready until the end of the month." After a pause he added, "I suppose they're making wild blackberry jam in the kitchens. Fresh bread and blackberry jam. If I ever become a fat country squire, it will be due to blackberry jam and fresh-baked—"

"Elgin," said Iris impatiently.

He looked around. "Hmm?"

"My drawers."

"I beg your pardon?"

She said, "They're missing." He looked shocked. When she said, "They didn't come back with the other laundry," he appeared more relieved than indignant. Then she said, "I thought we would be going to see my grandfather. Now it would seem that we're going to Kent, instead."

"Have you ever seen a donkey derby?"

"What do donkeys have to do with anything?"

"We've missed the donkey derby this time around, but we'll go next summer. It's a bit like Ascot opening day. The local boys ride the donkeys, though the beasts don't necessarily run, or trot, or even leave the post. You might like it. Have you ever watched charcoal making?" Before Iris could answer, he said, "I'll take you to see that, too. When it's nice we'll go to the beach at Brighton. Perhaps we'll even go to Paris and see if the chaps I met last year are still perfecting their diving apparatus."

"Elgin . . ."

"One of them stayed on the riverbank, you see, and pumped air through a leather hose to the man underwater. The one underwater had a metal tank sort of arrangement strapped on his back."

"Elgin . . ."

"The thing had a valve, and then a hose to get air to his mouth. Quite clever, really. He wore goggles. Had lead weights on his shoes to keep himself down. Thought I might like to try it my—"

Iris curved her hands around her mouth and called, "Elgin!"

He said, "We'll go to see your grandfather first. I'll tell him that we're married, which shouldn't take more than five or ten minutes. Then we'll go home."

"When will we do all this?"

"Tomorrow. Today we might go to Princess Victoria Park, if you like."

"There seems to be something else on your mind."

"Oh, just this business of hiding and seeking and all that."

"Oh?"

Elgin ignored the note of skepticism in Iris's voice, though he did have something else on his mind. Several things, actually. It was true that he found hiding unnerving, and the longer it went on, the worse it got. He had to put an end to it. They simply had to go home. Yet the closer they came to going home, the more he was afraid of what would happen after they got there. Home was wonderful, but it wasn't all that exciting, and he was afraid Iris would become bored after she'd been there for a while. Ever since they'd known each other, they had gone from one crisis to another. Even here in peaceful Bath life was high drama because they were still in hiding. They were even using assumed names.

At the root of it all was Elgin's suspicion that going from the heady excitement of the unmarried social whirl to a ho-hum married life might have been the reason his parents had come to fight all the time. When the wedding party was over and the excitement faded, the tedium set in, and they went on to boredom and fighting.

That sick, sweaty feeling came back when Elgin thought about growing up in a battlefield, and he wasn't sure that he could keep it from happening all over again. What would he do if Iris got that bored?

"Elgin, are you in there somewhere?" Iris was

shaking the sleeve of his dressing gown. "You did say that we'd walk in the park today."

He looked at her then, really looked at her, and saw the same dazzling blue eyes, the same mop of dark curls that never stayed put, though the haircut she had given herself the past spring had grown out considerably. When she smiled his heart skipped, and a shiver went through him when she tilted her face up for a kiss, her lips parted ever so little, warm and inviting . . .

And he knew that if they kept this up, they wouldn't see any more of the park than they had seen of Abbey Church.

Elgin pulled his hands from his pockets and wrapped Iris inside his dressing gown, holding her close. In her housecoat she was wonderfully soft. Lord, how he hated those stiff corsets, fashion be damned. Wisps of her hair got caught in the stubble on his chin when he kissed the top of her head. Honeysuckle. Her hair always smelled of honeysuckle and that always reminded him of home. Despite his apprehensions, he wanted to be home with Iris and swung her into his arms, carried her the few steps across the room, and dropped her onto the bed. The bed squeaked, Iris squeaked, Elgin grinned and went to the dresser to shave his whiskery face.

For a walk through Princess Victoria Park, Elgin wore an expertly tailored gray frock coat trimmed in lighter gray braid. Beneath it was a matching waistcoat. Below the coat and waistcoat were trousers of a small check identifiable as shepherd's plaid. His shirt was white, his tie was gray, his gold stick pin hardly showed above his high-necked waistcoat. Even his low-crowned top hat was gray. His shoes, the ones with the elastic insets, the same ones that he'd had to polish himself, were black. The gold watch chain and fob were quite right. Everything about Elgin was quite right, except for Iris.

For a walk through Princess Victoria Park, Iris wore her plain brown hat and second-best brown dress. So perfectly dull. She was saving her best brown dress for the visit to her grandfather at Huntington Manor. There she would collect her other clothes, nicer clothes, before going home with Elgin.

Iris's drab wardrobe had begun as a subject of amusement between the two of them. For the most part they ignored the disapproving looks they got from people on the street, who supposed he was a gentleman seducer of servant girls. Worse yet, he appeared to be a seducer who flaunted his lower-class affairs by parading the young women in public. It simply wasn't done. At least the part about being seen together in public. As for the private aspects of the arrangement, it was understood that a gentleman would have his needs. The female in question was simply a tart who lacked morals.

For that reason Elgin was becoming more and more resentful of the looks Iris was getting. Whenever someone raised an eyebrow in her direction, he felt a rush of anger that was surpassed only by the next withering glance she received. What had begun as something of a game was no longer amusing. Elgin forced himself to shorten his strides so that Iris wouldn't have to dash along beside him. He was possessed by the urge to run her back to the hotel, away from censuring eyes. But Iris seemed to be enjoying the outing, and they wouldn't be in Bath much longer, so he would stick it out.

Taking her cue from Elgin's subdued behavior, Iris tried to give him the solitude he wanted and turned her attention in other directions. Like the clothes worn by other women who were strolling through the park. So fashionable. Iris had to admit that she was getting tired of plain brown dresses, though these clothes did exactly what they were supposed to do. They turned her into a nobody. But it wasn't fun anymore. That's when she thought of her beautiful new hat in the round box under the bed at the hotel. Even the box was beautiful, all covered in flowered paper, with the name of the shop in gold. Oh, how she looked forward to wearing that hat, but not with a plain brown dress.

All around her Iris could see that the park was swarming with hats that matched fashionable two-color dresses. Little hats with veils and feathers and yards of ribbons. Hats of felt or woven horsehair trimmed in bright colors that were the same as the buttons and braid and tassels on elegantly draped mantles.

There were hats with birds that had flowing tails and spread wings. Birds in shades of green and violet, tints of blue and pink. Birds that were bigger than the hats upon which they were perched. Nothing like the birds that flitted through the trees in Princess Victoria Park.

Elgin was painfully aware of how quiet Iris had become. Iris, who was usually so talkative. It only reinforced his fear that they were running out of things to say, coming that much closer to arguing like his parents did. Common sense told him it wasn't so. On the other hand his parents never had made any sense. His lunch began to feel like a lump in his stomach.

Obediah Huntington tapped his pencil on the paper before him without having put down anything of use. He had intended to begin notations on the treasures from Crete, but his thoughts kept drifting to Iris. At the end of an hour he had produced a page of lines and arrows, circles within circles, and rows of things that might have been birds, but maybe not. The news that Bumpsted had remarried left him badly undone. He simply didn't know what he would do with Iris. It was one thing when he thought there was a market for the girl, but now . . .

Things were looking bleak, indeed, when Prudence, draped in widow's black, arrived with her little silver tray. On it was the customary doily. On the doily was a small china bowl. In the bowl was a mixture of dead-nettle that had been bruised, then mixed with salt, vinegar, and hog's grease. Over her arm was a white towel. Without waiting to be told, the squire carefully withdrew his bare foot from beneath the table and just as carefully rested it on the footstool Prudence pushed his way. There were footstools all over the house. While she fussed over the arrangement of a towel under his foot, avoiding any contact that would exacerbate the searing pain in his toe, her brother eyed the tray ominously and craned his neck to see what else was on the tray. All he could see was a paintbrush.

Wincing at a slight bump, the squire said, "My sources tell me that people are beginning to talk about Iris. When Farley brings her back, I suppose we could pack her off on a trip to the Continent." The squire adjusted his black armband, feeling a twinge of hypocrisy. All the men in the household, gentlemen and servants alike, wore this symbol of a family in mourning. "Such a trip would be logical at this time," continued the squire. Prudence dipped the brush into the warm grease mixture and ever so gently began to apply it to the villainous toe. He said, "Taking such an excursion would make it appear as though it was Iris who was accompanying you on a trip so that you might regain your peace of mind due to your recent bereavement. It's a common enough thing to do. Eventually Iris's absence from home and her tour will all blend into the same thing in everyone's mind."

"A tour?" said Prudence, staring up at her brother through wide, startled eyes. "Deary me. Do you mean the sort of arrangement where I would go from place to place, in carriages and trains and ships, to walk about and look at grand buildings and famous ruins and scenic wonders, in addition to the occasional site of a local miracle of greater or lesser significance? I was afraid that's what you meant." She returned to the painting of his toe with the greasy mixture.

"There will be gardens, too," said the squire. "Don't forget about seeing the gardens. Tours often include fine gardens. In fact, we might even find a tour that specializes in gardens. Any kind you like."

"Oh, dear." The thought of so much traveling and parading about didn't appeal to Prudence at all, gardens or not. She returned the brush to the tray and said, "Perhaps I could stay at a hotel while Iris did things."

"Who knows what sort of things Iris might do? I'm afraid it's out of the question to ask her parents to accompany her. Perhaps one of her sisters would go if you can't."

"Not her sisters," said Prudence, shaking her head. "The married ones who would make suitable companions are quite taken up with their families just now. Two of them are in a delicate condition, you know, or perhaps you don't know, though that's how it is. They have been sewing the dearest little caps and dresses. Carriage robes, too. And buntings."

"Perhaps there's someone we know who might be taking their own daughter on a cultural tour of the Continent. They might be willing to take Iris with them. That would certainly be acceptable."

"It might do nicely, if only we knew of such people, but we don't. That's one of the difficulties that has arisen from keeping Iris so isolated for so long. I'm certain she must have had some friends at one time or another. Of course, if she had a husband, there wouldn't be a problem about finding someone proper to take her on a tour."

"Prudence, if she had a husband we wouldn't have to send her on a tour!"

"Oh, dear. I see what you mean. That is a problem. My goodness."

"If only I could take Iris to Egypt. She would

love it. The Nile, the pyramids, camels—quite educational. Unfortunately, my toe makes such a thing impossible, so if you would rather go to Egypt than the Continent—" When he looked at his sister, the thought left his mind. It was impossible to imagine roly-poly Prudence perched atop a camel, and he cursed Bumpsted for getting married before they'd had an opportunity to trot Iris past him for consideration.

Scowling, the squire muttered, "For all the brainpower I've expended, I'm right back where I started."

"I'm afraid I don't quite understand you," replied his sister.

"Egad! It isn't as though there are long lines, or short lines, or anyone at all wanting to marry Iris. It was bad enough when she cut off her hair the first time marriage to Bumpsted was mentioned. Then there was that scandalous business with the razor, but we won't talk about that. Then there was the fire when she burned up that rubber thing her mother sent. And the gypsy. We won't talk about that, either. I hate to think about what else the girl has done or might do next."

"Well . . ." said Prudence thoughtfully.

"Never mind! I don't want to know." Her brother wadded up the paper with the lines and arrows and flying things, tossed it backward over his shoulder, then slumped deeper into his chair. Right there in front of him was his greasy toe. Though it smelled like bacon, and he liked bacon, it failed to cheer him. A kitten, a new black one, wandered into the room and sniffed at his toe. Prudence lifted the little creature onto her lap.

The squire stared off into space, then at Prudence, and said, "What if there's someone who hasn't heard about what Iris has done? Perhaps someone who's been out of the country. An unattached man from good family who would take her if the dowry was interesting enough. Maybe someone whose family has fallen on hard times. Those are the people who would understand the benefits to be derived from a generous marriage settlement."

"Obediah, I don't think such a plan will be as easy to execute as you would hope. Surely this husband will come to suspect that his new bride isn't . . . well, isn't quite as new as he had expected her to be, what with the time Iris has spent with the gypsy, you see. I do hope you see."

"Egad! You're right. I'd forgotten. And I still don't know if she is married to him. If she married him it wouldn't do the least bit of good to find another husband for her." The squire twisted around toward the desk and took up his pencil, then drew out a clean sheet of paper. Stretching his arms to get elbow room in his sleeves, he leaned to the task of making two lists in elaborate copperplate:

If Married To The Gypsy: 1) Change her name. 2) Get her out of the country. 3) A mission school—India, Africa, far away.

If Not Married To The Gypsy: 1) Get her married, but not to the gypsy. 2) Fast. 3) Where and how to find a husband. 4) Cost of convincing him.

After staring at the lists for a few moments,

the squire said, "Pru, I'm much afraid that it might not be possible to secure a man from a really good family, even with an impressive dowry. But we might find a willing man involved in trade." He hesitated on the word *trade*. "Perhaps there's someone whose business is floundering and Iris's dowry would provide the capital to survive. Even marriage to Iris would surely be better than ruin."

Yet the squire, for as much as he loved his granddaughter, had to wonder if such a marriage really would be much of an improvement over ruination. A man could recover from financial disaster. A man might never recover from taking a wife like Iris. Tossing the pencil aside, he sank back into the silence of his chair. The kitten lay in Prudence's lap, blissfully chewing on her handkerchief, a white one edged in black.

Eventually the squire said, "I'll contact my man of business. He'll have extensive connections on all levels of society, though putting connections together will take time. It would be quicker if Iris's father knew of a likely candidate, but her father might be inclined to have Iris locked up in a private lunatic asylum—under another name, of course. He might well think it was the most expedient thing to do, in addition to ensuring the most secrecy and least scandal." Before Prudence could comment, the squire said, "No, I don't think I'll mention this to him at all. The beastly thing is that I can think of the problems, but I can't think of the answers."

"Obediah, have you considered that Mr. Farley might be the very man to resolve this dilemma?"

"Farley? Egad, I believe you have something

there! Why didn't I think of it before? Farley knows everyone. I'll put the question to him, privately, of course, as soon as he gets back here. Yes, indeed. Farely is the man to find a husband for Iris. How long must I leave this grease on my toe?"

"The receipt didn't say, but Mr. Farley should be of considerable assistance, and I'll shut the door so the kitten can't get back in to tease your dear toe. I haven't named it yet. The kitten, that is. Not your toe. That would be silly, wouldn't it." Prudence bestowed a kindly smile upon her brother, and on his toe, and on her cat, and left the room.

· *Fifteen* ·

Prudence sat holding the telegraph message telling them that Iris and Elgin would be arriving in Little Woolton by train on Thursday. Folding and returning the paper to her pocket, she said, "No, it didn't give the least hint as to the time of arrival, only that it would be sometime today, providing that today is Thursday, and I'm quite sure this is Thursday. Is your toe any better?"

"Some," said her brother absently. "I'll have to be more careful where I drop my shoe." He'd been only half listening to his sister, his ear being tuned, instead, for the sounds of his granddaughter's arrival.

"Obediah, whatever will we say to Iris about the surgery that had been planned for her? She may be afraid that the threat will arise once again."

"Think! Prudence. Iris doesn't know about the surgery. How could she? By the time anyone went to look for her that day, she had already run off with the gypsy. She wasn't even here when the doctor arrived. And, since she doesn't know, I see no reason to bring up the matter now. Nothing came of it."

Prudence agreed that nothing had come of it, then said, "Obediah, how are we to behave? Iris has been gone for a long time without permission. Do you know what you're going to say when you see her again? It might be terribly awkward."

"Not in the least. The goal we must keep in mind is to get the girl respectably married. If we scold about past indiscretions she may bolt again—heaven forbid. There must be no mention of anything unpleasant. I won't even ask exactly where Farley found her or how he arranged her return. We will smile and be happy to see her. When all is concluded as I have planned, whatever Iris does will be someone else's problem. There must be nothing said that will upset the apple cart before we can unload the apple."

Prudence nodded and said, "How very sensible of you, Obediah."

An hour later there were voices in the hall, and a brown wren of a female entered the room. Elgin Farley was right behind her.

"My goodness, I almost didn't know you!" exclaimed Prudence. She embraced Iris and whispered, "Say as little as possible until we're alone."

The squire in his turn gave Iris an affectionate pat on the cheek, then shook Elgin's hand with businesslike efficiency. Once seated they all looked as if they'd rather be someplace else. Searching for just the right words to use in this delicate situation, the squire finally blustered,

"Well, Iris, were you actually married to that gypsy?"

There followed a stunned silence before Iris said, "No." She tried not to fidget, but knotted her fingers together all the same. "I was not married to that or any other gypsy."

Heaving a great sigh of relief, the squire said, "Thank heaven for living in sin."

"Obediah! What a perfectly dreadful thing to say!"

Elgin turned to Prudence and said, "The coachman told us of Chumbly's passing. May I extend my sympathy at this time?"

Prudence said, "Thank you," then asked Elgin if they'd had a pleasant journey and went on to make a great fuss over Iris and the clothes she was wearing.

Leaning toward Elgin, the squire muttered, "Chumbly's gone on to his last reward all right and tight—wherever that may be. He finally had too much to drink and popped off, with a chorus of monsters and devils at his heels."

Though it hadn't been intended that Prudence should hear the remark, she did and said, "Yes, it's all true. It was the bottle in his top dresser drawer that finally did it, but I poured it out so it won't happen to anyone else."

"Ha!" snorted the squire. "It took more than one bottle of whiskey to do Chumbly in."

"I know," said Prudence, "but the doctor doesn't want me to talk about it."

"And quite right he is," grumped the squire. The ensuing silence left the homecoming even more strained than it had been before.

Elgin noted Iris's white knuckles, felt her distress, and understood why. It wasn't as though she and her family had kissed good-bye before she left on a proper holiday. He said, "You look frightfully done in. Perhaps your family will excuse you."

Prudence sprang up and said, "Indeed, you do look tired, dear," and motioned Iris toward the door. "Perhaps it's that brown dress that makes you look tired. It might be, you know, though it isn't the brown of it, actually, it's the shade of brown of it. So muddy. You probably shouldn't wear brown at all. We'll get some nice hot tea, though your sister Kathy can wear brown and look quite well in it, but it's too bad of her to wear red. The new tea from Ceylon is simply delightful."

Iris stopped at the door and looked back at Elgin. He gave her a smile that told her not to worry. She returned a more hesitant smile that said she certainly hoped he was right.

Gaining the bedchamber she hadn't seen in ever so long, Iris flopped across the bed in her usual undignified fashion. On this occasion her aunt refrained from reminding her that a lady didn't do such things. The dear woman simply went to the wardrobe and began to look through the dresses Iris had left behind. She knew Iris didn't have a black dress, but did find one of dark green serge, the most appropriate one available for a household in mourning. She laid it on the bed, fluffed up the ruffles, and said, "Iris, are you truly as tired as Mr. Farley said you are?"

"Not quite, but I'm pleased to be out of there so that he and Grandfather can talk."

"Well, I have news for you, too," said Prudence. "You are indeed fortunate because your parents have washed their hands of you. They have decided to look for a foreign title, perhaps Italian or German, for one of your younger sisters, who seems to think it's a fine idea. Now, tell me, what have you been doing all this time? I know you weren't with a gypsy, for I sent dear Mr. Farley to the boathouse after you."

"I've been living with dear Mr. Farley," said Iris, unbuttoning her dress.

"Good heavens!"

"We were married by a minister friend of Elgin's, who loves to garden. You'd like him."

Breathing easier, Prudence said, "I'm sure I would, but I'm afraid that life is about to become quite complicated for you. By now your grandfather is making arrangements with Mr. Farley to find you a proper husband, since the marquis has remarried. At least that's what he said he was going to do, though I don't think it would be at all convenient to have too many husbands at once. I don't think Mr. Farley would care for it, either. And just think of the extra meals you would have to plan!"

Iris smiled. "I don't think it will come to that. Elgin is going to tell Grandfather that we're married. Then he and I will leave for his home in Kent. What I need is my traveling dress."

"I wouldn't be too sure of that."

As Prudence would insist upon the dark green dress, Iris wore it over the laciest petticoats she could find, then laughed because she had never thought of herself as a lady of fashion. A moment later she wasn't laughing.

"What's wrong?" asked Prudence. "Don't you like the dress? Let's pick out another." She opened the wardrobe doors again.

"It isn't the dress," said Iris. "I like it ever so much better than the brown one. It's just that my life really was empty before I went away with Elgin. I was contented enough, I suppose, but I wasn't happy, either. You don't think Grandfather could actually do anything to spoil it now, do you? I'm sure he means well with his plans for me, but I simply can't be what they all want me to be."

Prudence laughed delightedly and said, "Iris, I don't think you'll ever live your life the way other women do. And you're fortunate to have found a man who truly likes you. You'll both be happier that way. There was a time when I thought of becoming a doctor, you know. A doctor just for children, but I wasn't brave enough to oppose the wishes of my family. They said it was a positively indecent occupation for a lady, and they were right, of course. But if I'd been strong enough, and had someone like dear Mr. Farley with me, I think I might have done it. Now, tell me, Iris, what else would you like to do?"

"Vote."

Prudence gasped and clutched at her heart.

"I'd like to vote in an election for Parliament."

"Good heavens! Women can't *do* that. Don't let your grandfather hear you say such a thing. At least not for a while. Perhaps when his toe is better. I trust it will get better. I've used so many treatments on it. Voting. My goodness. Let's go downstairs and have our tea, shall we? Then we'll find out who it is that your grandfather has arranged for you to marry next, though it had better be Mr. Farley again, or there will be some profound complications, mark my word. What a day this has been, and my kitten got into Lydia's yarn, the naughty puss, and I believe we've run out of goutwort." After a moment of speculative thought, Prudence said, "Iris, do go out in the garden and I'll have our tea sent there. It hasn't rained all day, so it should be quite nice."

When Elgin arrived at Hungtington Manor with Iris, he had been prepared to deliver a brief speech about himself and Iris being married, be done with it, and leave. When the ladies left the drawing room, he was still prepared to announce the marriage, but the squire made it known that he had something to say first, so Elgin deferred to the older man out of good manners.

It was while the squire was expounding upon the importance of discretion in business dealings that the maid arrived with a vase of fresh flowers. She left quickly, but the interruption was more than a little distracting to the squire. No sooner had he resumed his monologue than someone else came in to clean the fireplace grates. Seeing that the room was occupied, she left promptly, but took any sense of privacy with her.

"We could do with less traffic," announced the squire and led the way to a quieter place, a territory of his own. When the door of the African Room closed behind them, they were enveloped by an air of furtiveness. There was also an air of turpentine, as that was the last gout treatment Prudence had applied to her brother's toe in this room. Leaning heavily upon an ebony cane with a dragon's head handle, the squire indicated the seat Elgin was to take. The man himself sat in his elephant-tusk chair and propped his afflicted foot on the now balding head of the tiger-skin rug.

Voice lowered, the squire said, "Farley, there's a piece of business with which I could use your assistance."

"Oh?" came Elgin's cautious reply. He'd been staring at the tiger-skin rug. The beast didn't look dead, exactly, but more like something monstrous had squashed the thing so it couldn't get up.

In turn the squire was watching Farley and said, "It shouldn't be too terribly difficult, not for a man in your position. You know so many people."

"I'm afraid I don't follow you. Is there someone of particular interest to you?"

"Yes. Someone who will make a suitable husband for Iris."

It was a moment before Elgin said, "Oh."

"You look surprised. Don't know why you should. I would have thought that by now you'd understand why we'll have to take what we can get to have her respectably settled. She simply won't behave. There has been talk, you see. Altogether too much talk about the fire she lit that smoked out a house full of guests. People I don't even know are now insisting that they were here at the time and saw the event for themselves. What nonsense. But other people listen to them nonetheless.

"Even so, perhaps we are fortunate that the

fire has given people so much to talk about," continued the squire. "That way they haven't noticed that Iris ran off with that gypsy, though
there have been whispers about the search that
was made for her the day she disappeared. No
one is inclined to believe that she had been
asleep in her room all the while." He shifted
around in his chair, flexed his foot, winced, went
back to the way he was. "Ah, me. It sounds complicated, I know, but never mind. With a bit of
luck we can put a stop to the wagging tongues by
getting Iris married."

Seeing his chance at last, Elgin said, "If that's
the only problem, then there is no problem. You
see, your granddaughter and I are better acquainted than you might—"

"That's it!" interrupted the squire, pleased
that Elgin had caught on so quickly. "That's exactly why I want you to find her a husband! In
addition to knowing who's available, you should
know Iris well enough to understand what sort
of fellow would be agreeable to her. If that's possible. If that isn't possible, we'll have to do something else. She didn't fancy the Marquis of
Bumpsted, and he was quite a catch."

"Was? Am I to understand that Bumpsted has
cashed in his chips?"

"No, nothing of the sort. He's just up and married someone else, that's all. Damned inconvenient, really. That's why we have to find another
husband for her. I expect you can recommend a
likely candidate. Someone respectable, though
perhaps financially strapped. Iris will bring an
impressive dowry with her."

"Sir, I'd like to say—"

"Well, don't. At least not now. We have important things to attend to."

With a shrug Elgin said, "If you insist." The fact that he was being asked to find a husband for his own wife had a theatrical touch about it that amused him immensely. But he couldn't very well appear amused. Yet the squire would go on and on without listening to what he had to say. As things were, Elgin thought it might be best to sit tight and let the man exhaust his plans for Iris. When the futility of it all became obvious, Elgin would tell him not to worry, because he and Iris were already married. So simple. Then he and Iris would leave for Kent and that would be the end of it. He thought the whole thing could be finished in a matter of minutes. Lord, how he wanted to go home with Iris. He wanted his own house and Iris across from him over his own table. He wanted to walk with Iris in his own gardens, and he wanted his own bed with Iris in it. And he'd given up any hope for a quiet peaceful life. Didn't know why he'd ever thought he'd like it.

"Well, then," said the squire. "Let's get to work. Tell me of the likely candidates—the ones in need of funds would be the best place to start."

Elgin puckered up and tapped his thumbs, sorting through a jumble of thoughts. Then a smile crept into those thoughts, and he said, "There's Piggy Horton. Titled connections, so you know the breeding's there. He's a jolly good chap. Has a good disposition. Easy to get along with. Everyone likes Piggy and he does need money."

"Why?"

"His allowance has been cut back. You see, Piggy has a brother who drinks too much. Now and then the fellow becomes impressively intoxicated and breaks up someone's furniture or something. It takes a bite out of the family coffers to pay for the damage he's done, especially when the damage has extended to a Rembrandt sketch. But everyone likes Piggy. The worst thing Piggy ever did was discover cream puffs and puddings at a tender age. The important thing is that he'd treat Iris well, though you might not want to turn her dowry over to him all at once."

"Why not?"

"Piggy has never picked a winning horse in his life."

"Egad! Who else is there? We might even consider a respectable family in, you know, a business of some sort."

"Do you mean someone in *trade*?" Elgin could see the old man cringe.

"If it's a nice family I suppose we might consider him . . . if we must."

"As a matter of fact there's a good man in the meat-packing business who's looking for a wife. The fellow hasn't got any real vices or even any undesirable relatives as far as I know. Very respectable. His name is Endive, Roland Endive, and he does need money. Had a fire in one of his warehouses, and the insurance wasn't enough to cover the losses."

"Will he be good to Iris?"

"Most assuredly so. Roland has been good to all his wives."

"How many have there been?"

"Only three. They keep dying off. Now he's got eleven motherless children. Or is it only ten? I lose count. But they're nice children, at least most of them are. Iris will probably love them."

The squire wasn't so sure. While he was pondering the fate of Endive's three late wives, a footman arrived to tell him that his presence was required in the library. After being convinced that it couldn't be postponed, the squire excused himself and hobbled from the room. As soon as he got into the passage, he encountered his sister.

"What is the problem?" he asked as soon as he had moved a little farther down the hall. "I'm on my way to the library."

Ever so softly Prudence said, "Never mind the library. I've been looking for you and sent for you myself. I suppose you and Mr. Farley have been talking about a suitable husband for Iris. At least that's what you said you were going to talk about, and as you made yourself quite private with Mr. Farley, just the way you said you would, I assume that's what the two of you were about."

"Prudence, is there something on your mind?"

"Oh, yes. Of course there is or I never would have interrupted you at a time like this, that is, while you were having private conversation of an important nature with a guest."

"Prudence, I—"

"Obediah, there is a great problem, or possibly a small problem, but surely a problem. I've sent Iris out into the garden."

"Prudence, we—"

"Obediah, have you considered that since Iris

has been in the intimate company of a man all this while that she may be in greater need of a husband than you had previously suspected?" Then she whispered, "Motherhood may be just around the corner."

"Egad! In the event that the possibility you suggest has already made itself manifest, Iris doesn't need a husband soon, she needs a husband now!"

"Whatever shall we do?" exclaimed the wide-eyed Prudence.

Leaning heavily on the dragon's head cane, the squire's eyelids dropped in cunning thought. Slowly he turned to stare at the door to the African Room. Elgin Farley was the only marriageable gentleman around, and he was sitting just inside. Granted, Farley wasn't his first choice as a husband for his granddaughter, but fate was like that. He said, "Pru, I think I may have the answer to this newest turn of events. Farley is about to discover that he's up against a man of iron."

"My goodness! Who is it, Obediah?"

"Me, you silly woman! Farley will be dough in my hands, though I'll have to proceed with considerable caution so that I don't overwhelm him and frighten him off." Squaring his shoulders the squire nodded confidently to his sister and returned to the African Room and his elephant-tusk chair.

"Now, then," said the squire when he was settled in among the ivory. "Where were we? Oh, yes. Iris. Arranging a marriage takes a great deal of consideration. I was about to say that these men you have recommended are undoubtedly fine fellows, yet it is difficult to decide because I don't know them personally. Can you recommend anyone I already know?"

After a moment Elgin said, "I don't believe so."

A ponderous "Umm" was followed by a longer silence while the squire tried to figure out how to proceed. He knew it wasn't any use to offer money to Farley. The fellow didn't really need any. Furthermore, he seemed to prefer the bachelor life. Yet there had to be something Farley desperately wanted, something he wanted so badly that he would marry Iris to get it. Every man had a price. He just had to figure out what Farley's price was. He had to think! And then he knew. As it was Farley was assured of a piece of ancient Roman glass, but he also coveted some other ancient artifacts. The squire's frown eased into a sly smile. He sniffed and said, "Something in this room is going to make me sneeze. I believe the air will be less conspicuous in the Egyptian Room."

It was true that the Egyptian Room didn't smell like turpentine. It had, instead, a strange musty odor that one could only assume came from the partly unrolled mummy. Though he didn't say it Elgin preferred the smell of turpentine. The squire directed Elgin to a chair, a chair with an unobstructed view of the mummy.

Pointing to it, the squire said, "Those things aren't as easy to get as they used to be, though the supply isn't exhausted. Tomb robbers are still about. It's a family business, you know. Generations of them. They aren't interested in the common mummies, the humble folk who went on to the hereafter without the benefit of valuable charms in their wrappings or treasures in their tombs." The squire wagged a finger in the direction of a case filled with just such things.

"No," he continued, "it's the other mummies those men want, the extravagantly prepared ones from the rich tombs. Then there are the mummies that go up in smoke as fuel in the fire boxes of the trains that run across Egypt. Yes, it's true. With so little wood over there the last remains of some ancient ones, if they're well coated with flammable resins and tar, get cut up like cord wood and stacked at railway stations. After they're stripped of their valuables, of course. Then there are the ones that get ground into powder to be used in medicines. Some of the old receipts call for powdered mummy as an ingredient."

Elgin, staring at the partly exposed mummy on the far side of the room, couldn't imagine consuming any part of it no matter what ailed him.

Seeing Elgin's interest, the squire said, "Mummies, that is to say the genuine mummies made in the old days, haven't been much used for medicines in a couple of hundred years. That's when the traders learned that it was easier and cheaper to have the dead collected from the streets and prisons, bury them in the desert for a few years, then dig them up and pour bitumen over them. I spoke with a doctor who went to Egypt and saw the things piled up in the back of certain shops like so many dried fish."

"I'll have to remember that," said Elgin somberly, resolving to inquire more closely into the ingredients of any medicine he took for the rest of his life. Especially if it was powdered. With that in mind he said, "What does this medicinal mummy taste like?"

"Salt or tar. A lot of compounds that are supposed to have mummy as an ingredient have only tar. No one seems to know the difference, actually, though the stuff must cost them dearly just the same." The squire laughed. Elgin didn't laugh.

The squire was sure that Elgin's reticence was an indication of the depth of his interest in the ancient things around him. With a wave of his hand he indicated shelves and boxes of more artifacts and said, "Tell me, Farley, what do you find of particular interest?"

"That mummy has given me plenty to think about."

"Has Iris talked about the mummies?"

"Among other things, like Roman glass, early bronze pieces, tiles, statuary. Her knowledge is impressive. Yours must be even greater."

"It is," agreed the squire, "though perhaps your own is almost as good?"

"No. Not at all."

"Don't be modest. How else will we be able to get down to business if I can't find out what a gentleman like yourself might like to see in a young lady's dowry? Man does not live by bread alone. Sometimes he has enough bread. Then he might need a piece of ancient glass. Or a mummy. Hmm?"

"Am I to understand that you're going to include things like that"—Elgin pointed at the exposed mummy—"in this dowry you're providing for Iris?"

"Ah-ha! Have your interest now, do I? Thought that would do it! You can't fool me. I know what a man such as yourself is looking for. The only trouble with you is your parents."

Profoundly confused, Elgin said, "I beg your pardon?"

"I don't like to offend, but your parents, both of them, are a pair of idiots. Good blood, but they're daft all the same."

Grim-faced, Elgin rose from his seat. The squire said, "Dammit, Farley, sit down. I'm sorry you're insulted, but it's true. I have no objection to you, personally, it's your parents. Their fights are legendary. Your father once pushed your mother's pianoforte out the window during a fight at their house in London. When someone asked why he did such things, he said that a good row first makes for better screwing after."

"Are you saying that they fight like that because they like it?"

"Like it? They positively thrive on it! Everyone thought they'd kill each other before they were married a year. I've always said it was a good thing they had each other so they wouldn't make two other people miserable. Not your fault, of course, though that doesn't make them any less peculiar, but we were talking about mummies, I believe."

"We were talking about my parents!"

"Not anymore. But you'll have to do no matter what your parents are like, because you're handy. Can you read hieroglyphics?"

"Are you certain they fight because they enjoy it, not because they're bored with each other?"

"Iris can read hieroglyphics," said the squire. "Not much call for it, though. Not like French."

"Are you suggesting that I should marry your granddaughter?"

"What else would I be talking about? I'll tell you what. I'll make that mummy"—the squire pointed at the great unwrapped one—"yes, that one, part of Iris's dowry. How does that sound to you?"

"A tad revolting, actually. And it hasn't got any feet."

"Drive a hard bargain, do you? If that's the way it's going to be, I'll add another mummy. An older one in perfect condition." Elgin stared at the exposed mummy, then back at the squire, but couldn't think of an appropriate thing to say. "Well?" demanded the squire.

Once again Elgin studied the withered thing devoid of its protective bandages. The whole of it struck him as rather grotesque and he said, "A wrapped mummy does have a certain appeal to it."

"I should say it does. The gold and precious amulets will still be in place among those wrappings, and you're trying to make me think that you're some sort of novice at this. What a joke! I know exactly what you're up to!"

"I sincerely doubt that," said Elgin. And he wondered how his situation had got to be so turned around. When he arrived at Huntington Manor, he had planned to tell the squire that he and Iris were married and then go home. He had expected a poor reception because he didn't have a title. Not even a little one. But it hadn't happened that way. Instead he was negotiating a dowry to marry his own wife! But things were going his way without any trouble, so why make a fuss?

"So it's settled, is it?" said the squire, looking altogether too pleased with himself.

"Oh, I don't think so," replied Elgin, not really wanting a partly unrolled mummy, wondering how he could give it back without offending the squire. The man seemed to think it was a wonderful thing, this mummy, so he should keep it. Elgin had heard that one shouldn't look a gift horse in the mouth, but with a gift mummy it was so much worse. "The arrangement could do with a bit of correcting," said Elgin as politely as he could.

"More, is it? Don't think you can get much more out of me, even for marrying Iris. I'll throw in a Roman amphora, a copper shield from ancient Greece—in prime condition I might add—and the figure of a goddess from Crete, though you'll have to keep her covered up, those goddesses being the way they are and all."

"That's not quite what I had in mind. You see—"

"All right! The tiger-skin rug. That, however, is my final offer, take it or leave it and Iris with it!"

"I'll take it, but—"

"No *buts*. Return here in . . . let's see. Posting the banns for three Sundays . . . Be here in two and a half weeks. It will be a simple, private wedding as there has been a death in the house. Say good-bye to Iris and be quick about it, if you please. There's no telling what she might do if she doesn't like the idea of this wedding, so you'd better get out of here quickly."

"Wait just a moment!" cried Elgin indignantly. "I have no intention of leaving here without my . . . my . . . *hat*," and mumbled something about it being a favorite hat. He had almost said he wouldn't leave without his wife. And he couldn't very well say that without making it appear as though he had deliberately set out to make a fool of the squire with all this dowry business. So he mumbled about his hat.

"In two and half weeks Iris and the antiquities will be all yours," said the squire. "Until then she and they stay here. What in hell did you expect?"

"Expect?" echoed Elgin. "Well, I thought I might stay in the neighborhood."

"And I thought you might go home. Surely your own family has to be told that you plan to marry."

"My parents are abroad just now. I doubt that I can locate them in time for the wedding."

"It won't break my heart or my pianoforte if they can't get here at all, though I understand that you have well-behaved sisters, and I have no objection to them. You also have to get your house in order for a wife, with or without your silly hat. Perhaps one of us should tell Iris what's been planned. Better you than me if she doesn't like it. Was there something you wanted to say?"

"Well, no, nothing of any significance now."

"I didn't think so."

As soon as Iris saw Elgin, she hurried up the grassy path, dry leaves crackling beneath her sweeping skirts. When they met she would have thrown herself into his arms if it hadn't been for the arresting gesture of his halting palm.

He shook his head and said, "Your grandfather still doesn't know that we're married. I'm afraid he wasn't inclined to listen to what I had to say. I don't know exactly how it was that things went so askew before the interview was over."

"I do," said Iris with a knowing smile. Elgin stuffed his hands into his pockets. She tucked her hand in the crook of his elbow and fell into step beside him. "Grandfather is like a steam locomotive when he gets his mind set on something. That drive has made him an acknowledged expert on antiquities, though it does tend to lead him astray on occasion. What was it this time?"

"At first he was determined that I should find a husband for you. Then he decided that I would do well enough for your husband, not that he really liked the idea. He doesn't care for my parents, you see. You know about my parents. Anyway, he wants you properly married before you run off with any more gypsies."

"How much was the bribe to get you to agree to marry me?"

"The dowry he offered included two mummies, some ancient glass, one naughty statue, and things I don't remember. Ever time I tried to tell him that it wasn't at all what I wanted, he kept adding more things to the list. All of a sudden it was take you or leave you, so I said I'd take you, which was ridiculous because I've already got you, with our marriage lines right here in my pocket." He patted the left front of his coat.

"Then," said Elgin, "the whole thing became so confused that it would have been impossible to undo it without causing your grandfather a great deal of embarrassment. I really didn't want to do that. Now, however, I'm supposed to be out here telling you good-bye, only to return in two and a half weeks to marry you, if you're willing to go through with it again. Otherwise I'll take you home right now."

Iris hugged Elgin's arm. "Thank you for not making Grandfather look foolish. He does mean well, in his own way. If you had shattered his dignity, you would have shattered the man. I love you all the more for your kindness to him."

They weren't even hidden by the ornamental shrubbery when Elgin stopped and drew Iris into his arms. He said, "You make me sound noble, but I'm not. I don't want to play any more games. I don't want to leave you here at all. Not for two and a half weeks, or even two and a half days."

"But you will, won't you?" Iris reached up and touched his lips, a delicate stroke that provoked another response. With that came thoughts of other intimacies, other times when honeysuckle perfume was the only thing she wore.

He took a deep breath and said, "How can I say no?" Then "I might be back sooner than expected. In the meantime, remember that I love you and *try* to stay out of trouble."

Iris would remember, for it was the first time Elgin had actually said he loved her.

After Elgin had gone into the garden to see Iris, the squire had gone to look for his sister.

She was looking for him as well when they met in the passage outside the ladies' parlor. Terribly pleased with himself, he said, "You see, Prudence, I told you that Farley would be dough in my hands. Didn't I tell you that?"

"Yes, Obediah. That's what you said. Now if you'll just step in here and sit down I have some barley mush for your poor gouty toe. The grain has been boiled with quince and vinegar and will be ever so soothing."

The squire seated himself on a spindly chair in the feminine room. Prudence put a towel on the floor and the bowl on the towel. As instructed the squire put his toes into the warm mush and said, "I'll wager Farley is convinced that he's made the bargain of the century. Ha! Little does he know that I would have given him the mummified crocodile, too, if that's what it would have taken to get him to marry Iris. But I outsmarted him! He isn't much of a spy, either. You see, Pru, it's all a matter of knowing what a man's weaknesses are, then pouncing on them to get what you want."

She said, "You are so clever, Obediah," and handed him a catalog to occupy his time. The corner of page thirty-four was turned down to mark a selection of cast-iron plant stands shaped like swans and mermaids and unicorns, made in Glasgow, delivered unassembled.

The warm fall days had been gobbled up by damp winter evenings. Before a cozy bedroom fireplace in a great old house in Kent was a tiger-skin rug. Someone had put a hat on it to cover the bald spot. Elgin rolled over, laid aside a book on hieroglyphics, and pushed the hat down over the tiger's eyes. He said, "I'm not at all comfortable with an audience."

Iris sighed contentedly and said, "I never would have known." A plain gold band glistened in the firelight as she trailed her fingers over Elgin's bare back. "Do you know how long I've been in love with you?"

"I hope I don't have to guess," he replied in a husky whisper.

"Ever since you rescued me from that apple tree in Rutherford's orchard when I was a little girl."

"It wasn't me."

"You must remember. My dress was stuck. You and Maxwell Rutherford and a dog came along and you climbed the tree and—"

"It wasn't me," repeated Elgin. "I just got the splints off a broken leg a few days before. I didn't climb that tree. I could hardly walk. It was Max who performed the heroics. You had your hands over your eyes."

"Oh, no!"

"Oh, yes! You've been in love with the wrong man. What are you going to do about it?"

She had such a sweet smile when she said, "Come a little closer and I'll tell you."

Come take a walk down Harmony's Main Street in 1874, and meet a different resident of this colorful Kansas town each month.

A TOWN CALLED
❧ HARMONY ❧

__KEEPING FAITH by Kathleen Kane
     0-7865-0016-6/$4.99

From the boardinghouse to the schoolhouse, love grows in the heart of Harmony. And for pretty, young schoolteacher Faith Lind, a lesson in love is about to begin.

__TAKING CHANCES by Rebecca Hagan Lee
     0-7865-0022-2/$4.99 *(coming in August)*

All of Harmony is buzzing when they hear the blacksmith, Jake Sutherland, is smitten. And no one is more surprised than Jake himself, who doesn't know the first thing about courting a woman.

__CHASING RAINBOWS by Linda Shertzer
     0-7865-0041-7/$4.99 *(coming in September)*

Fashionable, Boston-educated Samantha Evans is the outspoken columnist for her father's newspaper. But her biggest story yet may be her own exclusive—with a most unlikely man.